P9-CLC-930

# CHAINS
# OF
# GOLD

# CHAINS
# OF
# GOLD

## By
## NANCY SPRINGER

*ARBOR HOUSE*
*New York*

Manufactured in the United States of America

10 9 8 7 6 5 4 3 2 1

This book is printed on acid-free paper. The paper in
this book meets the guidelines for permanence and
durability of the Committee on Production Guidelines
for Book Longevity of the Council on Library Resources.

Library of Congress Cataloging-in-Publication Data
Springer, Nancy.
  Chains of gold.

  I. Title.
PS3569.P685C46   1986      813'.54      86-7875
ISBN: 0-87795-830-0

# CHAINS
# OF
# GOLD

# ONE

I first met Arlen of the Sacred Isle on the eve of our nuptials: Lonn, the comrade, and then Arlen, the sacred king. Being not entirely without sense or spirit, I had no intention of wedding this winterking or a summerking or a sacred king of any sort; I wanted no part of anything so fearsome. But my father, Rahv of the Seven Holds, sensed the mystic power of that kingship—power, even though the newmade kings did nothing but breed and die—and he wanted a snatch at it, through me, perhaps for the sake of the flattery of rival lords. Or perhaps he truly hoped to obtain the favor of the goddess. Whatever his reason, he brought me a long journey across the Secular Lands, past the yellow eskers that divided the de-mesnes, past tilled land and pastureland, past many stone keeps atop their mounds and many tower holds. Closer to the river lay only oakwood wilderness, for no one lived there, near the holy water. Rahv brought me to the river shore on the eve

1

of the winter solstice, and in that chill dusk I was sent over to the Sacred Isle.

Naga, the river was called, meaning serpentine, or Sacred Catena, the chain. It ran at the edge of the Secular Lands, the edge of the world folk knew; on the far side, it was said, only heroes trod. Down from Adder's Head far to the north Naga flowed, lake after lake and island after river island, for every lake a name and between every lake the river and the islands, and for every island a name and a tree hallowed to it. The tree of the Sacred Isle was the willow, for sorrow.

I had never seen the Naga, for I had been kept very much castlebound, and I stared at the water, expecting to see snakes swimming in it, perhaps, or a sheen as of scales on the river itself. It looked black in the dusk, rippling and glinting rest-lessly, as if it were indeed alive, as bards said it would become in the end time, when it would rise and slither away to join the glycon in the deep. For the time, it lay darkly, and great white flakes of snow dropped into it.

Near my ear, someone guffawed.

"Belly of the goddess, but the wench's look is as dark as yon water! See her scowl. Beware, Rahv; they are likely to send her back to you when they see the black brows over her eyes."

It was Eachan, the wretch who had wed my sister and then killed her, daring to gibe at my black hair and dark-skinned face. I glared at him, and he laughed; other lords standing nearby laughed with him. My father cuffed me on the side of my head, though not hard enough to bruise, not when my body would soon be on display for the Gwyneda's approval.

"She will do for breeding," he said. "Naught else is needed. Go on!" he ordered, sending me forward with a shove.

I stumbled into the boat that awaited me and sank to the seat, gathering my sable mantle around me. Before me rose the high head of a swan. I sat in a swan boat as white as the falling snow, and though my hands touched carved wood it was alive—already it skimmed of its own accord away from shore. Not even a steersman sailed with me. I shivered, and the others watched silently, all the lords and nobles of the Secular Lands with their bright pennons and pavilions and their warm campfires, their ladies lining the shore and staring at me. The swan boat swam quickly, and soon snow veiled them from me, or me from them.

Alone. It was a chance. Of course I had long since made up my mind to escape, but there had been no escaping from Stanehold, where my father had housed me; even in daytime I was not permitted outside the walls. And there had been no lack of guard on the journey either. I had only lowered my eyes when my father had given me news of my impending nuptials, but Rahv was no fool. Ever since, all the long way hither, I had never been left alone, not even in the horse litter, not even to sleep. Only in the swan boat, rushing across the black water, alone—but my stock of courage was small, after all the years of bullying. I contemplated the Naga a moment too long, and it was too late. Already turrets were appearing before me, looming through the twilight, and a gray haze of winter willow, all looping boughs and long branches writhing into the water.

The island grew thick with magic, I sensed that at once, a magic as wild and chill and thick as the great thickets of ivy and bramble that tore at the keep, a knotted and twining magic. Perhaps the whole Sacred Isle was entirely magic and essence of magic. Fearsome. The thought made me clutch at the wood of my seat. So still, so silent did the watchers stand, those who awaited me at the island, that I did not at first see them—the Gwyneda, the white-clad blessed ones. Soon I would be one of them.

White robes that hid their bodies, hard faces under white hoods that hid their hair. Without a word they seized me and hurried me into the keep. Entering, I saw only a vast dusk, like a dark maw. I stumbled, trying to look about me, and they tightened their grip on my arms, hurrying me forward. Up a spiral stairway, along walls of cold gray stone, finally through a doorway—

A bedchamber. The door closed behind me, and unceremoniously they rid me of the sable mantle, the ermine robe—black for mourning, white for a bride. Then the long bodice of blood-red velvet edged in miniver, so that I stood blinking in a silken gown, feeling denuded even in that finery, wondering if these white-robed strangers were, indeed, women. I had thought they were, but their faces stared so flat and still that I could not tell. They tugged the jeweled clips and gilt combs from my hair, tearing out long strands of it, and as I drew breath to protest the door opened and a youth stood there.

"Lady Cerilla," he said quietly, "welcome."

His voice was warm, his dark eyes candid and warm and searching as he faced me. I trusted him at once, he, the only warm thing within the cold stone walls, and I thought him very fair, with his gentle rugged features and those frank eyes, and I wished I could somehow confide in him and beg him to help me escape. Not with all the watchers. The Gwyneda looked furious—yes, they were women, for their faces had sharpened into the look of women's fury, their noses turning as frosty white as their robes. But still they did not speak.

"Are you hungry?" the youth asked. "Shall I get you something to eat?"

I stirred from my trance of hope and misery to violently shake my head. I had never felt less hungry.

"A cup of mulled wine?"

"No," I whispered. "Thank you." *Help*, my eyes signaled, and he nodded gravely.

"Call on me for whatever you desire," he told me, "no matter what the hour. My name is Lonn." He bowed and left, closing the door behind him.

The white-robed ones finished undressing me without a word, not leaving me even my shift. I held my chin high against their unspoken hostility. Perhaps they were mute, I thought. Only later did I learn of the rule of silence that kept them from speaking to seculars, the rule Lonn had broken.

The room where they stripped me was as cold as their

silence, as bare as my body, with gray stone walls lacking any hangings, an unshuttered window slot set too high to see from, a hearth fire burning sullen and low. No furnishings except a great grim bed. The white-robes guided me to it, placed me naked between the chill sheets. That done, they left me, taking my clothing with them.

"Wait!" I told them. I wanted to ask them questions, make them answer me. But I was not Rahv; my voice quavered. They closed the door behind them.

Alone again, I lay and looked at the door.

It bore neither bar nor lock, for sacred brides, like sacred kings, were supposed to come willingly to the ceremonials. I would not be killed or even so much as flogged: I was expected merely to bed a stranger, bear a son, and be cloistered the rest of my life. What matter that I had petitioned the goddess for a true love? It was an honor to be the winterking's bride. A bar on the door, or a lock, would have been admission of the wrongness of my being there.

I smiled sourly. Like my father, the Gwyneda were no fools, and they had taken my clothing as their surety. Also, perhaps there was a guard outside the door, or a white-robed figure skulking near the first turning.

I waited, watching the gray twilight fade from the window slot, the dying firelight fade from the room, until all was sable black. Sometimes footsteps sounded in the corridor, sometimes voices. I waited, listening, until all night noises seemed to be stilled.

I moved, waited, moved again. I got up, shivering, wrapped a blanket around me as best I could, and felt my way to the door.

In no way could I guess what punishment might be mine if a guard stood beyond the door. Punishments were erratic, in my experience, and severe. But a strong anger stirred in me, longtime anger urging me on. So my father thought he could barter me away like a whelp, give me where he saw fit, as if I were no more than a slave! I had heard a minstrel's song, once, about a faraway father who loved his daughter, and it had stayed in me like a knife tip broken off in a wound.

Softly I pushed open the door.

No guard. The corridor was dimly lit by rushlights held in sconces and smoking as they burned, giving forth more stinking gloom than light. No one stood near, as far as I could see through the smoke. Barefoot, I padded back the way I had been brought in, edged my head around the corner. A glimpse of white robe, sound of footsteps; I jumped back and ran on tiptoe in the opposite direction, under a shadowy archway, past—a serpent's head thrust in my face, the body spiraling up a pillar! I nearly screamed. But in a moment I saw that it was a carving, stone or wood, and shakily I went on.

For what seemed like a parlous long time I pattered about, choosing my direction at random, shying at corners, descending stairways when I found them, often forced to flee from shadows or footfalls. The carved snakes lurked everywhere, as was fitting in a place sacred to the goddess. I saw them on walls, on doorjambs and lintels, even coiled on the floor. Always I watched them narrowly as I passed, thinking uneasily that if a carved wooden swan had come to life, so might one of these—or perhaps there were real serpents about as well. Soon I felt other reason for unease. The hold of the goddess seemed huge, labyrinthine, far larger than it should have been, could have been, on that river isle. Sorcery, I grew certain. No wonder the Gwyneda had felt no need to guard me, had left me in bed like a child put out of mind for the night.

Silently I vowed that I would find my way out, even though I was likely to die in the freezing cold—already I was freezing within the walls, my feet completely numb. And there would be the icy water to brave, for I had no way to cross the river. None of it mattered. I had to get out.

Call on him, that youth had said, that Lonn. What nonsense. How was I to call on him?

Remembering his warm glance, his candid gaze, I felt resolve suddenly melt into despair—the mere thought of help had undone me. My eyes blinked shut against tears. "Lonn," I murmured to myself, "Lonn," and I continued to walk, blindly, very tired, not much caring any more what happened to me, whether I blundered into white-robes or fell down a stone spiral stairway or met with a genuine serpent. I no longer so much as listened for danger. "Lonn," I whispered.

Wind and snow on my face.

Astonished, I opened my eyes, saw a white blur of a night. I was out, unbeknownst. Snow hissed and seethed in the wind, curling against my ankles; I stood in snow and had not even felt it with my frozen feet. Nor could I remember passing any gate or entry. But I felt the wind plainly enough, and the stinging cold, biting through my blanket as if it were spider-web. I jerked myself out of astonishment and ran.

"Lonn," I whispered between panting breaths, "guide me again."

I could see somewhat, for even on the darkest night there is always a dim glow outdoors—ghostlight, folk called it. Faint spirit fire lit the white smother of snow, and ahead of me a dark building loomed—a boathouse, I hoped. I had run half the length of the isle, and water had to lie near, though I could not hear the rush of it above the wind. But would a swan boat obey me? Perhaps if I yet again invoked the name of Lonn. . . .

Whispering to Lonn, I found the door and slipped within, then stood hearkening in utter blackness as the wind howled and shrieked outside. This place was warm, blessedly so, and I sensed stirrings, and I smelled—horses? A stable?

But what could be the use of horses to me? To anyone, on this isle?

There was no bridge to the shore, I knew. But in a more unreasoning way I knew that I had been led to these horses. It would have been shameful to scorn such a gift, even though I had never sat on a horse in my life—riding was not permitted, lest I harm my maidenhead. But I had seen men riding away often enough, and suddenly I felt a fierce desire to do the same. I stepped forward, feeling at the darkness, searching for a bridle or halter, finding only the rough wooden partition of a stall—

A footfall sounded somewhere nearby. Panicked, I flung myself into the stall, banging against the hocks of an unseen horse. The creature gave a startled jump but moved to one side without kicking me, and I lay in the straw trying to quiet my breathing, trying to listen above the clamor of my heart.

"Lonn?" a voice said softly, a masculine voice full of beauty and ardor, as if a song echoed in it. An unaccountable thrill and yearning took hold of me at the mere sound of that voice.

He walked past me and stood at the door, whoever he was, seeming to find his way quite surely even in the dense darkness. Who might he be, there in the deep of night? He stood for a while as if waiting, and then he sighed, and I wondered the more. Idly he moved off, patting horses and whispering to them.

A light floated past the window, lantern glow, and the door opened.

"Lonn." The same melodious voice spoke, gladness and relief in it.

"Who else?" Lonn retorted lightly. He closed the door behind him, hung his lantern on a hook, and unshielded it. I flattened myself in terror of the light.

"I knew you would come." The other strode over to stand beside him.

"And I knew you would be here, taking comfort in the steeds. You have always been besotted by animals. . . . Arlen, have you yet found yourself a modicum of sense?"

I shivered with surprise. It was the winterking himself, he who was destined to wed me and die! Forthwith I moved, feeling that I must see him. Risking noise—the wailing of the wind masked most noise, anyway—I sat up, inched forward, and found a crack in the boards, looked through it. . . .

Great Mother of us all! No one had told me that he was

young and tall and beautiful; how was I to know? I had thought Lonn fair, but Arlen's extravagant beauty stunned me. Some wanton energy filled him so that his every move sang to me; he seemed godlike, almost shining, his very hair crisp and alive, as if he wore a crown of flame—it was red, that marvelous many-tinged red of a chestnut horse in sunlight. And the features of his face, surpassingly lovely, their symmetry, the fawn-hued sheen of his skin, and his eyes—his eyes were as green as green springtime grass. And I gasped in glad pain at the pathos of his sad, smiling mouth.

Arlen of the Sacred Isle. With an eerie insight I knew, even then, that I would love him till I died.

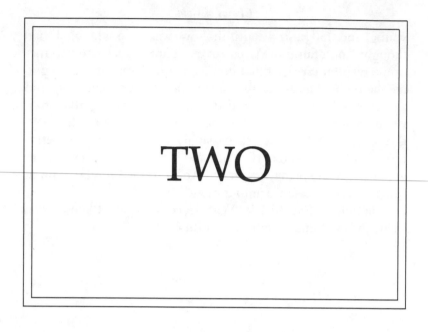

# TWO

"A modicum of sense?" Arlen said, and he shook his glorious head, his hair shining like a red hawk's feathers in firelight. "What has sense to do with what is happening?"

Little enough, I thought, gasping again with the pain of my thawing feet. Little enough sense. They had not heard me; my noise was lost in the sound of wind outside. Arlen smiled and sat on a barley bin, and Lonn sat beside him, looking commonplace next to his splendor.

"Even so, I must ask you yet once more to think," said Lonn in that warm, steady way of his, and Arlen glanced at him in annoyance.

"Don't badger me, my good friend, please. Not this last night that is given us to share."

"I must! Arlen, I cannot bear it. They will tie you up to that bloody tree, tie you with willow thongs and beat you until you faint—"

"I know," said Arlen.

"—and then they will put out your eyes."

Those incredible eyes. I shuddered and closed my own. I had not known it was to be so cruel.

"I know," Arlen said sharply. "Lonn, stop it."

"I cannot," said Lonn. "Then they will castrate you. And after the death blow you will be flayed—"

"Say no more, I tell you!" Arlen made a small, furious sound in his throat and sprang up, turning his back on Lonn, and patted several horses at random. I watched, seeing the anguish on his face, furious at Lonn in my turn.

"And then they will sever your joints," said Lonn, very softly, "and gut you, and hack you apart, catching your blood in a silver basin, and they will sprinkle us—" He choked, unable to go on. Pitiful pain in his voice—it was impossible any longer to be angry at him.

"Why?" Arlen spoke without turning around. "Why are you doing this to me? They have told us these things since we were striplings."

"They have told us so that we would not hear, not really know, not understand—how horrible—"

Silence.

"Arlen, go, flee," Lonn said softly at last. "Live."

Arlen turned back toward him, his face hard and fair, like a carving. "I would rather be dead than dishonored," he said. "A coward—"

"There is no dishonor in putting an end to madness."

"The sacred rites of the goddess, madness?" For a moment Arlen's green eyes blazed, but then he merely looked weary. "Lonn, I have no desire to quarrel with you. Please."

"All right," said Lonn stubbornly, meaning that it was not right at all. "If honor is of such concern to you, then think of the girl, *her* honor. She will be bound to know no man but you, one hour's wedlove in all her life and then celibacy. Suppose she has promised herself to a sweetheart? She is not here of her own will, any more than we are. Likely she will be foresworn."

I could have laughed or cried. Me, a sweetheart, in sterile Stanehold, with father standing guard? Arlen must have thought something of the same sort, for he laughed out loud, mocking laughter yet not unmelodious.

"A daughter of that precious Rahv? She'll be black as a crow and hard as flint, not likely to care for any lover or honor either. Save your concern, Lonn."

"But I think she is not of corvine sort, Arl," Lonn remarked with meaning in his glance.

"You've *seen* her? How in the many kingdoms did you manage—"

"I blundered in."

Arlen sat down again, sighing and shaking his fiery head, and Lonn spoke on.

"She is a gentle thing; I swear it from just my glimpse of her. No crow, Arl, for all that her hair shines black as the Naga. She seemed more like—like a dusky flower, a fragile blossom."

I snorted. Perhaps they heard me and thought I was a horse.

"Not that she lacked spirit," Lonn added hastily, as if I had reproached him. "She looked ready to bolt. You have seen the panicky glance of a tethered yearling. . .? But no flinty shell, Arlen. This—this horror, how is she to withstand it? What is to become of her?"

He spoke with an ardor that made me stare, forgetting any resentment, that made Arlen stare as well, made him furrow his fair brow.

"What do you want of me?" he asked Lonn quietly.

"Go away. Live. Let her return to her home."

"No one knows what would happen if the winterking did not come to the ceremony," Arlen replied, not in argument this time but in genuine keen-edged thought. "Likely they would slay someone else in my stead, and that one would not thank me. As for the lady Cerilla, they might be inclined to punish her in order to avert the wrath of the goddess." His voice was very low, with a stillness in it. "Indeed, they would be as likely to slay her quite slowly as to free her."

"Surely Rahv would not allow harm to come to her," Lonn said fiercely.

"I am not so sure," Arlen replied, and I knew that truth spoke in him, that he interceded for my life as Lonn interceded for his, and I shivered where I sat in the darkened stall.

They must have been friends, those two, ever since they were small boys. They sat gazing at each other, all the futility of the thing in their eyes, and reached a wordless agreement.

"I think we must settle for honor," Arlen said finally. "A winterking's death for me, and for her the life of a white-robe. She will make peace with it somehow. They all do." He shifted his gaze. The matter was closed, and new matter was needed. "What ails my gentle Bayard," Arlen murmured idly, "that he stands so oddly in his stall?"

He stood up and started toward me. I did not care to be found cowering in the soiled straw. With all the dignity I could muster I pulled my blanket tighter, rose, and stepped forward to meet him. We came face to face in the dim corridor between stalls, and I trembled in the lantern light like a dazzled deer.

"By the great goddess, a lass!" Arlen exclaimed. "Barefoot in the freezing cold and snow."

I lowered my gaze; I could not bear to meet the soft look of those marvelous green eyes.

"Who are you? How have you come here? Has someone mistreated you? Perchance we can set it to rights." He waited for my answer, and when none came he muttered, "By the holy oak, you are half naked." He took off his cloak and put it around my shoulders. "We will find you some clothing. Are you hungry?" Again he waited patiently for a reply. "Lass, will you not tell me who you are?"

I glanced up at him, biting my lip, not knowing what to say to him who was doomed to die. He met my look with a puzzled stare that melted after a moment into something warmer, a nearly trancelike gaze, and I answered it in like wise. Neither of us moved when Lonn came over to stand beside us, and he had to touch Arlen's arm to rouse him.

"Arlen of the Sacred Isle," he said in a carefully level voice, "may I present Cerilla, daughter of Rahv of the Seven Holds and Lady of Tower Stane."

Arlen seemed stunned. "Lonn was right," he murmured. Then he stepped back from me with a tight, hurt look. "Lonn was right," he said more calmly. "You have a lover; you were running away."

"No, my lord, it is not that at all!" Distressed, I spoke more than was my wont. "It is only—lord, please understand. My father cares nothing for my happiness. He gave my sister Rina to that toad Eachan, who killed her in his ill humor—" I stopped, gulping with emotion. "Lord," I appealed, "how was I to know that you are comely and kind?"

For some reason he winced, yet he stood silent.

"Surely I have no desire to see you slain, eat your flesh—"

The most horrible of the many horrors. He shuddered, but I felt suddenly calm, even bold.

"But I would gladly lie with you," I told him, with a proud lift of my chin so that I faced him more squarely.

"You do me great honor, lady," he said softly. "But—the one thing goes with the other."

"I know."

"It would be only the once, a single hour in the afternoon, and then—the bond is for life; the goddess sees to that."

"I know."

"I will find you boots, clothing, gold," he said. "Go, flee, save yourself."

"Leave you to face it alone?" I cried, with a passion that startled me. "But they will punish you!"

He threw back his marvelous head and laughed, a wild, ringing sound. "What can they do to me that they have not already planned?" he cried gaily.

"Both of you go," said Lonn, his tone vehement, and Arlen quieted.

"I have said that I will not be dishonored." He spoke softly, and his gaze was on me, softly. "No one will call me coward. But it is hard. . . ."

"At once. Go." Lonn stepped into the stall, took the blood-red Bayard by its tether, and brought it around. For the first time I looked at the steed rather than at the winterking, and a tingling shock went through me; the animal was alive with loveliness in the same odd way that Arlen was, every hair of its mane tossing on its crest, its eyes deep and feral and gold-flecked, fiery dapplings shimmering on its flanks. I wondered if magic had somehow touched me as well, if in a polished shield I could have seen it.

Arlen looked at me, at the horse. He shook his head, his hair leaping like sunflame. "I must stay," he said, and though the pitch of his voice was low I knew there would be no disputing with him. Lonn must have known it as well, for he turned to me.

"Lady Cerilla," he urged, "mount the steed. It will carry you across the water. After that, ride where you will."

I looked only at Arlen then, not at the horse. He answered my look without speaking.

"Lady," Lonn begged.

"I will stay," I said.

He fell to his knees before me.

"If you are his friend," I flared, "do not beseech me to go from him. I will stay to offer him what comfort I can. Before he dies."

Lonn stared up at me, and I glared back at him, and hope died in his eyes. "I have been his friend since we were babes," he muttered at last, and he got up and led the horse away.

"Your feet," Arlen said to me. "They are as blue as river pearls."

He gathered me up in his arms to spare me from walking any farther in the snow. Out into the dark and cold and snow and wind we went, his cloak and my blanket flapping about me, Lonn following us across the wide weed-grown courtyard with the lantern, his head bowed against the wind. But Arlen strode through the storm as if he had been born to it. Hold of the goddess bulked dimly before us, half ruinous, parapets showing jaggedly, like broken teeth, against the sky. We found a narrow entry. A dark passage led steeply downward from it, as if into the fundament of the fortress. Lonn unshielded his lantern, and after a moment we came out into a warm and cavernous room.

It was the kitchen, the great womb of the castle, deserted at this time of night. Arlen carried me across it and set me down on the immense hearth. Embers still glowed in the blackness of the gaping fireplace, and the brick of the hearth had retained the heat of the day's flames; I felt myself smiling because of the warmth. Arlen settled himself by me and rubbed my feet with his hands, his touch as warm as the hearth. Lonn stood his lantern on the table and found three earthenware cups, filled them with perry aand spices, and set the poker in the embers to heat for mulling them. Then silently he sat down on the floor by Arlen and me.

We talked of inconsequential things: the perry, and had it been a favorable season for fruits and liquors? The snow, and would it turn into a veritable winter storm? The talk, however trivial, seemed honey sweet. Lonn did not speak much, but I think he understood how precious this time was; he sat and did not hurry the preparation of our midnight cups. The poker still lay heating in the embers when, soundlessly, a white shadow stirred and one of the Gwyneda came into the kitchen.

Both Arlen and Lonn startled violently and blanched in terror. Then both slumped where they sat in relief. As for the white-robe, she stopped, then walked over to speak with us, her tread soft, as if she herself were afraid of being heard.

"All powers be thanked that it is only you, Erta," Arlen told her.

She answered him with a glance half amused, half rueful. Hers was a plain, comfortable face, square, pale of brows, with the freckles and blotches of age; there was no trace of the pinched and peevish expression I had seen on the other Gwyneda I had met.

"It is a harsh life for the white-robes," Arlen said to me. "They are never allowed enough to eat, they sleep on stone,

they rise early to tend to the dawn observances of the goddess—" He stopped, seeming to remember that within a day I
would be a white-robe myself. "They bear it differently," he
went on more softly after a moment. "Some keep to their
chambers as much as they can, others work like demons in the
gardens, others do stitchery, or divert themselves with friends
and enemies, or tend the children, or torment them. Most of
them are bitter in one way or another, and happy to cause
pain."

"And Erta is one of the few who are not," Lonn said.

"She is our mother," Arlen added, and both he and Lonn
laughed so that I saw it was a jest. Erta did not laugh, but she
smiled a little. Her eyes did not smile. She looked worried.

"Give the little one my greeting," she said to Arlen, "for I
cannot speak to her."

She meant me, I understood. "There is a rule of silence with
seculars," Arlen explained to me.

Still in awe of his beauty, I only gazed back at him. He must
have taken my glance as query.

"They are not allowed to speak to anyone not of the Sacred
Isle, not even their relations who come to the ceremonials," he
told me. "Nor am I, for that matter," he added with a sort of
wonder, and he laughed. "But there is nothing they will be
able to do to me after the morrow."

"There are some who are very angry with you, Lonn," Erta
said to him.

For speaking to me in my chamber, I understood. Lonn got
up, and poured a fourth tumbler of perry for Erta, spiced it,
and fetched the poker to heat it and the others, all without
speaking. He gave us our drinks, and we accepted them as
silently as he offered them. I felt quite warm by then, and
almost contented.

"It does not matter," Lonn said finally, and though he tried
to keep despair out of his voice it rang through hollowly.

"I would like for you to stay whole a few months yet," Erta
told him mildly.

He shrugged and would not or could not speak.

"You have strong magic," she said. "Let it help you in some way."

"What are you doing here at this time of night, Erta?" Arlen asked her. It was a foolish question, intended only as a diversion for Lonn's sake, and she knew it. She made a small noise that might have been a cough or stifled laughter, as if she were about to ask him the same. But she did not.

"I could not sleep," she said, and I never suspected the story that lay behind those words.

"We ought to see Lady Cerilla back to her room," said Lonn rather harshly.

Erta went with us, walking ahead of us, our defense and scout, but we met no one. It was a small hold, as I had thought, and we found my chamber quickly. Arlen and I looked at each other, but there was nothing to say, not in front of the others, and with a glance and a small smile we parted. I closed my door, flung my blanket on my bed, and crawled under it. Sleep did not come quickly—I heard the tolling of the bell for the morning ritual and saw the dawn of my wedding day show silver-gold through the window slot. The sun rose, sending out beams the color of orichalc, the glowing bronze of the mountains, strongest of metals. Chains of orichalc bound the glycon, the great serpent of the deep. . . .

My thoughts strayed, and after a while I dozed.

# THREE

I dreamed a strange and vivid dream.

I was hunted, running for my life; I was the swift and tawny deer that leaps between the spires of the Mountains of the Mysteries, and the hunter was an enigma, all flux and fear, first a horror, the flayed man, then a faceless being on a faceless horse, than a great serpent like the glycon. I ran amid oak trees and willow and rowan and golden apple, through mist and across rivers where women in white robes turned into swans and melted into seawater. I ran—and looked back over my shoulder to see that the rider was drawing nearer. It was a glorious youth on a steed of blood bay; it was Arlen. At the sight of the sweetness of his mouth I fell in love with him, and I stopped, turned toward him. But then I saw a rush of shadow, a monstrous, dark, swift-moving thing, unclear. And I realized that it was not he who had hunted me, that some horror pursued him in his turn—

I awoke with a start and could not sleep again. Within the hour the Gwyneda came to prepare me for the day.

All the forenoon was spent in lustrations and attentions that I bore with the best dignity I could command, though the Gwyneda were none too gentle. On first entering my chamber, they seized me and upended me to examine me. Only when they were determined to their satisfaction that I was what had been promised—that is, a virgin, and not bleeding at the time—did they release me. Then a bath of milk was prepared, and I was led to it and made to stand in it while pitchers of it were poured over me; it was cold. Only then, in the rhythm of the pouring, did the Gwyneda break silence, and they spoke not to me but to their goddess, in incantation.

"White goddess of winter," they chanted, and then their words followed the cycle of deathlife and the seasons.

> "White goddess of spring, the seed in thy bosom,
>     White goddess of summer, thy sower the sacred king,
>     Goddess of life, red reaper of death,
>     Great goddess of winter, white goddess, dark winnower,
>     Great goddess, hear us."

They went on in that way for a while as I stood amidst sheetings of milk. Then they progressed to petitions, begging the goddess for fertility of fields and heifers and women, for a mild winter without pestilence, for easy birthings among women of virtue, for a staying of the powers of death. Then they took me out of the milk bath and let me warm myself in the bed awhile and chanted over me there, surrounding me as if I were a corpse laid out before them. Meanwhile the milk bath was taken away and another brought; this time it was spiced river water, and I stood in it as before, and as before it was cold.

> "Great goddess of vengeance, whom blood of heroes pleases,
>     Dark goddess of death, with serpents in thy bosom,
>     See thou this naked one, nameless now before thee. . . ."

Imprecations! A thousand evil fates were to befall me if I were not a virgin perfect in purity before goddess and winter-king and the Gwyneda went on to detail most of them. Any punishments forthcoming from the anger of the goddess were to be visited on me and not on them, the Gwyneda. If my looks displeased the goddess, might my hair fall out, and if I had spoken ill of her, might my tongue cleave to the roof of my mouth and my lips erupt in putrefying sores. If I were not the purest of virgins, might I lie for a year in childbed, might my sexual organs rot and cause me agony. There was more, which I mercifully cannot remember. I felt no qualms concerning the matter of my purity; no man had ever been allowed to court me. But there was a malice in the women's voices that struck through my soothing thoughts and made me want to hide.

Erta was not among them. She could not have said such things so willingly.

Let them turn my whole body to ice, and a pox on them. . . . Finally they were finished, and escorted me into my bed again, and prepared the third and final bath.

It was of water with scented oil, and it was warm! I saw the steam go up and could scarcely believe it, not even when I stepped into it. Moreover, I was made to sit down in it, and lean back, and my hair was washed with a delicate scented lotion, and the fragrance of the warm oil was heady and most pleasant. And except for a muttered "Mother, comfort now thy daughter," all chanting had ceased.

Then the hearth fire was fueled into a crackling blaze which heated the whole room, and I was stationed in front of it so my hair would dry. By then I had realized that there was to be nothing to eat. Fasting was commonplace for them, I surmised. On this morning it would have been necessary for me in any event, for purification. And in truth, I felt different, my whole body faintly tingling in the warmth and somehow insubstantial, as if it did not belong entirely to me. Nothing seemed very real, and even my starving stomach did not tell me when it was noon and time for the nuptial ceremony. I had begun to think the morning would go on forever, and I was hazily surprised when they began to dress me.

Only a white robe—that was all they put on me. A white robe as simple as theirs, but of a finer stuff that floated like the river mist, and there was no hood, but a sort of trailing cape instead. They combed my hair carefully and fastened it up in loops and wound a garland of evergreen laurel around it like a crown. They tied a green silk sash around my waist, the ends of it fringed and embroidered with gold thread in the circle and spiral emblems of the goddess. Nothing for my feet. Barefoot as before, I walked out into the snow to wed with Arlen.

Name of the Mother, but he was beautiful! I had seen pageants of royal splendor and I had seen real lords riding out in all their jeweled adornment, but his beauty outshone theirs as the sun outshines the stars, and it was all simplicity: a milk-white tunic and breeches of doeskin and a crown of laurel and himself, glorious. He wore a green sash, like mine, and his feet were bare, like mine. His green eyes shimmered as green as the sash. He waited for me in a crowd of other youths, and I do not remember what any of them looked like; I saw only him, and went to him and took his hand, and he led me to the tree.

It was a pollarded oak, lopped into a stumpy shape, the very oak that within the day was to be splattered with his blood. We stood at its roots, and around us and the tree a circle formed, all around us the ranks of the Gwyneda and beyond them the youths and boy children who would go to the oak in their turn some day, some season. Lonn came and stood near Arlen's right hand. And beyond the dwellers of the Sacred Isle stood ranks and ranks of the secular kings and lords and noble ladies who had come that morning across the water to look on us. They would go the next day back to their servants and serfs and tenants, their garrisons and games of war, their vassals and their many strongholdings scattered between the eskers of the Secular Lands. My father stood there somewhere, and my

relations, and acquaintances. I did not look at them; I scorned
them all for what had been done to me.

> "White goddess of winter, behold now the winterking.
> Goddess of spring, behold now the bride."

More invocations. I did not listen, only stole glances at
Arlen as the chanting went on. He held my hand softly and
stood still.

"Bind them!" A voice said more loudly, and I stiffened. It
was one of the Gwyneda, and the others answered.

> "Power of the goddess, serpent power, bind them!
> Power of the goddess, glycon power, bind them!"

The white circle of Gwyneda moved, became a chain spiraling in and in on us, ever nearer. Hands to the waist of the one
in front of them, the white-robes shuffled closer and closer to
us, serpentined around us. I saw Erta and smiled at her, but
she did not look at me. She glided along with the others.
Tighter and tighter became their knot, coils looping around
us, until I began to breathe quickly in unreasoning fear, and
Arlen took me into his arms; there was no longer space for us
to stand side by side. The youths and young boys had joined
in, forming a darker tail to the great white serpent that surrounded us. The lords and ladies in their large ring merely
looked on—the chain was great enough without them, and I in
the midst of it seemed to feel the hot breath of an enormous
power, and the force of the great body or press of bodies that
threatened to crush us appalled me. I closed my eyes. Hot
breath all around me—

A warm touch on my cheek—Arlen's hand. He tilted my
head up and very softly kissed me on the lips. It was the first
such kiss I had ever known, and instantly everything else
dwindled to meager importance. I opened my eyes to look at

him, and as I blinked the serpent of Gwyneda uncoiled from around us, spiraled away, and formed a circle again.

"Power of the goddess, serpent power, go with them," the Gwyneda chanted. "Power of the goddess, serpent power, be in them. Bind them as with chains."

"Come," Arlen murmured to me, "this way," and he took my hand again. We walked forward. The circles parted before us like so many ring brooches, ring of white-robes and ring of youths and ring of noble onlookers. We walked through them and into the hold, and no one followed us. We found the chamber, my chamber with the bed—the only proper bed in the place, Arlen told me later. On the hearth cold meats awaited us, cold water and dry bread, the sparest of food.

"The feast will be after the butchering," said Arlen wryly.

"The feast is now," I said, and I reached up to put my arms around him. His breath seemed taken away. But then he loosened the robe from my shoulders and let it slip to the floor.

We lay on the bed together.

Ours was a blissful lovemaking, during that one short hour, ardent and effortless, like a dance or a dream. We were both virgins—to satisfy the ritual we had to be—but Arlen was much man, and magic was in him. As for me, I think the goddess possessed me as we embraced, made me bold and passionate.

"Rae," Arlen whispered against my cheek, "oh, Rae." That is an endearment, the name of the tawny doe that leaps on the mountains, and also name of the goddess, she who takes many forms, and she came to me; I flowered under his touch. There was no such thing as pain; all was sensation, ecstasy. Arlen kissed my eyes, surging over me, within. . . . "Rae," he whispered again. Afterward he held me, drew the blanket warm over both of us. I felt him quivering, and I knew that silently he wept.

"What is it?" I murmured, stroking his bare broad shoulders, his marvelous hair. A foolish question, since he was fated to die most unpleasantly within the day—but there are many aspects of death, and I ached to comfort him more fully. He sat up and faced me, tear tracks running back across his temples.

"I—Rae. . . ." He could scarcely speak. "I love you." His shoulders shook, as if earth had quaked within him; the words had undone his world. "I love you," he said more intensely, as if I could not possibly have understood. "I scarcely know you, but I have never loved anything as I love you now, this minute, anything, ever, and I want only to be with you, I want to— love you—and I have to—go off and—die on a filthy tree! . . ."

He sobbed, hiding his face with his hands, and I reached out to him and gathered him in, pillowed his head on my breasts. His sobs quieted quickly, I could feel how he hard- ened himself against them, but he lay motionless with his face pressed against me, and after a while he groaned.

"It is cruel!" The words burst out in a sort of desperate protest. "So cruel. . . ."

There were things that could have been said to him: how the red blood of the sacred king fertilized the earth of all the many kingdoms, causing the green crops to grow; how the goddess who gives us life demands payment in death—Meripen, she is called, death-in-life, and Mestipen, fortune-fate or destiny- doom, for all things are in her. Or how the seasons come full cycle and the great glycon bites its tail. In some sense he would live again, if only as grass. I said none of these things, but only lay still and held him and stroked his temples, feeling my own pain burn as deep as his, knowing the words would not have touched even the tithe of it.

"It is odd." Anger had left him, and he spoke only with a wry weariness, still nestled against my breasts. "Very odd. I had thought a coward was one who fears pain, as I do not; the blows and the blinding and all the rest of it—that is nothing. I would serve the goddess willingly in that way. But this love of you that calls me to live—pain of leaving you may yet undo me, Rae. Cerilla."

"I will love you as long as the goddess gives me breath," I told him. It was all I could do for him, and I could scarcely speak for sorrow. He lifted his head and drew mine down to his, to kiss me. Then we lay side by side, drawn close into each other's arms, until our hour was at an end.

At the appointed time the chamber door opened and Lonn came in, carrying a tall spear and a great frothing stoup of mead. He set the spear against the wall and came over to us, went to one knee to present the mead. He held the stoup in both hands. I could see that the draught swam thick with herbs.

"A potion," Lonn explained gruffly, "to take the edge from the pain." But as Arlen reached for it, Lonn hesitated and drew it back, a light coming into his face and eyes. "There is a change in you," he murmured. "You wish to live now."

"Yes, may the goddess forgive me." Arlen spoke tightly, holding back his grief. "For my lady's sake, honor or no honor. But it is too late for such thoughts."

"Think you so?" Lonn stood up, staring down at us. Then he laughed, a wild, enchanted laugh that flew like a trapped bird between the stone walls. "This cup is for me!" he cried, almost gaily. "And to think I never knew it!"

His voice had changed. The warmth was still in it, but so now was the echo of a song. I glanced at him, then stared, openmouthed. He seemed taller, stronger, greater in every way; his hair shimmered with golden light, a sheen as of sunlight lay on his face, and his every movement spoke of glory. There he stood, the hero, shining godlike. And his eyes, a glowing dark amethyst hue, the deepest hue of wood violets—how was it that I had not noticed them before?

"Lonn," Arlen breathed.

I turned to look on him and found him nearly a stranger. A youth like other youths, like a hundred youths I had seen beyond my father's castle walls, youths I had wished to speak to. A comely young man, fair but ordinary. Russet hair above a somewhat freckled face, anguish in his greenish hazel eyes. Still, with mingled consternation and relief, I found that I loved him ardently. The bond held strong.

Lonn raised the stoup to his own lips and quaffed the mead.

"You have done this," Arlen said to him, but Lonn seemed not to hear him.

"Where is that white shirt of yours?" he muttered. He was stripping off his own of wine red, and he tossed it at Arlen, his movements spellbinding, full of serpent power, his skin aglow with a golden brilliance. He found the white tunic and slipped it on, knotted the green sash. "Get up, Arlen, put some clothes on," he ordered. "You must lead the twelve, for a while. Dress yourself, take the spear. Already the white-robes are addled with mead, and as evening comes on they will be the more so. Let Lady Cerilla keep to her place and watch, and you lead the dance. When the frenzy peaks, go to your lady and take her and leave. No one will notice or know the difference until tomorrow, I feel sure of it."

"You have done this," said Arlen again, not moving, and Lonn shook his marvelous head, smiling.

"I? No. Power is in me, but difficult, unschooled; I could never by myself have managed this thing. This is the will of the goddess, serpent power working through me. . . . Get up, Arl. I will have need of you. If you but smite me a shrewd blow, I will go quickly."

He drained the flagon to the bottom, and wordlessly Arlen rose and dressed himself, put on Lonn's boots, and took up the spear with its head of wicked willow-leaf shape. From somewhere he had drawn courage; he stood in front of Lonn with the spear in hand, straight and stalwart, like a warrior, and they regarded each other. Their hands moved slowly to meet each other, touched. Fiercely they embraced, a warriors' embrace with no weeping in it. Then they went out together, comrades.

In a moment the Gwyneda came in to get me. Their faces were whitened with chalk, expressionless and as white as their robes. The sight of them disgusted me.

"Go away," I told them sharply. "I can dress myself."

They glanced at each other and said nothing, only came

over to me and pulled the covers out of my clutching hands, turned them back, and examined the bedsheets. Whatever they found there must have satisfied them, for they nodded and took hold of me. I made myself very heavy in their hands.

"Go away!" I shouted at them. "I am not a child; I am capable of getting into a robe by myself." I twisted away from them and kicked, and they were startled enough that they let me go. "Wait outside," I commanded imperiously, one fist in the air, and they looked at each other, shrugged, and withdrew.

I listened at the door, then dressed quickly, secreting all the bread and meat that stood on the hearth in the fold of my robe above the sash. I knew I would not remain indifferent to food forever; nor, I hoped, would Arlen. I tightened the sash to my utmost. That done, I took my time combing and arranging my hair, so that they would think I was a vain young fool, and then I appeared at my door, yawning. They greeted me with frowns and hurried me off to the oak.

Lonn hung there already, stripped and tied with willow thongs, his wrists bound to the lopped boughs on either side, his ankles to the trunk, and a bond around his waist as well. Before him stood twelve youths and striplings, eleven armed with darts or arrows and Arlen armed with the spear. All of the Gwyneda had chalked their faces, and they bore the scourges, the snakelike whips, their handles carved in the shape of serpents' heads. The nobles and ladies kept to their great circle, as before. It was as Lonn had said; no one had noticed any difference in the winterking—he was the one who wore the sheen, and that was all that mattered. I was hurried to my place at the fore, and someone shouted and swung a scourge, and it began.

I closed my eyes to most of what went on, and Lonn was good to me; he did not cry out. Still, there was the lashing of the whips to be listened to, and the brutal shouts, and every so often someone jostled me; they even tried to force a scourge into my hand. I stood stiff and still, letting the rites swirl around me like an incomprehensible storm. Great fires were being kindled to either side of me, fragrant fires of alder and cornel and applewood, for immortality. I could smell the spicy smoke, and when a serpentine dance began, in two loops coiling around the fires, I could feel it sweeping by me.

"Rae," said a soft, taut voice at my ear, "be ready."

It was Arlen. I mustered myself and slowly opened my eyes. Lonn hung before me, limp and bloody but still breathing—I did not look at him but a little to one side of him, seeing him as a red man, no more. The smoke stung my eyes, bringing tears, and I watched the dance, a blur. Faster and faster Arlen led it in the heady smoke, the youths spinning and leaping behind him, the Gwyneda circling and shuffling—tears had made tracks in the chalk on their faces, and smoke had begrimed it, and their white robes were disheveled, but they did not care; I could hear them panting. The look on their faces was not cruel, as I had expected, but merely entranced. Frenzy was building. Faster, faster, the dance, as the king hung on the tree. . . .

With a great shout Arlen leaped and turned and sent his spear flying. Swift and true it flew, transfixing Lonn to the oak, cutting off his life in one moment. The shrewd blow had been struck, and the youths loosed their arrows and darts, and the white-robes closed in on Lonn like so many hounds, wild for the taste of his young limbs. But Arlen ran around the fire and came to me, and we walked swiftly away. Straight through the ring of lords and ladies we walked, and none of them tried to stop us or so much as looked at us, so spellbound were they with what was happening at the oak.

Once beyond the crowd Arlen touched my arm, and we sprang forward and ran for the stable. I saw that tears streaked his face—from the smoke or from sorrow? There was no time to ask or comfort. We reached the horse; already saddled and bridled it awaited us, a comely dapple gray, Lonn's charger. The mane shimmered eerily on its deeply curved crest, and on its flanks the dapples glowed darkly, nearly purple, the color of

storm clouds. Winterking glory. . . . Arlen mounted and
helped me up behind him. He made no sound, but I felt him
shaking, felt his broad chest heave; it was sorrow.

"Do not weep," I told him softly.

"How am I to help it? I loved him as a brother, and I did not
somehow find a way to save him. I am a coward—"

"A harsh thing to say of the one for whom Lonn gave his
life," I reproved him.

A distant roar went up, the blood-shout from hundreds of
throats, and Arlen sent the horse springing forward. Down to
the shoreline it sped, through the willows, and out onto the
black water it leaped, and straight across the surface of the
Naga it galloped, sending up crownforms with its hooves.
Once I looked back over my shoulder. The Sacred Isle was a
nothingness, lost in winter mist; it might as well have never
been. And already day had turned to dusk.

We came to the shore of the Secular Lands amidst a crowd
of pavilions, and I realized that Arlen was riding at random,
scarcely knowing what he was doing, or he would have taken
us farther downriver, away from the lords' encampment. It did
not matter. The lords and ladies were all on the Isle being
sprinkled with blood, and the few servant folk who were about
merely stared at us. I recognized my father's pavilion close at
hand, its pointed top emblazoned with his sevenfold tower
emblem.

"Wait," I said to Arlen, "stop," and he did not question me,
only brought the horse to a halt. "Wait but a moment," I told
him, and I slid down and ran into the pavilion. My things
were there, packed up in a chest as if to be sold; I never would
have seen them again. I snatched up a pair of fur boots—
slippers, really—and put them on my bare feet. I found my
mantle—not the grand sable one I had worn to the Sacred Isle,
but my everyday one of brown wool—and fastened it on. I
gathered up some blankets. My father's manservant had come
in and stood watching me with his mouth agape. "If you say so
much as a word about this to anyone," I told him grimly, "I

will come back from my grave to haunt you." It was of no use,
I knew—of course the man would tell everything if Rahv
asked. No one could withstand Rahv.

I ran for the horse and handed Arlen the blankets.

He took them numbly, laid them across his mount's withers,
and helped me up behind him again. Day had nearly turned to
dark by then. We started off downstream along the riverbank,
and all the servants stood and watched us go without a sound.

Perversely, with the mantle gathered around me and the
slippers warming my feet, I started shivering. I pulled up my
hood. We followed the riverbank, guided by the faint gleam of
water in darkness.

"Will they pursue us?" I asked Arlen, and he came out of his
torpor sufficiently to answer me.

"The Gwyneda have no retainers that I know of, and they
themselves never leave the island—that I know of. But they
will be mightily wroth, I assure you. They might find
ways. . . . And your father, will he not come after you?"

He most certainly would, and not because of love, either.
With some thought of keeping our strength up—for I still was
not hungry—I reached into my robe and found a hunk of
bread. I offered some of it to Arlen. He shook his head.

"You eat it," he said, so I did. Gnawing at it, I found myself
suddenly famished and finished it all. I restrained myself from
eating any more. We might need it later; the night was dark,
and only the goddess knew what might be on the hunt for us.

# FOUR

It was a hyperboreal storm, as it turned out, that first emperiled us. Down from the frozen mountains to the far north snow came hissing, and stinging shards of ice driven before a mighty blast, breath of harsh Bora. At once we could see nothing, not even the glimmer of the river; the night was all befogged by snow. And cold! The numbing cold of the day had been nothing compared to this biting, strength-sapping cold at the fore of a thin and coiling wind. It struck through all my defenses of wool and endurance to whatever warm core was left in me, and I began to be afraid. The realms of death were in the north, folks said, and such storms were of the goddess's sending.

"Name of the goddess!" Arlen exclaimed. "We are in the water."

We had strayed into the river; we could hear it splashing about the horse's hooves. No wonder, as we could not see, and I did not understand the tone of shocked surprise in Arlen's voice until he spoke again.

"The—the power, it must be gone, somehow. The magic."

The horse was walking in the water, not on it. As long as we kept to the shallows, I thought, it did not matter, but Arlen seemed stunned. A stammer came into his voice, and he kept talking even though he could not have known whether I was listening.

"But—I—I have ridden all the way down the Naga's tail, down the Long Lake and over the spires of the lost city that lies under the water, and I have ridden up through the Blackwater all the way to the Lakes of the Winds, all of us lads, we used to go in procession—"

I could see them in my mind's eye, the doomed youths on holiday, laughing amongst themselves, fair tunics and bare throats and proudly lifted heads, riding their bright and beautiful horses upon the surface of the Catena. I smiled with wonder, even though my flesh had started to freeze.

"—though we were never allowed to set foot on any shore except our own, the Sacred Isle, we or the steeds."

The wind swallowed his words in a wild assault that made us both wince. We had to find shelter soon or we would both be dead. But how? The horse kept moving under us, but we could not see where we were going. Arlen must have had similar thoughts.

"I do not have a notion where—" he muttered. "Wait, a shore—"

We both felt the bump and the effort as the horse brought us out of the water, up a steep and rocky slope—my arms were locked around Arlen in a clutch as of a corpse, or I would have slid off backwards. Then the horse pushed a way into something that thwarted the force of the wind. Twigs against my face. . . . The horse stopped of its own accord.

"Yew," Arlen said, for there were small round leaves on the twigs even then, in the deep of winter. "By my body, I know where we are! Rae, get down."

I slid off, but my numbed legs would not hold me and I fell into the snow. It was not very deep, there under the trees. Arlen dismounted and dumped the blankets on top of me. I heard him struggling with the saddle and bridle, and he took one of the blankets for the horse, tying it onto the animal's body with the reins, but I did not realize that until later, for I was half in a stupor.

Presently Arlen found me, tugged me upright, and put his arm around me to steady me. "This way," he murmured. "Come on."

Out we went into the blast of the storm again, this time on foot. I followed him without question, leaning against him.

"Cerilla, walk," he said sharply. "I cannot carry you. It is not far. In fact, it should be close at hand."

The tone of his voice roused me, and I straightened. He was feeling about at what seemed to be the side of a hill. Then with a wordless grunt of discovery or satisfaction he took my shoulders, urged me down into a crouch, and guided me into a sort of cave or hole. I crawled in, silently cursing my long gown, which hindered me; I hitched it up to my hips, careless of the stones against my knees.

We were in a passage, I realized after a few moments, and it led downward as well as forward, and it was not large enough to stand in or even stoop in; nor did it seem that it ever intended to widen. Therein laired the darkest of all possible darks, and something in me rebelled against it. I stopped.

"Keep going," said Arlen, behind me.

"What sort of place is this?" I protested, an edge in my voice.

"It is an out-of-the-wind place, and a somewhat-warmer place," he replied just as snappishly—he was weary, too, and grieving. "Move!"

"It is a tomb," I said, and instantly the words sent a chill of fear through me. It was true, though I had not allowed myself fully to think it until I spoke. At any moment I was likely to find bones under my hands. Or any of the things that live in the underground places of the dead, something worse than bones—

"Arlen," I questioned, quietly this time, "have you ever been in here?"

"No. How could I? We were not allowed on any shore but our own. This is a crannog; it sits in the midst of the river, at a ford—"

I was not listening to him. "Great Mother," I muttered, "what is likely to be in here?"

"For myself, I really do not care." The despair in his voice wrung my heart. "If I could go before you, Rae, I would, but I came behind to stop up the entry somewhat."

But I had already started off again. I crawled doggedly, slapping my hands down hard, trying not to think of what they might find, not thinking at all until I banged my head against something made of stone. I stopped with a small moan.

"What is it?" Arlen asked from behind me, apprehensive.

"Nothing." Nothing but a squarish slab of stone, waist high. I felt to either side of me and found nothing but floor and air. Overhead, nothing either. The constricting stone walls and roof of the passage had widened, it seemed. Cautiously I straightened to my knees, then to my feet. There was room to stand. And it must have been warmer down there than I knew, for the pain of my bumped head was as a twinge compared to the pain in my reawakening legs. I gave up standing and slumped to the floor again, whimpering between clenched teeth. Arlen felt his way over to me.

"What is it, Rae? Have you found something?"

"No! I—am—perishing of cold, that is all."

"Well, here." He arranged the blanket on top of me, doubled it even, then moved away. I could hear him exploring our quarters as best he could in the utter darkness. The chamber was not large; the wall did not seem to be much beyond my feet.

"It seems to be a cenotaph, an empty tomb," Arlen said when he had found his way back to me. "There is nothing in here except us." He knew the questions in my mind. "Is the blanket helping?" he added.

"Not enough," I grumped. Now that we were safe, for the time, all my daring had left me. I lay shivering and sullen.

"Well, let me lie with you then, for warmth."

I hoped he had no thought except for that, for certainly I had never felt less amorous. He lifted the blanket, lay down close beside me, and I gasped—his flesh was icy, far colder than mine. Hastily I flung my mantle over him as well as the blanket, pressed myself against his chest, rubbing his back with my hands. Of course he would be frozen, he in only his tunic. I had thought it was his masculine hardness that had made him brave the cold without complaining, but I had been mistaken; so gripped was he by grief that he truly had not noticed. He might have died, not noticing.

"Flex your feet," I ordered him. "Bend your toes."

"Why?" He did not obey me. His head felt heavy against my arm.

"Arlen," I said, terrified, "do not go to sleep, or you are likely never to awaken again."

"It does not matter," he murmured.

"It matters to me!" I cried in his ear, startling him. I felt him jump. "It matters to me," I said again, more softly but more sternly. "Talk to me," I added.

"What is there to say?" He was going to be troublesome.

"Tell me about yourself. I pledged my undying devotion to you some several hours ago; I would like to know something about you."

I believe he nearly laughed; I felt a tremor in him. "There is not much to tell," he said. "We boys were raised on the Sacred Isle from the time of our birth, given as much as we wanted to eat and made to keep our bodies chaste and beautiful for the goddess, and sometimes the white-robes got a hand's turn of work out of us, but for the most part of the time we ran wild."

Wild lads, youths and lads, the lot of them riding on the Naga, down to the strand where the glain lie, the blue stone snake eggs of the great serpent in the sea. I smiled at the thought of such riding, wondered if anyone had ever seen them, had ever thought them a vision. But to find the glain, the talisman of seers, and never be let to set foot on the strand even to pick one up—my smile left me. So there was no magic in Arlen's steed any more, because it had set foot on a shore.

Arlen had fallen silent.

"Were they cruel to you?" I blurted to keep him talking, and instantly I could have bitten my tongue. It was a tactless question. But it made him stir.

"Sometimes." His voice sounded distant. "There were many ordeals, torments. We had to be tough—and they were always pitting us against each other, placing us on our mettle, so that we would vie for the honor—" He stopped.

The honor of being slaughtered. He was not yet ready to speak of that. "Tell me about your family," I said.

"I have none." He sounded amused, and warmer, closer. "No more than the Gwyneda do. The oracle gives them a new name when they come to the Sacred Isle, and after that they have none other, and to their families they are as if dead."

"Well," I remarked, "for me that would have been the one good thing about being a white-robe."

"Daughter of Rahv. Yes." He understood. "But do you not have a mother?" he asked me.

"She died somehow when I was younger. I do not remember that she was sick, and everyone has always been very vague about it." I shrugged. "I think Father killed her because she did not give him sons."

There was silence. I had stopped shivering and forgotten the cold; I felt quite comfortable.

"But you have a mother among the Gwyneda," I said presently.

"Perhaps. But I do not know which one it might be; none of us do. It was said that the white-robes do not know themselves, though I cannot see how that could be—but none of them ever gave a sign."

I kept silence, hoping he would go on of his own accord, and in a moment he did.

"There were always a few extra of us, a few more than might be needed for the ceremonials, I mean, though some died of fever and the like, and some were pockmarked or whatnot and—were sent away, I know not how, disappeared. For they were unpleasing to the goddess." He took a deep breath. "I was going to say, my mother might not have been a white-robe. But if she was, I always hoped she was one of the kind ones. Lonn and I—" He stopped with a choking sound.

He had been about to speak of Erta, I felt sure, but that meant speaking of Lonn. Speak of Lonn, I urged him inwardly, it will do you good. Grief turns to venom, unspoken. But I could not say such things to him, for I did not yet know him well. Instead, I kissed his face, since it lay close to mine. He shook his head rapidly, and his whole body tightened into a knot.

"Mother of torments, Rae, the pain!" he cried, panting. "Ai, why did you have to warm me?"

I thought he meant the pain of limbs coming to life, and so I suppose he did, in a way. I rubbed his shoulders to ease him, thought of reaching down to rub the calves of his legs. But then all in a rush between gasps of agony he began speaking of Lonn, none too connectedly.

"I could have gone, slipped away so easily—but no, then I had to stay and be with—Rae, the torment!" His arms were tightening around me, too tight, constricting. "I thought I was brave, but now I know better. That was why I wanted to go first, winterking, so I would not have to see—what he did not want to see—oh, no, Lonn, Lonn!" The name came out in a terrible cry, and his arms were crushing me, but I would not cry out, not then, not for anything. By far the worse pain was his, then.

"He would have been next," I whispered, with a small shock of comprehension. "Summerking. . . ."

"In a six-month. Yes." He went limp, releasing me, and lay beside me gasping or sobbing—the darkness shielded him, and I could tell nothing about him in that blackness unless he spoke to me. I needed his touch.

"Arl?"

His hand found mine, and he quieted.

"Are you all right?"

He did not answer me except by drawing me close to him again, gently this time. "Rae," he murmured, "how can I be so in love with you and still so heartsore?"

I brought the viands out of the placket of my robe. "Here," I said. "Eat."

He sighed, letting go of sorrow for the time, and sat up and nibbled at what I gave him. After a moment he ate ravenously and I sat beside him and ate as well; we were both hard put to stop and save some food for the morrow. Then Arlen went up to the entry and fetched the saddle pad, put it down to ease the hard, stony floor for us. We lay on it with the blanket doubled over us, close together for warmth, and exhausted as we were, immediately we slept. . . .

"Lonn?" It was a panicky voice, calling. "Lonn!"

I awoke to a feeling of cold and struggle. All was pitch blackness, as before, and Arlen was thrashing about beside me, half out of our bed, sitting up and letting in the chill. "Lonn! Rae?" he called in the same panicky way, and I reached over to touch him before realizing that he was still asleep; I was still half asleep myself. As soon as my fingers touched his arm he turned and seized me with such force that I cried out. But then he came to himself and pulled me to him more gently, held me with the passion of fear still in him.

"I am sorry, very sorry!" he exclaimed. "Have I hurt you? I thought—"

"It was a dream," I told him.

"I know. It is all very confused. I thought—Lonn was taking you from me, for he was the sacred king and his was the bride right. I saw him in all that unearthly beauty that was his at the last. . . ."

Mischief was in me, because I had been awakened so abruptly. "Did I go with him willingly?" I teased, and Arlen let go of fear with a laugh.

"No indeed, you did not!" I felt rather than saw his smile. "Moreover, I am a fool even to dream such a thing. Lonn would never—Rae, I may never again know such a loyal and honorable friend."

Sorrow was in his voice, but he spoke the name without tears, and for that I was thankful. He burrowed down beside me in our bed, pulled the blanket over us again.

"Ai, Rae," he murmured to me, "this has been both the worst and the best day of my life."

We made love. It was not much like that first incredible lovemaking, this time, for the glamour of magic no longer filled us, we were tired, and our situation was awkward, all constraint of cloth and fumbling in darkness. But I think, if anything, I cherished this time the more. It was us cleaving to each other, not winterking and sacred bride but us, Arlen and Cerilla, Rae, making a bond in the midst of adversity. Making a babe. I knew that, even then.

A peculiar thing happened as he lay atop me and within me. Something moved within that dark underground chamber of ours, a breath, a stirring, as if earth herself had breathed a small sigh around us or through us, the most gentle of exhalations. I felt it, that stirring, as if something were alive around me or in me, but it was a waft so small, so gentle, that it did not frighten me. I merely noted it with mild puzzlement.

"Did you feel that?" I asked Arlen.

"As if something just walked across my grave. Yes. The storm must still be blowing." He kissed me tenderly and extricated himself from me with care, rolling over to lie beside me.

"I thought you used the saddle to block the entry," I said.

"I did! But not entirely; we need air. Indeed, it is a very good thing that this cist faces northward and the wind has scoured it for us. Else it would be too stale for us to breathe, down here."

But the storm was not still blowing. Not some several minutes later, at any rate, when we had clothed ourselves and ascended. We no longer found our dark shelter oppressive but thought of it as a warm haven, a womb; we gladly would have stayed longer. But we could not tarry where Rahv might so easily find us.

Glow of pale winter light greeted us as we ascended the passage, afternoon light, and we came out into the white hush that often follows a snowstorm. The Naga flowed black between white shimmering banks where great trees, oak and ash and elm, stood with heads bowed under an icy burden, very still. Nothing moved anywhere, not even a raven; the only sound was the lapping water against the stonework that formed the shore of the crannog.

And a sort of bumping, very soft, very insistent. Our eyes found the source of it at once, and, unthinking, we took a few steps toward it—

A strange vessel, a sort of wicker basket floating like a boat, had come to rest against the stonework, held there by the current, and in it lay—a severed human head. Lonn's head. I recognized it at once even though the eye sockets stared up at me empty and hideous. By his brown hair lay a bloody, pathetic something else that I did not identify, for I was vomiting—hours later, I realized it was his genitals. Arlen made a retching sound, turned, and ran for the yew grove that flanked the cist, snatching up saddle and bridle on his way. He could not be gone quickly enough from this place now, nor could I. Hastily I crawled back inside the barrow to bring out our food and the blankets.

It took us longer than we had thought to be off, because Arlen had forgotten about the saddle pad and had to come back for it. So I stood for a while with my back to the bloody thing in the water, noticing other things, whatever met my eyes, to keep my mind from knowing what I had seen. I studied the stones at the entry to the cenotaph—there were some very old carvings on them, spirals, and after a while I realized that they might have been intended for coiled snakes, as they had a sort of triangular thickening at the center end, like an asp's head. I considered this very carefully. And I contemplated our horse. No longer the glorious animal that had left the Sacred Isle with us, it looked like any farmer's sturdy horse, a splotched gray suitable for the pulling of a plow, standing and stamping with cold and switching its tail, heavy-headed and sulky. Arlen's saddle looked too grand on it, but Arlen himself appeared none too grand, pale and unkempt, and I expect I looked no better.

Arlen had to fasten the reins back onto the bridle, since he had used them as a surcingle for the blanket, and he was making a botch of the job in his hurry, swearing under his breath, in a temper. I did not offer to help him, for that might merely have vexed him the more. By the time he had all ready at last—it took only a few minutes but seemed far longer—he was in a state somewhat beyond either panic or temper and nearer the realms of madness. He hurled me, rather than helped me, onto the horse's rump, and he sent the creature leaping off the crannog into the water and plunging across the ford, slipping and stumbling on rocks and ice; the river had frozen for several feet out from the shoreline, and the steed broke through at each jump, cutting its legs. When we made land at last, we were off at full gallop, breakneck fashion, over ditches and bushes and whatever lay in our way, and I hung on, too proud or stubborn to protest even though the horse's leaps nearly sent me flying. Only after the horse was in a lather did Arlen seem to notice what he was doing, and he soothed the frightened creature and slowed it to a walk.

"There," he murmured, "There, there, Bucca." I had not known the horse had a name. I cautiously loosened my grip on Arlen's waist, and we rode on in silence for a while.

"Rae," Arlen said presently without turning around, "I am ashamed."

I kept silence. Men were entitled to their furies, in my experience, but that did not mean I had to enjoy them.

"Poor Bucca. I ought to get down and tend to his legs, but I have to keep him moving for a while or he'll take a chill."

"But he's bleeding," I said. I could see the red smears on the snow.

"Horses have quantities of blood in them."

"So do sacred kings," I retorted, more sharply than I had meant to. Arlen stiffened and did not reply.

The day was far spent, for we had slept through half of it, and we rode through most of the rest without speaking again. Bucca ceased to bleed and walked stolidly. We passed out of the towering woodlands that flanked the Naga, found the beginning of pastureland and settled places, stone-walled hill-top garths. For concealment, we kept to the folds between the rounded uplands, folds where streams ran to hide Bucca's hoofprints. Shadows began to deepen, purple on the snow. Not until then did Arlen voice what was troubling us both.

"That thing in the Naga," he said. "It chills me."

I gave him a small squeeze to show I had heard. I, also, felt my flesh crawl at the memory.

"I feel as if it is going to follow me forever."

That note of wild despair in his voice—I could tell he was

going to take mothering. Fittingly so, he who had never had any.

"I never want to see that river again," he burst out.

"Very well," I said, meaning it. "But have you any idea where we are going?"

"None. Anywhere, so long as it is away from the Catena."

We rode on at random into the Secular Lands.

# FIVE

The land lay between long mounds of sand and loose rock, very long; from a promontory one could see them looping and wriggling across the moors for miles. Eskers, they were called, and no one could understand where they had come from. Some said they were the garth walls of giant men in times long past, and others that they were the nests of serpents, huge serpents, in the beginning days before such creatures had dwindled. And why might it not be so, if one is to believe in the immensity of the glycon that lives in the deep? Some eskers were longer and wider than others, and the narrower ones often attached themselves to the larger, like babes suckling at a mother, if serpents suckled in those forgotten times. But sometimes their nests contained boulders as well as pebbles and sand, and that puzzled me.

They formed boundaries of a sort between the demesnes and petty kingdoms, of which there were many. Once in every day's journey, or sometimes more often, there arose a square tower stronghold or a round keep on a mound, stony symbol of some lord's bid for power. We did not seek refuge or hospitality at any of them, for the lords were mostly in league with my father or else under his thumb. I knew of some few who were his rivals, worthy to challenge him, and we could have sought them out—but then I would have been a piece in a game of power again, a whelp to be traded, and I wanted no more of that. Arlen and I, we wanted only peace and a place to lay our heads.

For the time, though, we were very much at power's mercy. We knew that Rahv would be in search of us, or the Gwyneda, or both, and we kept on the move across the countryside, not knowing where we were going. This far north we traveled mostly moorland and peat bog and scrubby woodlot, land good for grazing and the hunt but not as fertile as the tilled lands farther south, and therefore sparsely settled. The few villages were clustered within the tower baileys. We could hope for aid only from outlanders, sturdy folk who fended for themselves and picked up the stones for their cottage walls from the eskers and moors. We would come upon their small holdings as we skirted the lands of the petty lords.

We thought we rode alone, but a presence traveled with us.

We did not sense it at first, but others did. The first freezing night after we had left the cenotaph, we gratefully stopped at a small stone cottage, and the folk greeted us with broad smiles—they seldom had visitors, they welcomed us, and of course they could see that we were young fools in love, runaways, and all their sympathies were with us. My white robe was so dirtied and bedraggled by then that no one was likely to think of the Gwyneda, looking at it. The goodwife, a round ruddy woman, merely clucked over it for a moment and bustled off to find a brown linsey frock she thought might fit me. They fed us a warm supper and spoke of giving us provisions in the morning and plotted where they might put our bed. But after we had sat by their fire for a while, their smiles faded.

"What is it?" I asked after some time had gone by and they had grown more and more silent and I thought I saw them drawing back from me. "If we have offended in some way—"

"Missy, ye'd better be off, ye and yer lad." It was the goodman speaking, his tone a mixture of belligerence and shame. "Ye'll bring ill luck upon us. Ye smell of death."

Arlen looked up blankly, thinking of our night in the cenotaph, I am sure, though there had been no stench there. "Why, let us wash, then," he said.

"'Tis not that." The man rose to his feet, looking ill at ease but determined. "There is death walking with ye; there will come pestilence upon us or some grievous ill fortune if it touches us. Out, now."

"But wait a moment!" Arlen stood up, incredulous. "You cannot turn us out into this cold night. We will be dead ourselves before morning!"

"Let us stay in the barn, then," I put in, seeing the dark cast of the man's face.

"And let the cattle sicken and die? I tell ye, go." The goodman reached for the poker.

"Our perishing will be on your account," declared Arlen hotly. "And if you think there is death here now—that is nonsense, but I tell you this: if I die this night my vengeful spirit will return to you and never leave you. I vow it." There was a reckless, burning look in his eyes.

"Husband!" It was his goodwife, frightened.

He was thinking. "Well," he said grudgingly, "I suppose there be's the shed. Naught in it but tools. I'll take them out."

"We'll need bedding," said Arlen, "if we are not to freeze."

"I'll put in some straw. For ye and the horse. I'll have the horse out of the barn—"

"There's no taint on the horse!" Arlen shouted. "Go smell him for yourself!"

In the end Bucca stayed in the barn, but we went out in the dark and slept in straw in a drafty shed and were glad of it. A small gift of food awaited us at our door in the morning, like a propitiation, but no one came near us. We ate and left feeling saddened and puzzled.

"Are all seculars like that?" Arlen wanted to know.

I had to laugh. "You have nearly as much experience of them as I! How should I know, who have spent my life locked in Stanehold?"

"Have you learned nothing useful at all?" he teased me.

"To be sure! I know several ways to embroider a napkin."

But it was beautiful, the snow on the moors, and neither of us had ever seen such a thing before, the long windswept slopes of land and the eskers snaking across them, and after a while the pale winter sun came out and touched everything with aureate light. Arlen, who had never been atop a hill in his life, kept shaking his head and exclaiming at every vista, and we could not be very sad, either of us, not with the horse surging under us and the heady feeling of freedom. We tried to keep to the hillsides blown clear and brown, but we could never hide our traces for long, not in the snow, and before the day was old we gave it up and struck out recklessly across the billowing wealds at speed. We laughed as we rode, and we forgot to look back over our shoulders as we topped each rise.

Came afternoon and nothing to eat, our good spirits abated.

"My stomach is pinching me," I complained. And a day before I had been grateful merely to be alive and at liberty.

"So is mine," said Arlen wryly. "They used to feed us well, back on the Sacred Isle—us boys, I mean. Scant fare for the white-robes, but anything we fancied for us lads, except love. . . . Bodies beautiful for the goddess. Meat being fattened for the slaughter." A note of longing had crept into his voice in spite of his bitterness—he was thinking, perhaps of dinners past. I paid no attention, for something inexplicable was happening within my senses and my comprehension.

"Wait," I said to Arlen. "Stop the horse a moment."

Bucca was glad enough to stop, and I slid down. We were at a level hilltop with a copse of tangled trees and something rumpled under the snow. Not knowing what it was, but following the guidance of a force I did not understand, I walked for some small distance, then stopped and scrabbled with my feet. The earth was peaty, friable even though frozen. I kicked at it and uncovered something that shone whitely—a turnip. I found a flat piece of rock and dug harder, with it and with my hands. There were withered stalks to be seen beneath the snow, now that I knew what to look for, and they guided me to more turnips and other things, I think they were parsnips, and orange roots such as I had seen in cattle mangers the night before—I did not care. If cattle could eat such things, so could I. On the instant I bit into one and decided it was tolerably good.

Arlen had long since tethered Bucca and come to help me. He was finding roots as well, but he took his first handfuls to the horse before returning to eat himself. I had sat down on a stone and was eating heartily. He stared at me in wonder.

"That is someone's foundation you are sitting on, I think," he said. "This was their garden; see the furrows? The house was destroyed by fire or war, I suppose, and they were killed or perhaps they went away. But the root crops survived. Cerilla, you say you know nothing, but you saw this place when I would have ridden past."

"I saw nothing," I said.

"Then how did you know food was here?"

"It wasn't me."

"Oh? Who then?" He smiled, thinking I was teasing him again, but I did not answer. I shied from saying what was true: that I had been told about this place, voicelessly, by something not myself.

Arlen gave up on getting any sense out of me, his gaze wandering. "Wait," he exclaimed. "Are those apples on yonder trees?"

They were, withered but still red and edible. We gathered as many as my mantle pockets would hold and we gave Bucca some. I am sure Arlen saw those apples on his own, without any strange prompting. But I had not so seen the fruits that lay beneath the soil.

We ate more roots and held some in our hands and took to horse again. Before we had gone far, the peculiar summons sounded through me once more. "Wait," I murmured to Arlen, "there it is again," and I slid to the ground and walked. When I felt compelled to stop, I searched beneath the snow and found a flat rock. Arlen had come up behind me expectantly. I turned the rock up—a squirrel's hoard of seeds and acorns lay beneath. We both broke into laughter. "No, thank you," we declared in unison, and we went on our random way. I felt the odd presence no more that day.

"Shall we try again?" Arlen asked as evening drew on, meaning that we should again ask hospitality of an outlander. I acceded. It seemed to me that the problem of the previous evening might have been their oddity, those folks, not ours. So when we saw a prosperous-looking holding in the fold of a hill we rode toward it, found the gate in the stone wall, and entered the yard. A woman met us with a smile. But even as we dismounted the smile faded and she backed away from us.

"Go on, go on your way. Please. It's early yet." she begged. And as we stared at her she ran inside and swung shut the heavy wooden door. We could hear her barring it and calling to her children to stay away from the windows, for the dead were riding by.

So ride we did. "The dead don't hunger," Arlen grumbled. "We should have asked for food."

There was another, poorer holding farther up the valley; we could see it in the distance, and we reached it in the dusk. A man with a lantern was coming in from his work in the byre. He brought the light close enough to look at us, then shouted and lifted his stick. Arlen turned Bucca and sent him out of the yard at the gallop. We both fell silent, feeling like lepers.

At least the night was clear; there was starlight to ride by. It was also cold. We took shelter finally in a sheep shed far up a long hillside, at the distance of a meadow from the nearest homestead, and we took pains that the folk should not see us in their sheep cot. It was a little, low stone building with the south side open to the weather, a shelter meant for lambing, perhaps. There was some soiled straw in it, and also there were some sheep. They stank, but we nestled down among them for the sake of the warmth of their wool. And Bucca had only the shelter of a thin whitethorn grove and a blanket on his back.

In days to follow we learned not to scorn the squirrels' hoards. When my signal unseen or voice unheard led me to one the next day, we took nuts and cracked them to have with our apples.

Those were not easy days; it would be untrue to say they were. We did not trouble the outlanders any more with the onus of our presence, but waited until they were abed and then took shelter in a shed or barn or byre, stealing a bit of hay for Bucca, or corn. For some reason, although we did not hesitate to take what the horse needed, we would not steal for ourselves. Perhaps we felt somehow to blame, while Bucca was blameless. Therefore we survived on gleanings, we both grew thin and haggard. And I had never known the world was so large, so awesome, or the hours of darkness were so long, away from lamplight and friendly hearth. Until we were settled in our rude bedding with our blanket over us and our bodies nestled together, the nights seemed full of dread mystery, as menacing to us as we seemed to others.

Perhaps because we needed it the more, the presence that traveled with us had grown stronger. Whatever food lay beneath the ground it would show to me without fail, even if it were only a single turnip or a few acorns—always to me, never to Arlen. But Arlen was beginning to sense the being of the thing too. At times one could almost see it; there was a sort of thickness in the air a few feet to the left of us. If we were separated, it went with me. On one occasion when it had led me off to some distance in search of carrots, I turned to see

Arlen watching with a peculiar expression on his face. Then he came slowly up to us. I say "us" because there verily was an other there.

"I wonder what it is," he murmured, gazing off to my left a little.

I must have been feeling particularly hungry that day, and bitter. "You could leave," I told him, as if he were stupid not to have thought of it himself. "Go off by yourself and join some lord's retinue, live like a proper person instead of a beast. They would accept you, for this thing would cleave to me; I feel sure of it. Go ahead."

If he had hesitated so much as to draw an extra breath—but he only smiled and took my hand. "Rae," he chided, "you are talking nonsense." And that was the end of it.

Hard days, but good. Arlen had never known women except for the Gwyneda, who were scarcely women at all in any natural sense. It was most sternly forbidden that there should be any contact of a fleshly sort between the young men of the Sacred Isle and the Gwyneda, even though some of the white-robes were as young as the sacred kings. The penalty for such passion was a most unpleasant death. So Arlen had known no lovers but me, and while he knew he loved me he hardly knew how to treat me, not in any usual way. More and more he came to regard me as a comrade, a fellow, and he confided in me much as he would have confided in—well, in Lonn. I did not entirely like this; I would have liked to have been wooed, courted, I who had prayed for a sweetheart. Still, I was a wife, and once a women wed, she stood at the mercy of her hus-band's fist; in this regard I was fortunate. Arlen had no notion of manly protection or a woman's place, but his equable love for me constrained him to keep from quarreling with me and I was glad of it, for he was mettlesome. I was grateful that the hot flash of his eyes fell on folk other than myself.

Being a comrade, I decided, had felt strange to start with, but better and better as time went on. Comradeship assorted well with freedom—another joy that had once felt strange.

Neither of us had a plan. "Where are we going?" I asked once, over his shoulder as we rode.

"I don't know." He laughed and nudged Bucca into a springing trot. "Folk think we are fleeing, but they are wrong," he said. "We are two seekers questing together. We are looking."

"Seeing the size of the world," I murmured. The vast world.

I was coming to know Arlen better—a bittersweet reckoning, for one who had dreamed of heroes. There was little of the hero about Arlen, but much to love: the moods that crossed his face, his warm way with animals, his occasional mischief, his mouth that stammered slightly when he was heart-touched or distressed—there were a thousand expressions about his mouth. And for all our happiness and Arlen's confidence I began to feel that he hid some deep hurt; something was bleeding within him, a wound that had not yet started to heal.

"What is wrong?" I whispered to him, late at night, just before sleeping beneath frosty stars.

"Nothing."

"I have sensed in you—not sadness, exactly. . . ."

"It is nothing, Rae."

"Lonn?" I asked softly, and I felt Arl shake his head, his hair brushing against my cheek.

"I have wept for Lonn. Leave it, Rae."

It was true, we spoke of Lonn often. I asked again, from time to time, but Arlen did not tell me what ailed him, and I decided he could not, that he did not yet know the name of it himself.

"Elderberries," he murmured once.

"What?" We were riding, and he spoke away from me, so I had not heard.

"Elderberries." He stopped the horse and pointed.

Bushes clustered thickly beside us, and the black berries hung in bunches from every bough. Arlen reached over and plucked himself a fistful, and my skin prickled in protest.

"Those are forbidden food!" I cried. The elder was the tree of doom and immortality, of death and the goddess; it kept its fruit throughout the winter. An infant laid in a cradle of elderwood would pine and die. The goddess only knew what would happen to a person who ate of the fruit of that tree. But before I could scream or stop him, Arlen put some in his mouth. There was a reckless look about those greenish eyes of his, almost fury.

"I am not going to starve. . . ." Though in fact he was courting death. He swallowed, seeming pleased. "Rae, they are good," he said offering some to me.

They were, very good, filling and sweet. I ate them because he had. I wanted to share his fate, whatever it was to be, and some of that angry recklessness was in me also; what new punishment could be in store for us? We would defy it. We ate our fill—and no ill came of it. Even looking back, I can discern none. After that we ate of the elderberries whenever we found them, and they sustained us better than any other food we could find. But we had placed ourselves far from other folk with that act, and we knew it and avoided them when we could, as they avoided us.

We traveled in this way for more than a month, heading mostly toward the north and east, away from the Naga and the seven holds of Rahv. There were two snowstorms; they covered our traces for a while and then caused us to leave more. The land grew more rolling between eskers, and more wooded, and even more sparsely settled. Nothing else changed.

So the greater was our surprise when, rounding the curve of a hill one noonday, we found dug into the side of it a house of earth, a soddy, not a stone cottage or a walled garth but simply a soddy set beneath the copse, and out of it came a man in dark clothing. And when he saw us—we were already quite close, having come on him from around the side of the hill because of its forested top—he walked toward us instead of away from us, and he greeted us.

"Arlen, is it not?" he said. "And Lady Cerilla?"

Arlen jerked Bucca to a halt, and we sat stock-still in astonishment. He looked up at us with bright black eyes. He was a small brown man, gnarled, as if he might be very strong for his size, and, oddly, he stood on brown feet quite bare in the snow. I could not think that I had ever seen him before.

"I have heard many rumors," he said, "of runaways from the Sacred Isle."

We had not thought that folk this far away could have heard any such thing, and we glanced at each other in consternation. The man saw the look and laughed softly.

"No fear," he said. "I am no spy. I only wanted to tell you. Look behind you."

"Thank you." Arlen cleared his throat, finding his voice hoarse with a stranger after all these weeks. "Could you spare us some bread?"

"Look behind you, I say." The small man turned away from us and went back inside his earthen home. Arlen and I glanced at each other, uncertain whether the bread was forthcoming, for the fellow's manner had been neither friendly nor hostile. We waited a moment, and then Arlen shrugged and sent Bucca trotting onward.

Before we had gone far we came to a windswept esker. The sand and rock of those mounds did not make good footing for a horse, and any other time Arlen would have skirted it. But this time he sent Bucca struggling up the slope, and when we topped the esker ridge we stopped and turned and looked back the way we had come.

No more than a mile distant a band of horsemen was approaching, more than a dozen in number, armed horsemen; I could see the glint of their helms. And they were coming on at the gallop.

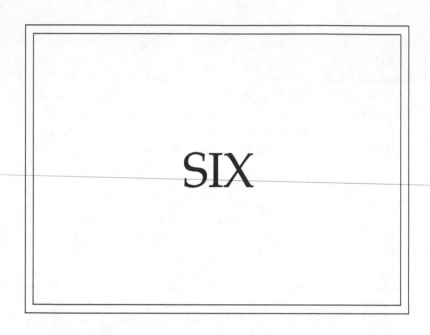

# SIX

There was no question of our outrunning them. Bucca was worn down from poor feeding and much work; he had become slow and sadly docile. We had to stand and fight. And I knew Arl was not yet so starved as to be docile.

He swung a leg over Bucca's neck and slid to the ground. Then he boosted me into the saddle and handed me the reins.

"Flee," he said. "Go, find safety."

"Nonsense!" I flared at him, and he must have known my refusal was final, for he smiled a little, grimly.

"Well then, go and see if you can find me a weapon." He started stacking some of the larger rocks together, making a sort of breastwork for himself.

There was a homestead beyond the esker, half hidden by a fringe of larch. I rode Bucca down there—I had never ridden by myself before, and I grabbed his mane for balance as we skittered down the rocky slope. but as soon as we reached the meadowland I kicked Bucca fiercely for speed, and he was a good horse; he did not fight me for mastery, but galloped me into the garth. Folk fled before us, and I did not waste time asking for succor, but looked about me. There were a pitchfork and a spade standing against the wall. Without getting down I was able to seize them, hanging onto the horse's neck, and after I had struggled upright again we were off. I stopped Bucca at the bottom of the esker and tied him by the reins to a thorn bush. Then I hurried up the slope afoot, using the handle of the spade as a staff to aid me, and was relieved to find Arlen where I had left him.

"They're just behind the copse, yonder," he said in a low voice.

"Have they seen you yet?"

"I think not, or they would have been here before now."

He was hunting about as he spoke, looking for sizable stones. A few large boulders jutted from the top of the esker, looking like fangs, and he had built a hasty wall around them. I put down the pitchfork and spade and started filling my skirt with egg-sized stones to throw. Then the horsemen trotted out from behind the copse and spied us, gave a shout. Arlen picked up the pitchfork as they charged toward us.

"If you have any sense at all," he told me, "you'll flee."

I glared at him.

"Rae—" It was a different tone, an endearment and a plea. I touched his hand, but I did not reply; how could I leave him to face sixteen armed men alone? We stood side by side, at the ready.

But at the base of the esker their charge faltered to a halt. It was bad footing for horses, I knew, but they turned aside before they touched it. What had stopped them? Horses milled about as the men sat them uncertainly, and one hulking man, he who must have been the leader, shouted furiously at the others to continue.

"It's that confounded aura of yours giving them pause!" Arlen exclaimed. "By my body, Rae, perhaps you had better stay with me after all."

I was not listening. I only stared at the captain, the big brute. "It's Eachan," I breathed.

"What?"

"My father's toady. That swine. The one who killed my sister." A taut, burning feeling filled my chest.

He had struck her down with his own ugly fists; only for that she had shown him some spirit, he had bruised and battered her and knocked her head against a stone pillar until she was dead. Then he had buried her with no more ceremony or sorrow than he would have shown for a middling-fine hunting dog. Now Father had sent him for me, it seemed.

"Here they come," said Arlen.

Eachan had bullied them into ascending the slope at last, but they came halfheartedly, the horses soon slowing to a walk. Eachan himself stayed below, lolling on his steed and watching—

The taut feeling in my chest tore open, and rage burst out. I flung a stone with a force that brought forth a yell of pain from somewhere in the ranks.

"Eachan!" I screamed, a witch's shrill. "Ea-chan! Coward! Coward! Murderer! Woman-killer—how many men does it take to help you kill women?" I hurled stones furiously, knowing that none of them could reach him, venting my rage on the men within range. Arlen was throwing stones also; one man had fallen from his horse, stunned, and others were cowering under our pelting. I was not satisfied; I wanted to hurt Eachan.

"Do you not care to murder women yourself these days? Must you have hirelings do it for you?"

His face had gone dark with wrath—and shame, I hoped. But there was no shame in his voice, only the hard edge of malice. "My orders are to take you alive, missy," he boomed.

"The Gwyneda want you for killing. Forward!" he roared at his men.

They heard the threat in his voice and kicked their mounts into a plunging canter, the steeds slipping on the pebbly terrain. Swords drawn and shields at the ready, they made for us. Arlen leveled his pitchfork to hold them off, and I swung the spade at them, screeching, slashing with the edge of it and hitting at their legs and the shoulders of the horses; I had not known such ferocity was in me. As for Arlen, his eyes burned with such reckless despair—or desperation—that I would have been afraid of him had I not known that something of the same sort was in me as well; he lunged fiercely, spearing his enemies with his awkward weapon. Some already bore wounds, and they fell back for fear of him.

"Surround them!" Eachan bellowed.

There was, indeed, no reason why they should not take us on all sides and not in the front merely, where our breastwork was. Some of them went around to come at us from behind, and I put my back to Arlen's back, defending him as best I could, swinging my spade as high as my arms would take it. But from time to time one of our enemies would reach over me to prick him in the shoulder. Never badly; each such attack gave me a surge of new force that sent them swiftly into retreat. But Arlen must have known I was tiring. He maneuvered us so that we each had some breastwork to one side, wheeling us around a quarter turn—and then I could see Eachan still down below, watching. The sight enraged me.

"Coward!" I shouted at him. "Murdering coward! Are you afraid to face me youself, you who killed my sister?"

He came up the slope like a charging bear. Once you have called a man a coward enough times, it seems, he is no longer afraid. Arlen saw him coming and leaped forward to meet him with a wild shout, spurned his own breastwork with his foot to send it scudding down the esker slope. It took the feet out from under Eachan's mount, but Eachan leaped clear as the beast came crashing down. He charged afoot, sword raised, and Arlen awaited him between the fanglike rocks. Eachan's men fell back a few paces, glad enough to leave the field to him for the time—

And Eachan broke Arlen's pitchfork with one blow of his sword.

I sprang forward, battering the brute with my spade, now blunted; he shrugged off my beating as if he had not felt it. And Arlen stood staunchly between his rocks, not yielding, fighting with nothing more than his bare hands. Eyes ablaze, no hint of fear in his face, trying to wrest the sword from Eachan's grasp, while I was hurling myself against Eachan from the side, kicking and clawing and tearing at him. We both fought like lunatics, but it was no use. Eachan was like a bull for strength, and he was cruel, teasing us. He gave Arlen a few wounds, cuts, shallow wounds to hurt and bleed, and then he gave him a few deeper, trying to make him cry out. And all the while Arlen withstood him gamely—and I broke my spade on Eachan's back—and then he ran his sword through Arlen's thigh, and Arlen went to one knee with the pain, his eyes afire with hatred. I stood woodenly, beyond screaming or clawing at Eachan and hitting him; I felt as if my heart had been torn out. Then Eachan stabbed Arlen in the shoulder so that he fell back on the ground.

"Belly next," Eachan said. And then—

And then I took a rock as large as a smith's anvil, picked it up in both hands, lifted it high, and smashed Eachan's head with it, lifted it high as I should not have been able to do and smashed it again. He lay on the stones, and I split his head open, and I stood on his body and continued to pound at his head with my monstrous rock until what lay there had turned to something other than Eachan. I ground my heel in what had been his brains. When at last I was tired, I looked up— Arlen! I had forgotten him, and he lay moaning in pain. I went to him quickly and pressed a fold of my skirt against his worst wound, the shoulder wound. Hazily I became aware that Eachan's men were sitting their horses all around us, and I looked up at them. It did not appear as if they were going to help me, so I dismissed them.

"Go away," I told them.

They shook their heads. "We are taking you to our lord," one of them said, meaning Rahv. "There is to be a reward for your capture."

I chose not to understand. "Go away," I said again. "I must care for him. Leave us."

Several of them dismounted and began to approach us from all sides. They moved slowly, cautiously, as if they expected me to be dangerous.

As, indeed, I suppose I was. But I did not feel dangerous just then; I felt exhausted, heartbroken and helpless. They were not going to let me be, they were going to take me away from Arlen, leave him there to die. I could not bear it. All powers that be. . . . There were no words in me. All was feeling, despair and plea, but the feeling was a prayer.

The rocks of the esker started to stir.

The men froze where they stood, some few feet from me. And well they might. For out of every cranny, out from under the boulders, out from between the rocks that had been our small stronghold, out from under Eachan's body, burrowing out of the very sand—snakes crawled, snakes, so it seemed, by the hundred. Most were small, but some bulked as long as a man and as thick as my arm, and they were black, shiny bead-black with golden eyes, and yellow like the sand, and brown, all hues of brown, dun, ochre, umber, and some were vipers, I could tell by the squat shape of their heads. I took Arlen's upper body into my arms with some thought of protecting him, but I was too spent to be very frightened, even though the snakes slithered right past us. They were all darting down the esker slopes, toward my enemies. And that presence was there too, that wavering thickness in the air, I had never seen it so plainly—with them, as if directing them. The men turned pallid, as ashen as corpses, calling back and forth to each other in voices thick with fear, some retreating slowly and some afraid to move.

And then a rumbling sounded from within earth itself. And the boulders rolled aside, and a shower of sand, a fountain, burst out of the top of the esker. And out of the cavity it left behind a forked tongue came forth, a tongue as long as a sword but sinuous, flickering; and then dreamlike, swaying and graceful, a serpent's head of a size to go with it, a head as large as a chest or a treasure casket, beautiful—I could not help but think it beautiful, though I knelt rooted with fear. For every scale on it was distinct to my sight, so close did it sway over me, like a polished shield, and all colors shimmered in them, bice blue and amber and verdigris and an earthy red as of clay, and its eyes were as large as a cloak brooch but more like giant shining jewels, rubies, blood red with black slits in them, like cat's eyes, except that when it moved its head the slit pointed always toward earth—it looked at all of us in that fashion, with a fixed gaze that seemed relentlessly to pierce us. There was no question any longer among Eachan's men of slow retreat. They yelled in terror and fled, most on horseback but a few of them afoot, for their mounts were as terrified as they were and had broken away when they could. They ran, and the sound of their shouting faded into distance.

I sat quite still with Arlen's head in my arms, for I would not leave him. He was breathing steadily, but his eyes had closed, and if he had seen the giant serpent of the esker he gave no sign of it. We stared at each other, snake and I—and as if for my benefit the creature sank from sight. The esker folded in on itself, sand and rock settled, and all was as it had been before. When I looked about me, even the smaller serpents were gone.

I got up, trying to rouse Arlen without hurting him too much. "Arl, come on," I begged, tugging at him. "Come, we have to get you onto Bucca."

The sound of my voice compelled him somewhat. He blinked and reached up to me, and I was able to help him to his feet, support him with his arm over my shoulder, my arm around his waist. We slid as much as walked over the top of the esker and down the far side toward where the horse stood tethered. But we somehow remained upright; and when I leaned him against the saddle, placed his foot in the stirrup, and boosted him he was able to mount. The effort cost him mightily; he groaned and fainted, falling forward onto Bucca's neck, and I had to grasp his hand to keep him from falling off. Blood on the hand, on his shoulders, his head, his thigh. . . . Goddess of mercy, help us.

I found the reins somehow and urged Bucca toward the nearest refuge, the homestead whence I had taken the tools. Folk looked out the window; I saw them. They could not see the esker beyond the larches, could not have seen the fighting or the great serpent, but they would see the blood if they were not blind and know Arlen was hurt. They had to help him.

They disappeared from the window as I drew nearer. No one answered my knock, and the door did not yield to my touch.

"Help us," I appealed to the blank boards. "He is wounded. He will die if you do not give us aid."

Silence, and the unmoving door.

"Open up!"

I could envision them clustered inside, pretending not to be there when I knew better, and the thought maddened me.

"Open up, or by the goddess I will curse you with the curse of the wandering dead who are denied—"

"I'll not open to ye nohow!" a man's voice bawled from within, interrupting me. "Curse all ye like; how can ye curse me with aught worse than what ye are, ye death-dogged wench—"

"Take him to the witch!" a woman shrieked. "Take him to the devil in his soddy, and let us be, and hap he'll be addled enough to succor ye."

The witch. The devil in his soddy. If it were the small brown man who had greeted us, he might.

"Curse you anyway," I muttered, turning and leading Bucca away.

It seemed that there was nothing for it but to go back up over the esker. I sweated with fear, doing that, now that I knew what lay beneath. But nothing stirred under my feet, and as we climbed my fear of the serpent gave way to a sharper and more stinging fear. Arlen's breathing had gone shallow, his face the color of old snow, his hand cold in mine, as cold as the cold winter wind.

"Mother, help him," I begged the wind as we hurried down the farther side, too fast for safety.

A stretch of snowy moorland, and then the copse, the dugout in the hillside just below it. The roof was of grass, the walls all of piled peat, smelling damp and earthy even in the deep winter freeze. I shall always think of that place when I smell the sod smell, and of that time, and of the spur of fear in me.

The door was of wood, and it stood closed. I rapped and cried out, "Please hurry—"

It opened.

Several sorts of feelings went through me in an unexpected surge: hope, gratitude, rage, desolation, maybe a few more, but mostly hope—even though the man had been called a witch, and even though the expression of his face was not promising, not welcoming, not anything of the usual human sort, merely brown and blank.

"A bed," I said incoherently. "He needs—help, some warmth, a healer—"

"There is no bed," he said.

At the time it seemed a setback beyond bearing. "No bed!" I shouted, fairly ranting at him. "Do you not sleep?"

"Not in the usual way." Nevertheless, he stepped back, opening the door wide to me. "But we will put something down for him. Bring him in."

"Horse and all?" I railed. I am sure I do not know why he did not despair of me and shut the door in my face. He was offering us aid, and I was so demented, I was shouting at him.

Nor did he shout back. Instead, he merely stepped to Bucca's side, took Arlen down in his arms, and carried him easily within.

# SEVEN

The soddy seemed very much like any cottage toward the front, except that the floor and walls were made of earth. Farther back, though, it began to get hillocky, with mounds of loose earth piled up and roots hanging down. I didn't care. It was warm. A peat fire burned on a small brick hearth. The man had me lay our blankets right before it, and then he put Arlen down on them, gently, and I began to peel blood-soaked clothing from him.

"Wait," the man said. "Boil water first. He is not bleeding any more; leave him."

How could I just leave him lying there? But the small brown man already had a kettle of water suspended over the fire, and he was crumbling herbs of several sorts into it. I suspected bitterly that he could care for Arlen better than I.

"And you," he said to the center of the room, "out. It is crowded enough in here without you."

At first I thought he was speaking to me, and I bristled. But before I could snap at him again I felt a peculiar sort of lightening sensation, a clarity, that I could not identify. It had come on me so gradually and had been with me so long that I took a long moment to comprehend: the presence was gone.

"It is waiting for you outside," the witch said. "Cold does not dismay it."

He spoke offhandedly, as of something he understood completely. I stared at him from my seat on the dirt floor. Here was one who would speak to me, vouchsafe me answers. The thought took my breath.

"But—what is it?" I whispered at last.

"Why, a dead person." He seemed surprised at my ignorance. "It has attached itself to you for some reason."

"But—what reason?"

"Why, you must tell. Is it revenge, perhaps? Have you been cruel to someone who has since died?" He spoke with complete detachment, as if it meant nothing to him whether I were a cruel person or not. But I had never had occasion or inclination to be a villain. I shook my head.

"Has a parent of yours been cruel to such a one? Sometimes such spirits are unreasonable in their vengeance."

Certainly my father was cruel. "But it does not seem vengeful, really," I said. "It has done me no harm except that folk flee from me when it is with me, which is a nuisance—and at times it has done me only good, showed me food, given pause to my enemies. I think it was by the aid of this—this death presence that my father's men were routed just now."

"Why, then," said the witch, "it must be someone who has loved you."

I could not think who, and my mind gave it up wearily. I watched him take the steaming water from the fire. He had found a clean cloth and was preparing to dress Arlen's wounds, and, unsmiling, he beckoned me to help him. He never smiled, I noticed, but neither did he frown. I did not care to wonder why he was helping us, but I did wonder who he was, or what. He seemed as dry and tough as a seasoned oak knot, moving about silently on his bare brown twisted feet. I could not begin to guess his age. "Do you have a name?" I blurted at him.

"Briony. Or Bri, if you like."

I did not like; I was half frightened of him. But his hands were deft and gentle as he washed and coaxed the stiffened clothing off Arlen's wounds, bathed the wounds and inspected them, and applied a thick, yellow salve. Arlen hardly stirred under his touch, even when he lifted and turned him. Briony took new bleached cotton cloth, washed soft but never used, and ripped it into strips for bandaging. I helped him wrap them on. Then he brought a goatskin of wine, and as he poured it into a noggin I saw it, black. That might have been because of the dim light, oil lamp light, but I caught distinctly the scent of elderberries, and I must have stiffened, for he looked at me.

"Yes," he said, "I eat them too. Here, hold his head up for me."

I had Arlen's head in my lap at the time, so I took it into my arms, steadying it while Briony held the noggin to his lips and made him sip from it by stroking his throat. Slowly, Arlen drank what Briony gave him.

"Elderberry wine is good for most ills," the witch added, as if in afterthought. "Would you like some?" he asked me.

I shook my head without thinking.

"Well," He sat the noggin down. "Arlen will do nicely for a while now, and I will watch him. You had better tend to your horse if it is not to perish."

Bucca! How long had he been standing in the cold? I hurried out. He had not even been tethered, it seemed, but he had not strayed far; he was pawing at the snow, trying to find some withered grass to eat. There was no barn by the soddy, not even a cattle shed. Nowhere to take him for shelter except up in the copse. I led him there and got the saddle and bridle off him and put my mantle over him for want of a blanket. There were some laurel bushes growing amidst the trees, too low to do him any good, but I considered that if I could make him a sort of framework and thatch it with boughs, anything against the cold wind—I felt absurdly anxious to care well for the horse, perhaps because I felt so helpless regarding Arlen.

I went in. Arlen lay as I had left him, and a good smell of meat filled the soddy; Briony was cooking something in the kettle.

"May I take the ax," I asked him, "and cut some limbs and bushes to make a shelter for him?" Meaning Bucca.

"What is the steed to eat?" Briony asked, his face expressionless as ever, and I shook my head. I did not know. Briony continued to stare at me, though the stare was not at all hard.

"Where is that dead one of yours?" he asked me. "Did it follow you about, outside?"

"No!" I stood dumbfounded. Gone, the presence was gone! Just when I was beginning to think who it might be—

"If you were to take the horse to the neighbors now that you are without your death dog," Briony said, "I believe they might put it in the barn for you."

Too stunned and spent by the events of the day to feel diffident about facing them again, I turned forthwith and started out to see to it.

"And be quick," Briony said. "Dark is coming on, and I smell the beginnings of a storm."

All the more reason to get Bucca under roof. I closed the door, but he opened it after me.

"And borrow some bedding," he said, "if you want to have any, for there is none here."

"Very well," I muttered, breaking into a run.

If even the bridle had been on Bucca I could have scrambled on somehow and ridden him, but I had dragged and heaved his gear into the soddy, and I was not about to go back yet again. So I led Bucca rather than rode him, with my green sash looped around his neck, and we trudged off into the gathering darkness.

Over the esker yet once more, by the mighty Mother, too tired this time to be very much afraid.

Briony had deemed rightly. The outlanders at the homestead seemed embarrassed rather than afraid to see me, willing enough to help me, anxious to send me away in a state of goodwill. They put Bucca in the barn and heaped his manger with hay and corn. They brought me blankets, a pillow, a straw tick. They were quick about it, but wind was rising and daylight gone when I set off again. I noticed that none of them offered to see me back with a lantern, big brawny folk though they were. They smiled nervously, and I guessed that their fear was not all gone.

No matter, I thought. It was not far to the soddy.

I had no more than topped the esker when the storm struck with force. Hissing, seething, coiling, stinging wind—the old stories say that the winds are disembodied serpents from out of the four linked lakes of the Catena, winged vipers, asps out of the Afterworld, and I believe it, they chill one so. And snow came with the wind. I could feel it prickling me in the night, and at once I could see nothing, and I was no longer sure in what direction the soddy lay, for I suspected the wind had pushed me off my path. Wind be cursed. This was the cold north wind again, old Bora, goddess in windserpent form, and I hated her.

I trudged on, facing the wind, not very afraid, for I had an armload of blankets—I could survive the night by wrapping up in them once I found the lee of a slope or a coppice. But I badly wanted to find my way back to Arlen's side, to know how he was, to bring a pillow for his head. I blundered on into the storm long after a sensible person would have turned aside to find shelter. And just when I was beginning to pant with frustration I spied a light, off to the left and some small way ahead, a soft whitish light, and I quickened my lagging steps as I turned toward it.

High, keening note in the storm's clamor—

I stopped where I stood, my heart pounding and sweat streaming down between my breasts even in the freezing cold, and in that instant I learned the feeling of unearthly fear. It was a spectral light, corpse white, and the spector was the sow, the hideous old sow who eats her own farrow, the young she has just given life. I saw the small leg of one hanging out of her mouth, the blood of it running down her jaw. She was as red as of clay or the reddish moon, and I saw her great dugs hanging down by the dozen, and the farrow squealing about her feet, and the black moon-marks on her hams, and her white ears. Then she turned on me the glare of her eye, a small, bloody, baleful eye, and I turned and ran. The night was full of the sounds of death to me then, the blackness of night the color of death, all of earth a great tomb of death and snow its shroud.

Sheer weariness slowed me to a walk soon, but I had lost my way, and if indeed I had ever known where I was going I no longer did. I stopped and stilled my weeping, hearkening and trying to think.

Then a light blazed out in the darkness, far brighter than the other and from a different place, too bright to be a lamp— and even if it were a lamp it could not be from the soddy, I felt sure, not off in such an unlikely direction. No matter. I trudged toward it, the wind to my back now, a great ragged moth drawn to the flame, blankets trailing like brown frayed wings. It seemed quite distant for such a bright light, and when I drew closer to it at last I could not believe the blaze of it, like no other flame I had ever seen, unwavering—

It was a lamp in the window of the soddy.

A magical lamp. Briony had placed it there to guide me, and as soon as I opened the door and he saw me he got up and snuffed it out; the ordinary flame of the oil lamp seemed dim as midnight by comparison. He went back to his place by

Arlen's side, and I stood just within the doorway, panting.

"Death is out in the night," I said. "I have seen her."

"I know," he said. He held a bowl of broth and was trying to feed it to Arlen. I put down the borrowed bedding and took off my wet mantle and went to help him, but Arlen's head seemed lifeless in my arms, heavy, his face hot and fevered, his pulse a fluttering thing, a dying lacewing. No, not dying—my mind denied it. But he seemed very far from us, and he was not taking the broth for all of Briony's urging.

"Arl!" I begged him.

The sound of my voice moved him somewhat, for he stirred slightly and took a spoonful.

"Keep talking to him," Briony said.

I coaxed and pleaded and called to him, and we got some of the nourishment down him at last. I laid down the soft pallet for him, the pillow for his head, and we moved him onto them as gently as we could, but we need not have been fearful of hurting him; he was far away again and did not so much as moan. I took away our old dirty blankets and covered him with the cleaner ones from the homestead, and then I sat looking at him, wishing there were something more I could do.

"Eat," said Briony, offering me a bowl of broth and a hunk of bread. But I shook my head. "Eat," he repeated. The tone of his voice did not change, but he put the things into my hands. "It is no use you should starve yourself, Cerilla."

It was true. I would be of no use to Arlen if I sickened. I nibbled at the bread, took tiny sips of the broth. The food went down slowly, for fear clenched my stomach against it. Briony must have seen my fear, or perhaps he felt fear himself, for he sat beside me and talked to me about Arlen.

"There are no vitals hurt in him," he said. "Flesh wounds all, painful, and he has lost a quantity of blood, and the loss weakens him. And there is always the risk of contagion. But he is young and strong, and he loves you with a love that would send him leaping through fire. I see no reason why he should not soon be well. The old sow will have to stray in the storm tonight."

I glanced up at him in shock muted by weariness. "How did you know?"

"I know nothing. It is only a manner of speaking."

"But you put the lamp out, you knew I was wandering—"

"Anyone would get lost in a night like this. And it is no great trouble to say the appropriate spell." He shrugged and got up to settle himself on the hearth by Arlen's side. "Cerilla, you are spent, and I have had nothing to occupy me for some days now. Sleep well. I will watch Arlen this night."

I laid out the saddle pad for myself and covered myself with our well-used blankets, but I could not go to sleep at once, not without Arlen by my side. My body ached, every fiber of me, with a grief and a dread I could not reason away. I trusted Briony to look after Arl by then, I wanted to go to sleep, I knew I needed sleep, but something within me lay crying, and as exhaustion took me I knew what it was: the child who had cried when my mother had been put into the ground. Mind tried to calm me, but heart knew: Arlen was in deadly danger.

I slept raggedly and awoke in the morning not much the better for it. At once I knew that Arlen was worse. His face was flushed, clammy and feverish to the touch, and all his wounds were swollen and sore and oozing through their bandages. Briony was sitting by his side with a wooden bucket of cold water and a square of cotton cloth.

"Is he in pain?" I asked, going over.

"He does not seem to be. I would take more comfort if he were; it would show that he was fighting the shadows. He has been shaking with chills half the night, though his face is hot. And he does not seem to dream or struggle. Here." He handed me the wet cloth and took up the bolt to tear more bandaging.

"Folk come here for charms from time to time," he added, though I had not asked him why he tore up good cloth for Arlen, "and they pay me in whatever they have to offer. I have no need of this cotton right now." He took the old bandage

from Arlen's thigh and threw it into the fire. The wound
looked and smelled worse than I had expected, and I gagged.

"Contagion," Briony muttered. The word sent a shudder
through me.

The next few days passed in a haze of misery. I sat by
Arlen's side for the most part, talking to him from time to
time, pleading with him or exhorting him or sometimes even
scolding him; none of it had any effect that I could see. Laving
his hot forehead, putting peat on the fire, guarding him from
chills, helping Briony change the bandages. Briony cooked,
mixed potions; I am sure he tried every remedy he knew of.
He made spicy, aromatic plasters, which he placed on the
wounds to draw off the heat, and he burned incense to purify
the room. He brewed possets and ground yael horn to put in
the wine for strength, but within days Arlen had slipped away
to the point where he would take neither broth nor possets nor
wine.

"Let me sit with him tonight," I said to Briony one evening
by lamplight. I felt sure he was tired, for all his day had been
spent in nothing but nursing Arlen, and that to no avail. I
noticed a crease between his bright black eyes.

"Perhaps some better thought will come to me," he admitted, "if I refresh myself. Call me if you start nodding." And he
went off into the shadows at the back of the soddy, where the
earth formed such odd hillocks and piles, where the roots
reached down from the copse above, forming an entanglement. I soon lost sight of him back there, and I did not know
what he was doing. Nor did I care to know. I chose to assume
that he lay down and slept. Sometime during the night he
came out again, and I went to my bed and dozed for a while.
But no new thought had come to him, and Arlen was no better
with the next day's dawn.

I took the burden of nursing on myself, insofar as I could,
once I had learned the ways of the house, the wheres of water
and wine and pans and the like. Busying myself with such
things helped me contain my distress somewhat. Briony

mixed more poultices, and then out of a chest he brought forth books, a weighty herbal and a smaller book with a black cover, a spell book. Most of the day and into lamplight again he searched through them, and evidently he found nothing of use, for he put them down at last with a sigh.

"You say you do charms," I suggested timidly; it is a bad business to anger a witch, and I had stayed away from talk of magic until then. But I was becoming desperate. "Is there nothing you can say, a spell—?"

"A mandrake can only do so much!" he burst out.

I gaped, and he turned away sharply, having said more than he intended.

"A *mandrake?*" I exclaimed.

"Yes. A mandrake," he responded sharply, turning back and striding a step or two toward me, as if I had accused him of something. "Why do you think I live in earth? Most men are not so fond of dirt." He touched his low ceiling. "But I go back there, amongst the roots whence I came, and burrow in earth to my knees, to my neck, cover myself with it if I can, for it feeds me better than meat. Are you dismayed?"

I shook my head, my mouth still agape. "It is just that—I have never seen a mandrake, and I did not know they became so—alive."

"I am a rather vital one. Rumor has it I am sprung from a hanged man's semen that spurted onto the ground. His death seed. I am expert with aphrodisiacs." He grimaced, mocking himself. "You and Arlen do not need that of me."

"But, Bri—" I had not called him Bri before, and I stopped, confused.

"What? What is it?"

"I do not care if you *eat* dirt," I told him earnestly. "You have been good to us."

"I have my ethics," he said stiffly. "No heart, not in any human sense, but I have loyalty, ambition, pride in my craft. And right now I have frustration."

"So there is nothing more you can do for Arlen." I said it

because it would have hurt him to say it, perhaps as much as it hurt me. I felt the pang like a lance head of despair.

"No." He got up, swinging his sinewy arms, brown, knotty arms much like the tough roots that hung down not far away. He faced toward them, and away from me, as he spoke. "I am good for all the everyday magics," he said, sounding dry, toneless. "Charms for colic and clubfoot and pockmarks, spells for crops or childbirth or calving or spitefulness or the return of unrequited love. I am especially competent in regard to love. But the great things—" He gestured, arms lifted. "—death and healing and redemption—they are not for me. The goddess has charge of them."

# EIGHT

Arlen was dying. I did not know how I could bear it, but there was no way to doubt it, no room left for hope. He no longer responded to anything, not even my voice, not even the pain when Briony lanced his wounds as a measure of last resort. He lay as if he were already dead, his face no longer flushed but pallid, his breathing shallow and out of rhythm. Briony and I both sat up with him that night, though we knew we could not help him, though he was not even aware that we were there.

"He should not be taken away for those wounds!" Briony burst out when the hearth fire had burned down to embers, shielding us with shadows so that I could not distinctly see his face. "He should not be dying. The cuts were clean and not very deep. He is young, strong, comely enough for all normal purposes and very much in love with one who is worthy of all love—"

I looked at him, startled by the sudden anger or yearning in his voice, by the way he fell silent abruptly, as if he had said too much. I wondered if Briony had ever known love, he who dealt in spells of love. How or whom does a mandrake love? A flame flared briefly from the embers to show me his face, but as usual, I could not read it.

"One who returns his love," he went on more collectedly. "He has a life of love ahead of him, everything to live for. I cannot understand why he is failing. He is no coward; he fought armed and mounted men for your sake, fought them like a berserker. Why is he not fighting this death that lies on him?"

We sat in silence for a while.

"I have never understood men," Briony exclaimed into the darkness with a passion I had not expected from him. "If I were he, I would be fending off the serpent with my bare hands and all the strength in my body."

"Do not rail at him," I said, though not sharply.

"I am not! There must be a reason, if only I could understand—Cerilla, tell me about him."

That awoke a vague wonder in me. "You seem already to know all about us," I said. "Our names, how we fled from the Sacred Isle—"

"I hear the talk of the underworld, that is all. It travels fast, but it is no more than gossip, rumors. Tell me the things you truly know."

There were so many things, the seemingly inconsequential things that had made him not a winterking but Arlen to me, Arlen my beloved and sometimes my vexation. The way his ears itched so that he drove me to distraction with noises and scratching, and the way he always had to hug something to go to sleep. The way he swaggered when he was tired. Things even less definable: the glance over his shoulder when we were riding, hands twirling locks of Bucca's mane—if there was an essence about Arlen, how was I to tell it to Briony?

"Cerilla," he urged.

"Animals," I said, for want of anything better to say. "He adores animals. Whenever he sees an animal, even a coney or a squirrel, he looks at it, he points it out to me. Kine, swine, he sees them all with such excitement. . . . Well, I suppose there could not have been too many animals on the Sacred Isle, and he looks at other things too, the countryside, and exclaims; sometimes he is like a delighted child. But animals—he wants to touch them, to be with them. When we are in a barn, he goes from stall to stall, even if it is only cattle or donkeys there, chirruping and giving water and washing sore eyes. When we are with the sheep in the field, he plucks the parasites off them."

"Why animals?" said Briony softly.

I shrugged. "Why not? From what I have heard, the beasts are far kinder than most folk on the Sacred Isle."

I felt him looking at me, so I went on.

"They did terrible things to the boys sometimes, to toughen them. They give them whips and set them against each other, or all against one, which was even worse, though Arlen said— Lonn would never strike at him, not even if it meant punishment, but Arlen struck at Lonn once because he was made to, and then he wept and could not sleep afterward, though Lonn forgave him."

"Lonn?"

"His friend—" I swallowed. "Who died in his stead."

"Arlen has been favored with such a friend? Few of us ever find a true friend or a true love. Arlen has both! And yet his has been a terrible life." Briony sounded dazed.

"Yes." I plunged on. "Twice a year, in preparation for the ceremonials of sacred kingship, they would have the boys over the age of ten taste of a mock death to harden them against the real death to come. They would hang each one by a noose around the neck, hang them until they swooned and then take them down, and when they revived they were mocked if they had struggled, and sometimes a puny one was not taken down, so they never really knew, beforehand—" I stopped, feeling sick. "I can speak no more of this."

"Nor do I care to hear much more." Briony got up and gave fuel to the fire. "Yet, if I only knew. . . ."

"Knew what?"

"Knew Arlen, truly knew what it was like to be Arlen." He sat down beside me again. "If I could somehow enter into his heart and mind, to understand him, I wonder if I could not somehow help him. . . . Cerilla, you should have taken him to a better witch. I have been envying him." The admission came out harshly.

"Great Mother of us all, why?" I was astonished.

"He has—everything, youth, his freedom, your love. . . . But he has paid." Briony got up abruptly. "I believe I had better go think."

"Bri—"

He would not look at me, but he listened.

"I do not understand him either. He has never told me, but—I have sensed a despair, a dark wound, a bleeding—within. . . ."

Briony went back into his earthworks to be by himself.

I sat with Arlen, quite alone. He did not move or moan; he required nothing of me. From time to time, feeling helpless, I would speak to him, whisper his name, but he did not respond to me, did not even stir. I decided I need no longer forbear from hurting him, and I got down on the pallet with him, took his head and upper body into my arms, rocked him, held him against my breasts. I could hear him breathe, shallow, gasping breaths, but he hung as limp as a lifeless doll in my arms, and anguish set me to weeping. I held him and wept until dawn, and with the dawn he was no better. Dim silver-gold light showed me his face pale and still, and though I yet felt a pulse in him there was no touch of color to his skin; he might as well have been a corpse. Something in my mind crackled angrily, and I called on the dead.

"Lonn!"

I whispered it at first, then spoke up more urgently. He had helped us once, maybe more than once. Perhaps he would help us again.

"Lonn!"

A thickening came into the air of the soddy, and a heaviness. That familiar presence. I knew it, I should have known it before. He had been with us since the cenotaph. He had never truly left us until Briony had sent him away.

This time, since I had called him, I could almost see him. Wavering, insubstantial, not truly connected with the earthen floor or anything around him, but still—I thought I could make out a human figure, the shadow of a face. He stood there, or shimmered there, unmoving.

"Lonn," I appealed, "you had power, you could have been a great wizard. Help him! You have saved him from death before. Save him yet this once more."

Nothing happened except that Briony came out of the back of the soddy, looking earthy and weary.

"So," he remarked, "he loved you too."

I could not comprehend at the time, thinking it was Arlen whom Lonn loved. "Lonn," I pleaded, "speak to him, send him back to me."

I could not clearly recognize the shadowdrift of a face or see the look on it. But it seemed to me that Lonn, or whatever answered to the name of Lonn, stiffened and moved back a trifle, as if discomfited.

"He is incorporeal," Briony said to me. "He cannot speak. Moreover, it is of no use to call on the dead to heal the living." He came over and sat by me to take the sting from his words. "Everything about the dead calls us to death."

"Then you mean—" I whispered, aghast at what I had done.

"No, no, it is of no great harm, having him here." Briony hastened to reassure me. "He has been with you for weeks, so one more visit is of small moment. It is only—Lonn is dead, so how is he to comprehend that you wish Arlen to live? That Arlen should live?"

We sat numbly; we sat and Lonn waved in air, as the

morning light grew stronger, aureate, showing us Arlen's fair young face so still, so shining pale. Gold and russet lights touched his hair. With an odd clarity I noticed the curve of his eyelashes, shining the color of bronze, of orichalc, very fine over his lidded eyes. How lovely he was, almost as if the winterking glory were on him again.

"Do the dead love death," I asked Briony wistfully, "as the living love life?"

He stirred to answer, but then he sat up arrow straight and stared at me. And then he leaped up with a shout and darted across the room, brushing aside Lonn's presence with the haste of his passing, making for the worktable where he kept his herbs and powders and the stone slabs and tools for mixing them.

"Cerilla, you have given me the answer!" he shouted, frantically concocting. "Love, life—they were never allowed to love it, these sacred kings, don't you see? Half hanged, mocked if they struggled—" He reached up to snap off one from a bundle of dried roots. "And love spells I can do. But what is life?" He turned on me suddenly, his black eyes glinting. "What are the things that make life? Cerilla, quickly!"

"Why, everything," I faltered. "The animals. The horse. . . ." Moving with sudden unreasoning sureness, I went and found a horsehair on the saddle pad I had been using for a pallet, a long gray hair from Bucca's mane. "Here," I said, handing it to Briony.

"And one of yours." He took it from my head with an odd tenderness in the twist of his deft brown hand. "All right. What else?"

"The world. . . ."

"A pinch of earth from outside. And a blade of grass, and a twig or a leaf if you can find them. Make haste."

I ran to fetch the things. I had not been outdoors in so long, I was dazed to find the snow was melting.

"That will have to do for now," Briony said when I brought

him what he needed. "I could do better with a little more time, but we will put the rest in words. Now, the wine—"

I brought him the elderberry wine, poured half a tumbler full. Briony added his potion.

"And we are going to get this down him if it kills him," he said grimly.

We nearly did kill him in stark fact, administering that draught. He choked on it in his stupor, and Briony had to beat him to make him breathe again. Then he swallowed, and groaned—and then I breathed; I had been holding my breath and pleading with the goddess. Then he swallowed the rest of it, slowly.

"Sunshine," Briony was saying, "and the way it dapples through leaves, and there will be the first buds of leaves in a month or so. Trees. Oak, ash, willow; the whitethorn will flower in May. Birds. The robin and the little crowned wren. Swans on the Naga, are there not? Soon the swallows will return and nest. Horses, are they not beautiful? So curving their necks. And the broad sweep of the moors, so much sky, and sunrise and sunset—have you ever seen the heather in bloom, Arlen? Have you?"

Arlen stirred and muttered as if in pain or protest.

"Arl!" I called to him.

"You talk to him, Cerilla," Bri said.

"But I have never been in the world much—"

"Surely you have dreamed."

"I dream of people. Of love, friendship."

Briony turned away and went back to his worktable.

"Do you feel that too, Arl?" I appealed to him. "The warm hearth fire, and the cup of the house served to the guest. It need not be a grand house, not a tower keep, only snug, a cottage. And a dog by the fire, a dog with warm brown eyes, and some chickens by the door. And—a cradle. . . . And the corn growing nearby, golden. Arlen?" I waited. "Arl, can you hear me?"

He moved one hand just a flicker and whispered something.

I could not hear what it was, but I nearly wept with joy, for I knew then that he was going to be well.

He moaned and muttered and whispered from time to time all day. Bri and I took turns talking to him, and sometimes he seemed to move or speak in answer to my voice. Toward evening Briony gave him another potion—a better one, stronger, he said, as it had had more time to steep. And he said a sort of charm he had composed about swans and swallows and the little crowned wren. Briony told me to sleep that night, but Arlen kept me awake with tossings and groanings and senseless mumblings; sometimes he nearly shouted. The sounds were as sweet as birdsong to me, sweet as bells that hail the dawn after the long dark night.

In the morning we gave him broth and bread and wine as well as a potion, and he took them all eagerly, though he seemed hardly to know where he was. Then he slept, now that the time for sleeping had passed and I was waking. But sometime before midday he opened his eyes and looked at me.

"Rae," he said, holding out a hand toward me shakily, and I went and drew him up toward me to kiss him.

"Ooch," he said, "that hurts."

He was too weak to talk much, and he spent that day eating everything that we would give him. Some of the color came back to his face. And we changed the bandages; the swelling had gone down, and the wounds looked as if they were beginning to heal. I believe Arlen had not been aware, before, of his many injuries, and as he took accounting he seemed shocked and sickened, although he had recalled himself sufficiently to refuse to cry out in pain. We could see that he was not entirely indifferent to it, however. Afterward I went to him and took his head in my lap, auburn hair and white wrapping, and he lay there and looked at Briony and asked what I had not dared.

"Why are you helping us?"

"Professional challenge," said Briony crisply.

"Love of craft," I remarked wryly to Arlen, "has made him

devote days to us, turn away others, lose sleep for your sake, spend his winter's supply of food on us. . . "

Briony stared straight at us with a flat brown face and black expressionless eyes, as if daring us to think otherwise.

"Something hurtful has changed," Arlen said to him at last. "Thank you."

The next day, when he was stronger, he told us what it was.

"I felt as if—all reason argued against it, but I felt somehow that I had failed. That I had betrayed my calling, that I was a coward and a renegade for not dying. Lonn's death reproached me. He and all the others had died. Why did I deserve to live?"

"Arl," I exclaimed, "there is no deserving about it! Only living."

"I know that now."

"But why did you not tell me how you felt?" I sat holding him in my arms again, head and upper body cradled against my shoulder, my bosom.

"I did not understand it myself. It was all so—unthinking."

"You were feeling as they had taught you to feel," Briony said.

"Yes. But now I feel differently." Suddenly he sat straight up, out of my arms and unsupported, and he looked hard at the apparition that wavered at the center of the room.

"Lonn," he said to it, "I am going to leave you behind."

"How did you know?" I marveled.

"I always suspected. It seemed so apt that he should haunt me. But now it no longer seems fitting. For, let the dead think whatever they like, the reward is mine. I am alive. Alive!" He suddenly gave a great fierce shout of laughter; defiance rang in it, and joy. The presence of Lonn shrank visibly from that joy.

"Alive, breathing, loving, beloved!" Arlen cried. "With a body for pleasure and a true love to cherish and the wide sky for riding under. It is all mine, for any reason and no reason, and I embrace it." He sank back against me, his strength gone for the time but his green eyes shining. "So leave me to it."

The presence of Lonn went out, leaving the air of the soddy clear again.

"He was your friend," I said to Arlen, puzzled. "Why would he wish to trouble you?"

Arlen shrugged, then grimaced with the pain of his shoulder wound and lay back with a sigh. "I do not think he means me any harm," he said. "It is only—I do not know what he wants of me. Perhaps nothing. Do you know, Briony?"

"I suspect he does not desire anything of you," Bri said, "any more than I do." His words seemed plain, but the look in his black eyes was opaque.

# NINE

We stayed with Briony until the warmer days of springtime came. Arlen was up and about within a week after Bri's cure, but he did not regain his full strength soon, for we had both been worn down by winter. And it was a joy to live within the warmth of the soddy, to sleep on a soft pallet, to cook good food on a fire—I learned to cook somewhat, those days, when I was not coughing. For as soon as Arlen was on the mend I took cold. Briony showed no inclination to be rid of us, so we stayed.

Our good mandrake gave us the freedom of his home, and sometimes he left us to tend it. Every fortnight, on the eve of the dark moon or the full, he would step out into the dusk and be gone as if whirled away on a horse of air. And with the dawn he would return, exhausted, and spend the day buried in earth in the deepest shadows of his soddy before emerging to speak with Arlen and me once more.

Arlen was fascinated by Briony, his craft, and his books, especially his herbal. He had never been taught to read, not on the Sacred Isle, but I knew how, for reading was one of the useless things that ladies learned. So, as Briony had no objection, I would sit by the hour and read the herbal aloud to Arlen. Afterward he and Briony would have long talks, and they would stand about studying the dried plants that hung from the rafters. When the early spring herbs began to sprout, Briony would go out into the copse or onto the moorlands to look for some he needed, and often Arlen would go with him.

Spring. The trees budded, ash and oak. The heather bloomed. The swallows returned to nest, as Briony had promised they would. The winter, which I had felt might go on forever, was over. White birches put out pale green crowns.

One day, when the sun shone as warmly as I had felt it since—before everything, since I was a maiden and my father's pawn—on a sunny day I went out to draw water for washing. My cough had left me, so I had been doing a great spate of washing, our clothes and everything we owned, including ourselves. And as I brought the wooden bucket up out of the dark opening of the well, there lay a small snake inside, coiled up in the water, a serpent as green as an emerald and as sparkling bright, and it raised its head to look at me. I went rigid for a moment with the shock of seeing it there in the bucket, but then I realized it would not hurt me, for it was not an asp but some other sort of snake, graceful and very beautiful. I took the bucket softly and poured out water and serpent into the heather; it looked at me a moment longer before it slid away. Then I knew that it was as I had suspected, that I was with child.

I gave up thoughts of washing for that day.

"We are going to have to decide what to do," I said to Arlen that evening at supper. "We cannot stay here forever."

"Especially," Briony put in, "as you are pregnant."

I glared at him in surprise and vexation, for I had planned to tell Arlen that myself, later, in private.

"Well," Briony said mildly, "if you *are* going to leave the messengers of the goddess lurking about. . . ."

"Are you really?" Arlen was looking at me with his chin hanging in an uncouth way. "I mean—I know nothing about it, but are there not—indications. . . ?"

I felt suddenly embarrassed, and I blushed. "I thought at first it was because of—the cold, the bad food, everything," I mumbled.

"You mean—you have been? Since our first times—together?"

I remembered those days, that passion, and wished I had not remembered while Briony's inscrutable gaze was on me, and flushed still more hotly. Arlen looked stunned.

"Great goddess," he said, and then he grinned. "As if we did not have trouble enough already," he teased me.

Briony brought out the wine, and we had a small celebration. Arlen gave me a ceremonial kiss, for fertility, and one far less ceremonial, for my own sake. But after that was done with, Briony called us to order.

"Arlen spoke more truly than he knows," said Bri darkly, "concerning trouble."

We sobered and sat one on either side of him at the table, listening.

"Rahv and his men will be hard after you, once the weather favors. Indeed, rumor has it that already they have set out, though the spring floods have not yet dried."

We sighed. "Another season of riding," Arlen said.

"Well," said Briony, "if you will accept the advice of a mandrake. . . ."

We turned to him attentively.

"Ride north and east, toward the Mountains of the Mysteries. Few folk dwell there, even fewer than live here, for those are awesome lands, too wild to be readily put to the plow. Also the mountains form a barrier, and there are other barriers less defined. . . . For many reasons, those lands are neither farmed nor traveled for trade, and so the region lies feral, of no interest to lords or even robbers. You may find some strange folk there, but no lords and no petty kings. And land is free for the settling."

"You think my father will not pursue us there?" I asked, too eagerly.

"I have no way of knowing where your father will or will not pursue you. Cover your traces more thoroughly this time."

As there would be no more snow, that might be possible.

Arlen's eyes looked moss green, for he was thinking. "How long will it take us to get there?" he asked Briony.

"Not overlong. If you ride quickly, you should arrive before Cerilla is too big to fit on the horse with you." He barked out a noise that might have been a laugh and walked back into his earthworks to sleep, if what he did there could be called sleeping. And Arlen and I went to our bed.

My news put a surge of energy into Arlen. The next morning he arose betimes, before the dawn, checking gear and packing the provisions that Briony gave us. And as soon as the sun was up he took our borrowed bedding and walked to the homestead to return it and to fetch Bucca—he went instead of me, for I would not cross the esker if I did not have to. I had told him what had happened there, but though he did not doubt my word he could scarcely believe me—an irrational state, but human. He did not remember the serpent, at any rate, and went fearlessly, and brought Bucca back without incident. Bucca looked glossy, well fed, and more than a little troublesome. Arlen also brought gifts of clothing and food, appeasements from the folk who had refused to aid him. We bore them no grudge, but evidently they bore some against themselves.

While the day was still cool we were ready, and Briony stood at the doorway to see us off. I went to him and embraced him and kissed him on the cheek—the first time I had touched him, and I felt sure he would not know what to make of my affection, as indeed he did not. He looked utterly startled and did not know how to return the kiss. Then Arlen hugged him as well.

"Great goddess have mercy," Bri said.

"A thousand thanks." Arlen gripped his brown hand, the mandrake hand that had brought him back from death.

"And a thousand good wishes go with you, Arlen. And with you, Lady Cerilla."

"May the powers be willing," I told him, smiling, "I'll be no more a lady."

"Why, then," said Briony, with some small touch of mischief in his voice, "you'd do well to take a less ladylike name. Should I call you Rae?"

"It is the best of names," I said.

"Call her what you like," said Arlen, "and I will never dispute you." And from that time forth I took the name of Rae, with him and with all others, and Arlen found other endearments for me.

We rode away, waving our thanks and our farewells. The springtime days were warm, the nights pleasant, and we had food and everything we needed; we rode steadily, and as we asked no favors of any folk we left no trail of rumor, or very little, for we avoided even the workers in the fields when we could. Nor did we leave much trail in fact, for we took a twisting course around the eskers, keeping to the stony ground to hide Bucca's hoofprints. As we traveled on, and the horse's hooves did not crack, and no one seemed to notice us or pursue us, our hopes grew that all would yet go well.

It was not until we ran out of food and needed to ask for hospitality that I realized all was not as I had thought. We approached a woman planting in her garden, and she looked up at us with a smile—but within a moment the smile became a puzzled frown, and even as I gave her greeting the puzzlement turned into a grimace of terror. She ran into her home, banging the heavy door into place behind her, and began to wrench at the window shutters, panting and gasping in her fear. I looked at the air a slight distance to my left. The presence had come so gently again I had not noticed it. Or perhaps I was so accustomed to it that I no longer noticed. No matter, for there it was.

"Lonn's back," I told Arlen.

"I know," he said grimly, turning Bucca away toward the open moorland, where we would trouble no one. Once we had gone a little distance, though, he stopped and swiveled around to face the Presence.

"Lonn, go away," he said, levelly enough. "You are turning folk against us."

Nothing happened. It was only a watery place in the air, a sort of shimmer or thickening, and it stayed there.

"Lonn, go!" said Arlen more forcefully. "Go back where you belong."

He stayed.

"What are we to do?" I whispered to Arlen. "He went before when you ordered him to."

Arlen shrugged and lifted the reins. "We'll ride," he said. "He went before because he wanted to, for some reason. I thought as much at the time. I have no sorcerer's power and never did. But Lonn was mighty in magic."

"Well, how did he come to be so mighty in magic?" I grumbled, vexed.

"The tale has it that a serpent crawled into the cradle with him when he was a baby."

That silenced me. Such, indeed, would have been a mighty conferring of power by the goddess.

"Perhaps he will grow tired of following us," Arlen said after we had ridden for a while.

I am afraid I snorted scornfully.

"Confound it," Arlen burst out, goaded, "how am I to spurn him, even in death? He is—you know what a friend he is. What he has done."

"He is a nuisance," I soothed, "but nothing worse."

Few folk lived in those parts, at any rate, who could have

given us food. We foraged. We came out of moor and esker into a moist, woodsy country, where wild asparagus grew along the shady slopes above streams, and a plant with a single folded petal of green or purple. Lady's hood, Arlen called it. Acting on a strange prompting one day, I dug one up. The root was large, and I rubbed the dirt off it and kept it.

"We should cook this and eat it," I said.

"How do you know?" Arlen asked. "I thought you were kept always castlebound and ignorant of anything practical."

I sighed, oddly reluctant to tell him the truth. "Lonn showed it to me," I admitted. "Things under earth seem to be in his province."

"Oh." Arlen sighed also, then accepted it, digging up more lady's hood himself. "Well, as a matter of fact, I think Lonn is right," he said. "I have been told these thing are famine food."

They were tolerable, boiled. But I did not see how we were to last so, foraging, all summer.

Those were pinched times. The going turned from farmland and pastureland to woodland, with not even a byre to plunder for cattle feed—I, for one, was not above a bit of thieving by then. There were brown mushrooms growing in the loam, chainmail mushrooms they were called, and we would cook them with the wretched lady's hood. Also, we learned to eat greens. That was all.

And so, by degrees, and not even knowing it, we came into the primal forest.

Knowing came to me with a chill one day when I heard the yap of a fox at midmorning and looked about me. My arms tightened around Arlen as if in a spasm, and he stopped the horse, startled.

"Arl," I whispered to him, "this place is the wildest of all wilds."

All was dim, mossy, ivy-twined. The most immense trees loomed, towered, as if they had been there forever, and the great butts of ancestor trees had fallen in the shadows and were rotting with an orange glow amid thickets of bracken. Ivy chains trailed down, touching us; I shivered and shrank from that chill touch.

"So much the better," Arlen said bitterly. "There are no Gwyneda here, or lords' henchmen either, to harass us. Only beasts." He sent Bucca onward.

We fought our way through ivy and thickets and around the great logs, trying not to break branches, trailing one that broke despite us to scrape away the hoofprints in the soft forest loam. Soon we came to rippling fens where the trees stood white and skeletal, dead, and the midges swarmed. We gave up trying to hide our traces, leaving deep tracks as we found our way around and through them. And beyond them at last, on firm ground when evening fell, we heard the howling of wolves.

"Sleep," Arlen said wearily, for we had nothing to eat. "Sleep, and never mind my cousins, the boys with the silver whiskers. They will not harm us."

We slept, even all bitten as we were, for the midges had been feeding on us; we lay close together under our blanket and slept as deeply as if we had been drugged. And when we awoke at dawn the wolves were sitting about us in a circle, with the sunlight of the new day sending up silver lights off their thick fur. They sat, respectful, and we lay and looked up at them in profound respect for their gleaming teeth and powerful jaws. Then, seeing that we were awake, they got up and trotted away. In a moment nothing more could be seen of them in the greenish shadows.

"Look!" Arlen pointed.

At our feet lay a brace of rabbits, freshly killed.

We made a fire and cooked them, so impatient that in the end we ate them half raw. And we found some greens and cresses to have with them. When we had devoured them, we traveled through what remained of the day. But the food seemed only to have awakened our stomachs and set them to grumbling, and by evening we were ravenous. A rabbit ran in front of us and we watched it, hungry and helpless. Arlen had never learned a hunter's craft, no more than I had, for the

killing of animals lay of all desires farthest from his heart—
though, being human and full of unreason, he loved to eat
meat.

The rabbit bobbed away into twilight leafshadow, and we
sat watching after it as if entranced. Where it disappeared
stood a stubby hazel tree—no. It moved. A mouth opened,
and a laugh more eerie than a hawk's scream echoed through
the dusk. A stocky old woman in a rough brown peasant's
dress stood there, her shoulders stooped and rounded as if by
toil, her weathered face creased in mockery and merriment.
As we blinked she was gone, as if swept away on a horse of
wind like Briony, and her witch's laughter floated behind her.

"Ride!" I hissed at Arlen.

We rode until we could no longer see the way, and went to
sleep hungry. The next morning when I awoke, there was a
bear sitting at our feet, a great grizzled bear with curved black
claws. The bear lifted a forepaw when I stirred, and the sight
of the shining claws made me catch my breath.

"*Arl!*" I shook him awake, and he blinked groggily at the
bear. It greeted him with a querulous growl.

"What is it, grandfather?" Arlen got up, went vaguely over
to the bear, and began to examine it for parasites. The creature
lowered its head to him.

"Oh, I see, the ears." Arlen set to work. There were dozens
of ticks to be plucked off. I lay still under the blankets until he
was done.

"Thank you for the gift, grandfather," Arlen told the bear
gravely.

Food! Letting go of caution, I sat up to look. A large fish lay
at my feet. At once I began to think of gathering firewood.

"But we are very hungry, very, very hungry," Arlen went
on. "If in your kindness you could find us something
more. . . ?"

The bear muttered darkly and slouched off. Nor did it bring
us anything else; that must have been a lean season for everything but the bloodsuckers. We ate the fish and were glad of it.

But by evening, still riding through forest, we felt faint with hunger again.

"Am I dreaming," Arlen murmured, glancing about him, "or do I smell the aroma of a roast? Seasoned with scallions? I must be going mad."

"What is that shadow," I whispered at the same moment, "moving yonder?"

It could have been anything, in the dusk. A young deer, perhaps. Something tawny and slender. It slipped away, and a moment later, a little farther on, a weird light appeared: faint and greenish, rather like a very dim star somehow fallen to the forest floor.

"Wisp light," I gasped. "Do not go near it!"

"I swear, I smell cookery," Arlen declared, and he sent Bucca forward. The wisp bobbed on before us.

"Stop!" I protested. "Or turn aside."

"Rae," Arlen said, "have you never noticed how all things go to contraries for us? We eat elderberries, wolves and bears bring gifts—what else can we do but follow this—envoy?"

We followed.

Within a few moments there shone many such lights in the dusk, ahead of us, clustered and orderly, almost as if they illuminated a structure, a castle. And as we drew nearer I could see what it was. The immense jagged stump of a great old tree, an oak, lighting-felled, and all about it, growing up from the roots and from the stump itself, a coppice of new shoots—for the oak is one of the immortal trees that never truly dies. And upon the stump and sitting in the branches of the coppice were many small folk with their oak-apple lamps filled with wisp. They wore tight leathery garments of brown and green, their hands were twiggy, their faces sharp and snaggletoothed and too big for their small bodies. With much merriment and a great spate of talk they welcomed us—I could not understand a word of what they said. And there was the aroma of good cooked food, and a feast spread before us.

I slipped down from Bucca, and Arlen got down and unsad-

dled him. When the horse was cared for he seated himself on a
grassy hillock, and the oak elves swarmed about him, petting
him and bringing him sweetmeats. But I stood uncertainly.
Food, the choicest of food, lay within reach. Yet something in
my mind urged me away. No, not my mind! A summons
exerted *on* my mind, within my mind, by something not me:
Lonn.

"I don't care," I told him aloud. "We might as well die of
treachery as starvation." And thrusting my hair back from my
face, I seated myself. Arlen was right. It was time to take the
bold course. And, angry, I grew determined to oppose Lonn
for once, to test the limits of his meddling.

So, though he continued to pester me, I ate. Arlen ate. We
ate for hours, feasting on viands that could not possibly have
been there, in the midst of a vast forest, with no hearth in
sight—we knew that and gave no further thought to it. We ate
roast capon, roast venison, roast lamb dressed with mint
leaves, roast duck. We ate poached fish, braised veal, boiled
sausage. We ate freshly baked buttery breads, sweet green
grapes, strawberries, apples out of season. We ate soup and
trifle and custard. I ate the creamy porridge my mother had
prepared for me as a child. Arlen claimed it was currant jelly
on one of Erta's scones. How could that be? It did not matter.
None of it mattered. Sleep did not matter. We would eat all
night. . . . From somewhere came the sound of the most
exquisite music played on lutes and pipes and viols.

When dawn touched us, though we had ceased to eat, we
were still sitting on our hillocks, staring at the remnants of the
feast.

Wisp lights were gone. Platters, merriment, music, oak
elves, all had faded away. Before us lay piles of fungi—
toadstools, redcaps, the bracket fungi that grow on the trunk
of dead trees—all the most poisonous sorts, as venomous,
some of them, as asps. Broken bits of them lay about us, and I
held a large orange one in my hands, half gnawed.

I dropped it slowly, looked at Arlen. One would think we

should have been shocked, horrified. But not so—nor were we much frightened, for in a perverse way we had known all along. The oak elves are the vengeful spirits of the felled tree; everyone knows that. By their glamour they disguise dead leaves as dishes, the creaking of insects as music, deadly mushrooms as delicious food.

"I feel quite full, very satisfied," Arl said softly to me.

"So do I," I told him. "Quite content."

"Well then," he asked, "shall we ride? Or must you sleep?" He spoke stiffly, formally. We felt foolish.

"Let us ride." I did not wish to stay any longer in that place.

We rode, and made a long day of it, and it was dusk before we spoke any further of our feast. We had found a dry dingle to camp in, and Arlen was looking wistfully at the shoots and bushes that surrounded us.

"Contraries being what they are," he said, "do you think we could eat all sorts of things and they would nourish us?"

"I would not try it," I said sharply. "Perhaps the wolves will bring us more game."

They did, from time to time. But it was a long passage through the wilderness, and we were often hungry. Forever Forest, I named that place in my mind.

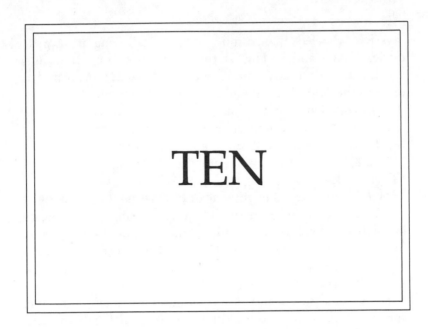

# TEN

The leaves had thrust entirely out of the bud before we came out of the deep forest and onto meadowland and open woodland where herding animals roamed.

"Look," Arlen gasped in greatest wonder. "Yaels!"

A herd of perhaps a dozen of them, a sort of white deer, or nearly white, with amber mane and tusks like those of a boar and tall, curving horns, which they could turn in any direction at will. Small and fleet, they ran swiftly away before us, bounding out of view. We never saw them again.

But everywhere grazed the wisent, great brown lumbering beasts with cleft hooves and short horns; they neither challenged us nor fled. I watched them warily as we rode, but found we had more reason to be wary of the aurochs, the huge black wild oxen with their long and wickedly forward-curving horns. The first day we came upon a cluster of them beneath some trees, and they bellowed and charged us, those horns coming at us like so many lanceheads.

Arlen wheeled Bucca and sent him galloping in a wide circle, fleeing and seeking at the same time to continue onward. But the aurochs would not be outflanked; they veered at us from the side. Bucca could not outrun them, no matter how Arl chirruped and urged him, not with two riders on his back. The wild oxen were as fleet as he and perhaps even longer of leg, for they stood as tall as a horse and were all bone.

"Wait," Arl murmured, more to himself than to me. "There's a lame one."

"*Arl*," I protested, knowing already what he was thinking.

"We cannot outrun them. There is nothing for it but to brave them. Moreover," he added, "these are only my cousins, the ones with the sharp toes. They shall not hurt us."

I felt not nearly as sure as he seemed. But Arlen would be Arlen; it was no use to reproach him.

He kicked Bucca and circled around to where the lame aurochs lagged, then pulled the horse to a quick halt and slid off, leaving me where I was, only slightly safer on the horse's rump than I would have been on the ground. Arlen took a few steps forward, and the lame aurochs floundered in panic at his approach. It was a cow great with calf, and her foot evidently caused her much pain for she could scarcely walk, but she swung her black head at him and bellowed in threat.

"There, now," Arlen murmured, walking over to her. "Hooo, now."

The herd of her fellows thundered up and plunged to a halt, surrounding us with a circle of sharp horns. Bucca flung his head up and trembled with fear. I spoke to him softly, trying to calm him, quiet my own tense breathing, soothe the wild kine crowded all around us, pitch black except for white gleam of horns and rolling eyes. Aurochs stamped and snorted but did not move as Arlen approached the hurt cow.

"Easy, now, my lovely," he murmured as he reached her, and, sweating and trembling, she let him lift her heavy foot. Caught between the halves of the cloven hoof jutted a flint, cutting sharp and so firmly wedged that with all his strength

Arl could not dislodge it. He groped down and found another
stone with which to knock it loose, and all the while none of
the aurochs moved. Blood and pus dripped from the swollen
flesh of the foot once the flint fell away, and Arlen would have
bound it, but the moment he loosened his hold the cow lunged
away, still limping. He forebore to follow her further.

"You should soak that in cold water," he told her, and he
came back to Bucca. I helped him mount. The herd of aurochs
parted and let us pass.

"The cut is full of contagion," Arlen muttered. "I hope she
has the sense to lick it clean."

"I am sure she will," I said curtly—danger made me short-
tempered. "Those wisent, I suppose they are your cousins
too?"

"Certainly. The lads with the brown beards."

I found myself hard put to be civil with him that night.

The next day we came in sight of the mountains. In the
distance we saw the odd, aspiring shapes of them, dark storm-
cloud gray against a blue sky. But it took a week or longer
before we reached them, and there were no more gifts of food
from any of Arlen's "cousins" or other kin, only what we could
forage for ourselves, and that was little enough. We grew
weak.

"Mountains of the Mysteries, forsooth," Arlen grumbled,
though in a hushed tone. "It is a mystery, I suppose, how they
came to be here."

They rose as abruptly as a wall from gently sloping woodland and meadowland all around. I thought of the eskers and
forebore to wonder more.

The mountains loomed gigantic, towering so far above our
heads that we could not take them in, the greatest of great
rocks, sculpted by weather into dizzying shapes, curves and
hollows and caves and arches and spires. Balanced on some of
the spires and sculpted edges were boulders the size of wisent
or larger, poised so delicately that one would have thought a
stray wind would have sent them crashing down, and yet they

had been there, I suppose, nearly forever. Under them ran
terraces where wood violets and ferns grew and small trees—
or perhaps the trees only looked small against the vastness of
the gray mountains, the peaks that soared until they faded into
mist or sky. We could not find a limit to them, and I, for one,
felt very puny.

"Well, now that we are here," Arlen continued in peevish
tones, "where are we to go and what are we to do?"

He was not asking me, just voicing a plaint in case the
powers of sky were listening. Hunger had made him irritable.
I, however, felt a nudge and answered him.

"This way," I told him, starting off to the left and upward.
We were afoot, looking for food, with Bucca trailing along
behind us, making his way riderless over the rough terrain.
Though verily I believe the terraces made better going than
the wilderness had.

"Why this way?" Arlen grumped.

"Why not?" I countered. I was not willing to tell him that
Lonn was leading us.

We toiled upward for some time before the way put us featly
under one of the balanced stones. As we approached it I could
see that it was moving, forsooth, slowly rocking in its perilous
place. Stiffening slightly, I hoped Arlen had not noticed, for I
had made up my mind not to turn back. But he gave a shout
and stopped so suddenly that Bucca blundered into him,
sending him stumbling forward.

"It won't—" I started, annoyed.

"A face!" Arlen declared.

I looked where he pointed, under the lee of the gently
swaying rock, and saw nothing.

"It—it's gone," he stammered, pushing me. "Go on, hurry,
before—"

He shoved me out from under the swaying stone, and I
believe we went onward only because it would have taken too
much time to turn Bucca somehow and go back.

"Before what?" I flared, vexed by his fear. Before something sent that stone down on top of us, he had meant. Such nonsense. But he would not answer me, and I did not fully comprehend until I had seen one myself.

It happened the next day. We had to pass under a teetering stone again—no wonder folk called them rocks, I jested dourly with myself—and just as we drew abreast of it I glanced up and saw—a face, a small, gray face right under the slowly moving rock, peering over the edge of its pedestal at us, a glance as hard as the stone itself and as barren. Then it was gone as if it had never been.

And there above us shivered a stone the size of a small cottage, balanced on the edge of fear, and mind had to wonder: Would a touch really send it down on us? And I stopped and stood shivering like the stone.

"Go on," said Arlen grimly in my ear. "Going back is no better than going on."

So we went on, and the rock teetered and did not fall as we passed under it and left it behind us.

"Briony said we would meet strange folk," I remarked after a while.

"We are insane to come here," Arlen burst out. "This is a guarded place, a forbidden place, can you not feel it? The forest, the aurochs, and now these—whatever you call them, that dwell under those uneasy stones—"

"Call them logans," I said for no reason, walking in a trance of hunger.

"All right, logans. The goddess only knows why they are letting us pass. Probably to lead us to a worse fate farther up. We are out of our minds."

"You call me insane?" I cried with unnecessary heat. "You, who banter with wild beasts?"

We quarreled, a meaningless quarrel. Greens suited Bucca, but they left us snappish, half starved, and there had been nothing else to eat for days. The starvation made us feel always cold—or perhaps it truly was cold, for it was wet; whenever there was not fog or mist there was rain, those days. And although we found caves and niches to shelter in at night, they felt as damp as the outdoors, and there was little wood for burning, and none dry. We shivered through the nights without a fire, wrapped in sodden blankets, not taking much comfort even in each other. I slept fitfully, and in my dreams I saw gray faces.

We have that miserable weather to thank for saving us from my gentle father, Rahv. I learned later that he had reached the edge of the Forever Forest and a herd of hostile aurochs before turning back. He could see nothing for mist, least of all a gray horse on a gray mountainside. But if we had been able to light a fire I am sure we would have, wretched as we were, and it would have led him straight to us. Him and a dozen men.

Not knowing our own good fortune, we felt heartily sorry for ourselves. My head reeled with hunger, my unborn child feeding on me, my belly beginning to swell but the rest of me very thin, haggard. Arlen could have felt no better, for he had been giving me the larger share of our meager food throughout the journey. When we had strength to speak, we quarreled, blaming each other for being where we were.

"We could have gone around," Arlen said in smoldering tones, "but no, we needs must climb up past teetering rocks, wearing out what little strength is left in us. With the horse, yet! Now there is no way out."

"You are the one," I pointed out, "who always took the contrary ways. Eating elderberries. Following wisp lights—"

"Following a death dog? It is Lonn who leads you, admit it!" He sounded savage.

"Jealous," I coldly retorted, "of a dead man?"

"Belike leading us to join him."

So small wonder that, when I took a notion to go crawling into a crypt, Arlen refused to have anything to do with such folly.

It was on the day when wet had at last given way to a hazy sunshine that cast gray shadows. Lonn, the voiceless urging, led my eye to the entry within one such shadow. I saw the spiral snake design carved on a rock, as I had seen it once before at a certain cenotaph, only this time it was mostly hidden by a leaning slab, and in my light-headed state I would never have noticed it on my own. "Wait," I said to Arlen, and I went over to it. There was a low dark crevice of an entry in the shadow of the slab, and I grew excited. "Arlen, come here!" I cried. But instead, he sank down to sit where he was.

"Come here!" I demanded again. "We have to go in where this passage is."

"Speak for yourself," he said rudely. "I am not moving unless it is to go on."

I turned to glare at him. "But there is food or something in there!" I shouted. I felt sure there was, for Lonn was nudging at me.

"What food could be in that hole?" he retorted. "I am not yet so desperate that I wish to feed on old corpses."

That did not even make me shudder. I, who had balked at entering the cenotaph some few months before.

"The air will be too foul to breathe," Arlen added.

"How can you know for sure?" I stormed. "Come here, or I will go in myself."

"Go ahead." He stayed where he was.

*Brute*, I fumed inwardly. With my pregnant belly, I had come to expect help and protection, forgetting that protection takes away freedom. And in truth, the swelling was yet modest. Thin as I had become, I was able to slip behind the stone and twist and stoop into the entry.

"Don't shout for me if you get stuck." said Arlen sourly.

So he was not going to help me or try to stop me. The callous lout. Thoroughly on my mettle, I started to crawl in, then stopped within a heartbeat, motionless with fear. Two serpents lay coiled there just within the entry, coiled in symmetry one facing the other, spiral coiled, like the carving on the rock outside. On their backs shone the chain markings of the serpents most sacred to the goddess. They were clay-colored, and their eyes were of golden hue. They raised their heads and looked at me, stared with a sort of cold wisdom as I met their stare mutely. Then they turned their heads and,

again in symmetry, they slid away from me, rustling back into
the rock somewhere.

I do not know why I did not turn back at once, except that
Arlen's churlishness goaded me, urging me onward against all
reason. And there was Lonn prodding me as well. And,
against all wary instinct, I think I sensed truth: that those
serpents, the guardians, had given way before me and would
not harm me. So I crawled onward, into darkness, that dense
under-earth darkness that will not admit to seeing at all.
Fearing at any moment to put a hand down on a snake or a
bone or something worse but not, somehow, expecting it.
Short of breath. The air was, indeed and truly, very bad.
Onward, down, dark. It was not a long passage, not as long as
the cenotaph's entryway, but more strait, therefore more fearsome. I wriggled my way through, feeling squeezed and sick,
all anger against Arlen lost, hoping only to see him again. . . .

My hand came down on cloth.

No breath to spend on outcry. Numbly I sent my fingers
forward, seeking further. Bones, dry bones—I could bear
that—and something of rotted wood, a chest. And a spill of
cold that slipped and slithered and rustled under my fingers
like a nest of serpents, but it was hard. Metal. No time to
think more of it, my lungs were dying—

I took a handful of it at random, turned, and started back
the way I had come.

Very nearly I did not make it. A heavy smothered feeling
took hold of me, as if I were drowning in earth, and even the
daylight at the end of the passage looked dark to me, and I
blinked at it twice before I could comprehend Arlen's frightened face looking down at me, his hand reaching toward me. I
moved my own left hand the few needed inches to meet it, and
he hauled me out like a great fish. I lay gasping.

"I never—I never thought you really would," he was stam-
mering. "I didn't understand—Rae, I could have lost you. I
am such a brute, I couldn't be bothered—"

"Balderdash," I interrupted, still fighting for breath. "I am an idiot. What is this stuff?"

I lifted my clenched hand, and we both stared; trailing down from it there shone bright chains of gold.

I folded my legs to make a basket of my skirt, and over it I slowly opened my hand. The things shimmered down like sunlight.

There was a clasp of white gold jeweled with sapphires to keep the wearer from evil influence. There was a brooch of red gold, round, like a little shield or a sun, studded in a flame pattern with beads of gold; and there was a smaller brooch, a triskelion. There were three small loose gems, of what sort we were not sure, for there are many jewels of reddish purple hue, and there were two beads all in bright colors of enamel laid between threads of gold. And there were the chains, some thicker than others, bold chains, red gold and white and pure aureate gold, chains fit for a king or the most esteemed warrior among kings, he whose lord gifts him with golden chains, the gifts of loyalty.

"Treasure," Arlen breathed. We both sat as if stunned. Then he looked at me sheepishly.

"Well," he said in a tone that struggled for sobriety, "I am convinced, Rae. I will go down and see if there is more." He got up.

"There is. But Arl, wait. . . ." I needed the help of my hands to sit up without his support. "The snakes. . . ."

"What?" He stared at me.

"The guardian serpents. They let me in, but how are we to know they will do the same for you?"

He stared. Then he came to me swiftly, knelt beside me and took me into a tight embrace, his faced pressed against my neck.

"Rae," he whispered, "you are the treasure, the true treasure."

# ELEVEN

We got it all out within the next few hours, the gold, or as much of it as we could find by groping about in the utter blackness of that tomb. Arlen was forced back on his first attempt, not by the serpents but by the foul air. But as he learned the way he traversed the passage more swiftly, and on a third trial he was able to bring out a heavy load, dragging it in a sack made of his shirt. Then I went down again and found a little more, feeling for the chill hardness of metal and jewel on the chill hardness of stone. Then he made one last raid and came up with less than I, and by unspoken consent we considered the matter done, the unknown king sufficiently plundered, and we sat and stared at our booty spread out around us. No crown—perhaps the king had been no king but a great warrior, proud in his many chains, for they were great chains, heavy and intricately linked. Also there were amulets of gold and silver, moon crescents of silver and sun disks of gold, and there were tiny animals made of gold—a seated dog, a reclining deer, a perched and hooded falcon—and there was a small golden boat with sail and oars, and a miniature of the sun chariot, all of gold, with leaping horses and great wheeling sun riding behind them. There were surpent rings and serpentine torcs biting their tails, jewels for eyes, and there were loose jewels beyond numbering. . . . We sat amidst it all, and suddenly Arlen lay back dizzily and laughed up at the sky, laughter with a hard edge, yell after yell of laughter.

"Rae, we are a pair of poor sillies," he whooped. "What is the use of all this to us? We cannot eat it."

We were, indeed, starving where we sat. I felt a sudden chill of fear, of doubt that we would be able to get up, to journey onward, and I saw Arlen looking back the way we had come, where there lay only miles of mountain and woodland and wilderness, where all the gold in the world would not buy so much as a bowl of gruel. He was still laughing as he looked, and the tone of his laughter frightened me all the more.

"Stop it!" I shouted at him, and I struggled to my feet and tugged at him to make him get up also. His laughter stopped and his face grew grim.

"Let the stuff lie," he said

"No. Lonn wants us to have it." We would have been churlish indeed to refuse such a glorious gift.

"Why? So that we may lie upon it? So that it may adorn us in an unmarked grave?"

I was too weary to be angry with him. Nor could I too sharply disagree with his thought that we might die. But something had grown stubborn in me, and I began to gather up treasure by the fistful and put it in Bucca's saddlebags. And after a moment Arlen did likewise.

"Lonn be cursed," he said, scraping up jewels as if they were pebbles. Then, our footsteps painfully slow, we started onward again, up the mountainside terraces toward the place where we thought we had discerned a pass to whatever lay on the other side. More wilderness, most likely.

We reached it just at sunset. Great peaks towered on either side of us, but between them lay a patch of soil, level and gentle. It grew larger as we plodded ahead, soft grass underfoot and copses of slender trees scattered about us, and the trees were full of the whistlings of birds as the dusk drew on. So benumbed were we by hunger, and exhausted, that it took us some moments to realize that where there were birds, in the spring of the year, there were likely to be eggs. But when it struck us we gave each other one glance and left Bucca where he stood. He dropped his head to the grass and ate, and we ate also, sucking the eggs raw from the shells; there were plenty within easy reach on all sides. Frantic and greedy, we wandered farther and farther in search of them the more of them we found.

"Look!" I called to Arlen. "Lights."

Mouths egg-smeared and agape, we stared. We had come to the far side of the Mountains of the Mysteries. Their flanks went down in grassland and moorland as much as in rock, and clinging perhaps halfway down was a village with the lamplight yellow in its windows, glowing in the quiet dusk. Velvet purple dusk. I thought I had never seen anything so lovely, yellow lamplight and the yellow of gorse in bloom catching the last glimmers of the day. And there were other lights, more distant and so seemingly smaller, other villages farther down the mountainside, and farther yet, a dim and bulky something that might have been a castle.

Arlen drew a bit of gold chain from his pocket and looked at it dazedly. It also glinted yellow in the last sunlight of the day.

"Rae," he blurted, "do you realize we will be able to trade for what we need?"

"I dare say." I faced him, and he has since told me that I looked intolerably smug. "Lonn has not led us so badly after all."

"I suppose not," he said, too full of gladness to resent or dispute it.

There was food in my stomach; already I could feel some small strength coming of it, and there would be more food on the morrow. I lay down where I was, lay down on the soft grass and went to sleep within the moment, never feeling the chill of the mountain air in the night. When I awoke to a misty springtime morning, Arlen lay beside me, and he had placed the blankets over us.

There was a spring trickling out of the rock to the northern side of our haven. We drank. There were chainmail and treasure-chest mushrooms, good food both, and we ate them. Arlen ate them impatiently. "Now," he said, "for more proper viands." He started to saddle Bucca and looked at me curiously when I did not get up to help.

"You go," I told him. "Trade for what we need or what you can get, and come back here with it. I will stay here with Lonn."

"Oh." He glanced at the blur hovering near my left hand, as if seeing it for the first time in weeks. We had both grown so accustomed to Lonn's hazy presence that we had forgotten it, accepting it as we accepted the presence of the air itself. But others would not accept it so readily.

"There is no need for you to stay behind," Arlen said. "The gold will speak more loudly than our voiceless specter."

"Perhaps. But there will have to be much showing of gold, and they will envy us for it afterward, and hate us for frightening them, and some of them may plot to steal it from us. And I want no one's hatred and no one's envy." I shook my head vaguely, feeling that I had somehow ventured beyond a single day's plans. "And I am tired, Arl," I said.

"I wonder," he murmered, looking about him.

He wanted to stay too, I knew it then. Stay in the small plot caught between the mountain peaks, where wild blackberries grew and the birds sang. The mountain walls made it seem like the strongest of havens, shielding us from all harm, like a very private paradise, our own special place where no one had ever come before—though of course we knew better—and pursuit might be close behind. . . .

"But we cannot run forever," I said, as much to myself as to him.

"The way is narrow, where we came up," he said. "I could perhaps block it with stones. . . "

"It is spring. We could plant a garden."

"Well," he said offhandedly, as if it were but an idle thought, "I might as well leave these things with you, then." And he removed the saddlebags full of treasure from Bucca's back, gave them to me, and took instead a single gold chain, one of the smaller ones, and pried it apart into links. Each link was as good as a gold coin, and he might yet have to pound some of them into halves or quarters. He put several links in his pocket and gave the rest of the chain back to me. He kissed me. Then he rode away down the gentler slopes of the northern mountainside.

I spent the day drinking at the spring and eating what I could find and sleeping beside our gold.

When Arlen came back at sunset he brought freshly baked bread. I could smell it as he came up the mountainside. He carried a spade across the saddle in front of him, and in his left arm he cradled a lamb, a fleecy white lamb, quite young. He rode up to me and handed the spade down to me and himself got down without letting go of the lamb, holding it tenderly.

"Are we to eat that?" I asked, staring in a predatory way. I must have been parlous hungry. Arlen glanced at me in mild shock and amusement, then put the lamb down on the grass; it lay flat and still, as if it had forgotten the use of its legs. His hands freed, he began to draw viands out of the pockets of his tunic and out of the slack above his belt. There were rounds of bread and hunks of cheese and, so help me, meat pies still warm from the oven. I grabbed one greedily.

"Those are what took me so long," he explained. "You eat. They have been feeding me all day."

"They were willing enough to take you in? No taint?"

"No taint. They seemed somewhat in awe of me, though. They could not believe I had come over the mountain." He shrugged, looking bemused. "I was hard put to make them accept payment for their hospitality. They are friendly folk."

He was bent over the lamb, handling it gently.

"This little one is sickly. And I think, from my memory of Briony's herbs, I might know the one that could help it. If I can find it hereabouts. . . ."

He wandered off, searching in the fading light, and I ate my fill, and there was more left for the morrow.

Arlen healed the lamb. I have never fully understood his craft or his gift, only that it takes time and thought and much caring. But within a few days, when we were in need of food again, it was gamboling about on its long woolly legs in the manner of lambs that are well, and when he rode down to the village again he took it with him to return to its owner. When he came back, he bore not only food but seeds for the garden plot we were digging, and a chicken and a clutch of eggs.

"Is the chicken ailing?" I asked.

"No, the chicken is well." He smiled, looking faintly shamed, as if he had somehow been bested. "It is for us to keep, and if the eggs hatch there will be more. The man set high value on that lamb."

I will not tell you the whole story of that spring and summer, for it would be only a tale of the ordinary things, hard work in sunlight and good food afterward and days passing one after the other as we made our house. We built it out of stones gathered from the mountain slopes, near the spring and flush against the rock of the northernmost peak for the less labor and for protection against the winter storms. It was only a cottage of a single small room, with a dressed stone for a hearth and a roof of slate, but to us it was home, our first true home, no prison but a haven such as Stanehold and Sacred Isle had never been. Under a sort of half cave or overhang we built a shelter for Bucca, faithful Bucca, who was learning to draw a plow. The chickens flocked everywhere; daily I hunted the eggs. And as the summer drew on there was a heifer. Someday there would be milk for us and for the babe and milk to spare, to set out for the logans. For the time, I left them bread and sometimes an egg, and the gifts were always gone in the morning.

Arlen had given some gold for the heifer, but mostly it was a gift of gratitude from a man whose cart ox he had healed. His fame as a healer of animals was spreading. Every time he went to the village for supplies there was word of another homesteader with need of him, and he would travel to see what he could do. He even went as far as the castle to tend to the lord's lame charger—the lord, he told me, was fierce, but folks in these parts knew nothing of either Rahv or the Sacred Isle, and we were glad of it.

I stayed in our mountaintop haven, my belly swelling with child, and never went down into the village at all. Arlen's new friends knew of me, for he made no secret of it that he had a wife, but I would not go down among them, lest my death dog go with me and frighten them and set them against us. Nor did any of them ever come near me, for the village folk would not come up the mountain. It was a forbidden place, they said, the home of otherfolk and the oracular dead, and they feared to set foot there. I think they whispered among themselves about Arlen, that he was divinely sent to them, a demigod, even. His speech was somewhat different from theirs, he told me, and they seemed awkward with him at times, half in awe. But no one could long be frightened of Arlen, good heart that he was.

In time, as more folk felt need of him more often, he took to going to the village every day in case some messenger awaited him. I would wave him on his way. And through the summer I gathered beans from our garden and made bread from the grain we had bought and gathered blackberries and felt the movement and the growing of the child in my belly.

"Have you noticed," Arlen said to me slowly one evening near autumn, "how the rats and snakes never take our chicks from us, as they do to others? And the cutworms have not been in our corn? And our spring continues to flow even though the season has been dry?"

I had not particularly noticed. But then, I had not been out of our small holding to see how things went elsewhere.

"Lonn has been with us in the best sense," Arlen said.

I did not feel so sure. If we had indeed been blessed with abundance, it could have been the logans looking after us, or the goddess, or even sheer blind luck. But it was like Arlen to feel kindly toward Lonn, and a long step from the bitter Arlen of the springtime, so I smiled.

He was looking around our beloved cottage as if he had a great confession to make. A fire, some stools, a kettle on the hearth. Not much, but it meant a vast amount to us.

"All that we have we owe to Lonn," he said.

I nodded. It was true, if only because he had shown us the gold.

"He died so that I might live and have you. He saved my life, there at the esker. He has fed us from his underground stores when we would have starved, otherwise. He saved us, somehow, from the spite of the oak elves, and sent the beasts with meat for us. He gave us the treasure which has bought us all we hold—and, the goddess willing, it will buy us what we need all our lives."

Had it, indeed, been Lonn who had done all these things? Some of them, perhaps. The cutworms, even, since they work underground. But the oak elves, the wolves, seemed hardly in his province.

"If he had not been with us to start with," I said dryly, "it would not have been necessary for him to feed us."

"But feed us he did. And if he had not been with us, so that we hid ourselves from folk, perhaps your father would have had us after all. Captured us within the month, even." Arl leaned forward earnestly. "Rae, I am ashamed of myself, that I have felt harshly toward him sometimes."

"I have felt harshly toward him myself," I said.

"I suppose." He hesitated. "It must be very lonesome for you, up here by yourself always."

I shrugged. I had always been much by myself, and one grows accustomed to the conditions of one's life, whatever they may be. "You could not send him away if you tried," I said.

"I know." He paused, sheepish. "I wish there were some way we could have his blessing and aid and not his taint, that is all. But one cannot have everything. Rae. . . ?"

"What?"

"Have you considered how we are to manage, when your time comes? No midwife will come near you."

I crossed my hands atop my massive swelling of belly and wrinkled my nose at him. It was true that I was afraid—how could I help but be afraid? Women died in childbirth sometimes, and it was a horrible way to be taken. But fear was of no use. And I knew Arlen's gentle ways with the mares, the cows, the ewes in lambing, and I knew his stock of herbs, and I felt sure I would be as well off with him as with any midwife.

"We will manage well enough," I told him.

"May the Great Mother bless us with an easy birthing," he said. "Rae?"

"What?" I asked again, with all the patience I could muster. He was very much like a child sometimes.

"When the baby comes, if it is a boy—let us name it after Lonn."

I gave him one quick, curious glance, trying to fathom his reasoning. Was this his way of propitiating the goddess, through Lonn, for continued good fortune and an easy birthing? Or did he really believe that Lonn could give us these things by himself? Or was it his hope, perhaps, that Lonn would be so pleased that he would consent to leave us? In the next instant I was ashamed of those thoughts. All I saw in Arl was love of his lost friend, to whom we owed so much. In

truth, the name of our firstborn was a small enough re-
membrance to give to him. I had sometimes thought myself of
giving the name of Lonn to the babe.

"It would be fitting to do so," I said. And in the same
moment I hoped that the babe would be a girl, and wondered
why I felt dismayed.

# TWELVE

It was a boy. And the goddess was gracious to us and gave me an easy birthing. One day in early autumn as I pulled the ripe gourds in the garden my waters broke, spilling on the warm earth, and by the next day, after a night of lamplight and panting, I had my babe. Arlen drew him from me, gentle, breathless until the infant breathed—and the baby did not cry, but merely breathed and smiled. It was the sweetest of smiles. I was as wet with sweat as he was with birthing when Arlen handed him to me, and I put him at once to my breast, where he suckled. The goddess was good to me still, for within two days my milk came in, so the babe had nourishment in plenty, and I did not fall ill with the birthing fever, but healed cleanly and was strong within the week. We were indeed blessed, Arlen and I and the little one.

We did not call him Lonn at once. That was not the custom, for children were taken away so frequently, the little visitors,

118

that most often parents waited to see if they planned to stay, not naming them until the moon had come round again, to save themselves from so much hurt. But I think Arlen and I would have been slain with sorrow if this baby had been taken from us, name or no name. Indeed, we gave him a pet name, calling him Spriggan, our little elf. And how well I remember that first evening, when he had been bathed and warmed and dried, and the soft hair floated on his head, red-gold in the firelight, as fine as swansdown. I held him, and Arlen sat on the hearth beside us both, gazing as if awestruck, as if the goddess were there and he would fall down in worship.

"Touch him," I offered. "Go on. You delivered him from me; you need not be shy with him."

Arl put out a hand toward us, and tiny fingers curled around one of his. "So golden," he whispered. "No—pink. And soft as a rose petal."

"Pink and golden both." I had my face against the baby's hair, and I sniffed the top of his head, rubbed my cheek against it. "And—the fragrance, like nothing else in the many kingdoms. Like the most delicate of spices, and—earth . . . ."

"Like a baby," Arlen said.

"Like all babies, and yet like no other baby either. I think I would know him anywhere just by the sweet fragrance of his head."

"Would you, now." His mood of wonder had changed to one of gentle amusement. "Well, I think I would know him better by this."

He touched it softly. Along the baby's small left shoulder lay a birthmark, a purple stain, as dark as blackberry wine, nearly as dark as elderberries. It was a looping, mottled thing, indistinct, rather like a knotted chain or perhaps the serpentine of the Sacred Catena.

"It may go away," I said, though only for the sake of argument, for I did not consider it a blemish but a blessing, the kiss of the goddess.

"I warrant it'll stay. Anyway," Arlen added, "all powers be

willing, you'll never have to go wandering about sniffing him out, like a brachet with a lost pup."

Little did we know.

For a month all went well with us. Autumn deepened. The babe was a babe like any other: our Spriggan, our very special own, to be sure, but much like all babies everywhere. He was troublesome by night and slept away the days in his cradle by the hearth—a cradle made by his father's own hands, made of birch, the wood of inception and springtime growth. He sucked greedily at my breasts and smiled toothlessly afterward. Dark came earlier each evening, as days shortened toward winter.

Four weeks to the day after the baby's birth, as was the custom, Arlen took him down to the shrine of the goddess in the village to be named. I did not go. That was *not* as was the custom, but it could not be helped; there was a shimmering presence in the air to my left, and I dared not venture where other folk were. I gave Arlen a honey teat made of sweets and cloth to soothe the little one should he become hungry, and I sent father off with child and waved after them and watched them on their way, and I watched for their return through a long afternoon, restless and lonely.

With the coming of dusk I could hear the baby crying. All the way up the mountainside he was crying in great frantic gasps until he was hoarse with his bawling, and though I tried to shut my ears to it for the sake of whatever lies Arlen had told the villagers, in the end I could not stand it. I bolted out of the house and ran to meet them, nor could I rest or speak until I had taken the babe from Arlen and put him to my breast. Sucking, he quieted, though from time to time a sob still shuddered through his small body.

"Well," said Arlen wearily, "little Lonn is duly named."

"Was he like this all the time?"

"No, only lately, after we had started home. The naming went well enough."

"And was there a fuss?" We stood on mountain rimrock, looking down at the village.

"Indeed there was, though a friendly sort of fuss. No one knew I had a son, we have kept your condition so secret, and so of course it was a great surprise for them to see me with him, and then every goodwife in the village wanted to know why you had not come down for the naming, and when I told them you were still weak from childbirth they talked of venturing up here to help you with the chores. But nothing came of it, for they are afraid. Perhaps someday—"

I was not listening, but looking at the village, and my eyes widened, and I gasped. "What in the name of the goddess is that?"

A blaze, a fire, in the village square. And as we watched it grew greater, and another sprang up beside it, and on the summits of the foothills and moorlands all around sprang up others, in pairs.

"It must be—we have lost reckoning. . . ."

It was the day of the quarter year, between winterking and summerking, or rather the eve of that day. And the village folk were preparing to celebrate the festival of the dead.

"We had better get within," Arlen said uneasily. Spirits were wafting through that dusk, for the portals between the now and the afterlife stand wide open on the eve of that day. Folk took refuge between the fires and made propitiation of burned beans, spirit food. We went inside and stirred up our own hearth fire and sat beside it, and we burned a few beans ourselves. But we found it hard to feel very afraid of the spirits of the dead. We had lived with one of them for so long that we no longer noticed him.

The next day, as I sat and sorted wool in my lap and rocked the cradle with my foot, the baby spoke to me. "Rae," he said indistinctly. It was a weird, husky voice to come out of that flower-petal mouth, and I was quite startled. I stopped what I was doing and stared. The baby smiled at me, a winsome, toothless gape. The voice had been a fluke, I decided. A meaningless murmur, a burble of the stomach, even. I turned my eyes back to my work—

"'Rilla," the baby said. "Rae. La-dy Ce-rilla."

I jumped up and retreated a few steps in shock and horror, the wool tumbling down on our dirt floor, unheeded. "Stop that," I said sharply, my voice trembling. "Stop it, or I won't feed you!" I am grateful still that Arlen was not there to hear me. Though of course Lonn had chosen to speak when Arlen was not there. And on the instant I felt ashamed. To offer to starve a tiny babe, my own firstborn, whom I dearly loved—

"Go to sleep," I muttered, caught between guilt and anger. But the baby cried until I took him up and comforted him. When he was sleeping I picked up the wool and put it away; my hands were shaking too badly to work with it any more that day.

It is odd how one can manage to ignore ill chance, even the worst of ill chance, for a few days. Hoping, I suppose, that one might be mistaken, that circumstances might not be as vile as they seem. By the time Arlen came home for his dinner, I had almost convinced myself that nothing had happened or that, if it had, it would pass. He knew I was distraught; he could tell it by my silence and my restlessness, and he asked me what ailed me, but I told him nothing. What was I to tell him? That our Spriggan was possessed? Perhaps it would pass with the passing of the day.

"Lady Cerilla," the baby said to me the next morning, more plainly; and I ran away so as not to have to face what was happening, ran into the coppice by the house with the tears streaming down my face and stayed there for the better part of an hour, and then I was ashamed of myself again. But when I came in the baby did not speak to me any more that day.

On toward evening I left the little one asleep in his cradle before the fire and went out to help Arlen with the heifer in the byre, and he helped me gather eggs. When we came in together, he turned first to the infant, as he always did. I watched Arlen's face to see the smile in his eyes, but the smile stopped before it had well started—a shocked silence came there instead, and he sharply drew in breath. And when I glanced at the cradle, there, sleeping with the baby, beside him and draped and looping all over him and about him like an oddly patterned blanket—it was a serpent, the most sacred amber-golden serpent with the brown chain markings on its back, a serpent of great size; its head, beside little Lonn's on the pillow, was as big as my hand.

I could not help it; I had been through too much. My nerve broke and I began to scream. Arlen grabbed me and put a hand over my mouth to hush my noise; I did not struggle against him, but I kept screaming, the sound muffled by his fingers. The baby stirred sleepily, and the serpent raised its great head and regarded all of us with eyes as green as emeralds. Lidless, expressionless eyes—remorseless, I thought. There was wisdom in serpents, but no mercy. Whatever they did, their reasons were their own. Still, it did not hurt us, any of us, but merely flowed over the edge of the cradle and out before the baby was fully awake. And then with great dignity, with its head raised regally, it rippled its way to the door and out into the dusk.

I kept screaming. I have never been so out of control, before or since, and Arlen could not comfort me, though he attempted to soothe me in every way he could think of, holding me in his arms, rubbing my back and shoulders, talking to me, trying to make sense out of me—nothing helped.

"Lonn!" I kept shrieking, "Lonn!"

And he kept saying, "But he is all right! Look at him!" meaning that the baby had not been harmed.

But I was screaming because Lonn was there, Lonn whom the goddess had gifted with the gift of serpent power, and I did not want him in my cradle; I wanted my own sweet Spriggan back again.

Finally in simple exhaustion I stopped screaming, but I could not eat or sleep, and Arlen was worried about me. He did not leave me alone the next day. But as nothing more happened, I became calm and ate some supper toward nightfall, and on the following morning he went off to the village to tend to an ailing milk cow.

As soon as he was well gone the baby looked at me. "Lady," he said in his deep man's voice, and I jumped up from where I sat with a cry.

"What do you want of me?" I shouted, and at the same time I covered my ears with my hands because I did not want to hear. But I heard well enough.

"You," Lonn said.

I snatched up an earthenware bowl, meaning to fling it at him, but how could I hurt a baby, my baby? I flung it against the wall instead, where it broke. The look on my face must have been fearsome.

"I found you food," he reminded me. Speaking seemed difficult for him, but easier than it had been two days before. "When you were hungry. And—gold."

It was true, all too true. Curse the gold, I thought vehemently, but I did not say it. I did not know what to say.

"I—love—you."

I had never wanted love less, not of the perverse sort he was offering me. Man's voice, dead man's voice out of the body of a baby—it sickened me. In the name of all that was sacred, how was I to tell Arlen? I could not tell him. Perhaps I was somehow mistaken, or perhaps I was insane, raving. If I were not already, certainly I soon would be.

"Lady Cerilla—"

"Be silent," I told Lonn savagely. The baby started to wail with fright or hunger, and after some hesitation I put it to my breast. It was the baby, I told myself, the sweet baby, not Lonn. Those tiny hands feeling at my breast were the hands of an innocent—or were they? Lonn had spoken from the infant's mouth. How much of this small body I held was itself, and how much was Lonn?

Arlen returned in the early afternoon while the baby was sleeping, and I passed him in the doorway.

"Stay here, tend the little one," I ordered. "I am going down to the village."

"What?" He was utterly taken aback, as was to be expected, for I had never gone down to the village, and we had always said I never could; I would turn the folk against us with the taint of death that followed me. But now I strode off amidst Arlen's startled pleas for an explanation, and I would offer him none, and I would not think clearly even within myself just what it was that I expected to find.

It seemed odd, very odd, to approach the village and step within it after having regarded it all those months from my far vantage. I felt as if I were stepping into a tapestry. Perhaps it was only because nothing seemed real, those terrible days. Woodenly I walked between the houses, wondering at them, that they seemed so upright, so solid. I came to the square, where the women stood and chatted around the well. As I approached they turned and looked at me, the stranger, and I stopped, waiting for them to grimace, to shout in shock and terror, to run. Hoping they would.

They did not. They came up to me, curious, trying not to seem too curious.

My tongue would scarcely move. I had to moisten my lips before I could speak. "I am Rae," I whispered to them. "Arlen's wife . . . ."

On the instant there was a spate of happy talk, deferential, even. Was I, indeed, and had I come down at last, and was I well; they were happy to see me. And would I come and have some soup and a scone. So good to know me at last after all this time, and they gave me their names, Treva and Nissa and Peg, and they valued my husband and all he did, such a generous heart he had, and he was so good with the animals, and never sharp in his dealings, not at all. And they hoped we had enough and to spare, and that the season had favored us with good crops. And my little one, the baby, was all well with him?

I startled the women by bursting into tears, and they became alarmed.

Was the baby sick? Surely Arlen could help him. Or was it something dreadful, the smallpox, the plague? No? Was I overwrought? Should they—and here they hesitated—should they come and lend me a hand at the cottage?

I turned and ran from them, back through the village street and up the steep slope, panting and gulping and grasping at the prickly gorse, never feeling it sting. I dare say they thought I was mad. They stood and put their heads together, not attempting to follow me. I came back to the cottage at last, gasping and blown, and I must have looked wild, for Arlen got up from where he sat at the table and came to me.

"Lonn," I said hoarsely, standing just within the door.

"He's all right," Arlen told me in a tone meant to be soothing.

"No!" I stamped my foot at him. "Lonn is—there!" I pointed at the cradle, trembling, and Arlen stared at me in perplexity.

"Not here!" I waved my left hand about in the air and tried to explain; I was beyond sparing him any longer. "No more presence, Arl. No wavering thing by me, no death dog. The women down below, they greeted me. Lonn is not in air any more. He is there." And I pointed at the cradle again.

Arlen's face had sobered as he listened to me, beginning to understand, but he did not yet share my panic, my despair. "Perhaps he has merely left us for a while," he said gently, "as he has done before."

"No! He is—in the baby." The words choked me, and I started weeping again. Arlen came and comforted me in his arms, but I could tell he did not yet entirely comprehend or believe me. How could he? I scarcely believed the horror of it myself.

"I—" It was too grotesque, I could not manage it. I turned to Lonn and shouted at him. "Go ahead, tell him! Speak, show him what you have done! So clever—talk, you wretch! You do to me often enough!"

The baby, of course, merely started to cry, and Arlen took a step back from me.

"I am not insane!" I flared at him.

"I have not said so," he replied levelly, and he picked up the little one and soothed him, since I would not. "The baby talks to you."

"Yes."

"What does he say?"

"He calls me by name. He says he—loves me . . . ."

I faltered. It sounded so harmless, so sweet, even, coming from my lips. Arlen was regarding me in a quiet, watchful way that infuriated me.

"Look! Look at his eyes!" I shouted, pointing a shaking finger again. The baby's eyes had gone from their middling gray color to a deep purple shade I remembered well, dark amethyst, the deepest hue of wood violets. Arlen scarcely glanced at them.

"Babies' eyes change color," he said. Reasonable, not ungentle, but I wanted something more of him.

"You do not believe me!" I accused him.

"I do not know what to believe. Perhaps only that you need rest." He sighed. "But yours is the breast that feeds this little one."

I took the babe and gave the breast, but he could see my revulsion as I did so, and for the rest of that afternoon and all the evening he studied me, studied the babe but mostly studied me, and I could not eat under his gaze, and I slept only from exhaustion. The next morning Arlen gave me a searching glance, kissed me, and strode away to see again to the ailing cow.

As soon as he was well gone, Lonn spoke to me in his dark

and husky voice. "You should not have told him, lady," he said. "It was to be our secret."

Speech was coming to him more easily now, it seemed. I did not jump up and scream this time, but sat numbly, ignoring him.

"But it does not matter." A small note of spite slipped into the voice. "He thinks you merely mad. He will leave you, and then I will have you to myself."

"You think poorly of your friend," I retorted briefly. Though the very thought of Arlen's leaving me wrenched at my innards.

"I will have you—"

"The friend you died to save." He did not want to speak of Arlen, I saw. Or of that past time, that sacrifice.

"I want you. I will have you to myself."

"And what will you do with me," I asked sourly, "poor little thing, you?"

"I will not always be little. I will grow. My hands will learn to grasp, my body to stand and walk. I have time, all the time in the world and the afterlife; I can wait. I will grow strong in body, as I am already powerful in magic. I will have you in the end. You will be my bride."

His words, the inexorable tone of his voice, chilled me.

"And if I say you nay?" I flared, striving to hide my fear. "You think you will take me perforce, then?"

"I will force you, yes. Bed you by the king's right. Take you as is my due—"

"Not while I have strength to defend her," said a quiet voice, a strong voice of this world. Arlen came in at the door, knelt by my chair, and put his arms around me, and I laid my head gratefully against his shoulder.

# THIRTEEN

It took us some few days to decide what to do about Lonn, and during that time Arlen stayed with me constantly, to spare me Lonn's importunities and give me comfort. Grotesque as was our plight, it eased me greatly to have Arlen by me, my ally. As was his nature, he first took care to heal what lay wrong between us.

"I thought you were turning against the child," he admitted, eyes downcast. "I thought—it is foolish, I know, but I saw how babes were treated on the Sacred Isle, and I never wanted such things to happen to mine . . . . I came back to spy on you."

"And I am glad you did," I told him.

"But—I should have known better."

"What were you to believe, you who have never known a loving mother? The truth is harder to believe than the other. I wake up most mornings not believing it myself . . . . No, do not ask my forgiveness." I forestalled him. "There is no need of it." I was so heartened to feel his love, it was not hard to be noble.

We would have made love, I think, were it not for the weird presence of Lonn in the cradle. He was asleep, but he had a way of awakening quickly and looking at us knowingly with his violet eyes, those all too corporeal eyes. He awoke and looked at us in that way even as I thought of it.

"Hands off what is rightfully mine," he said.

"Rae is no man's property." Arlen did not move except to embrace me more tightly. "You gave me the gift of life, and love followed . . . ." Arlen shook his head, some part of him still caught up in painful denial. "Lonn, I do not see how you can have changed so badly, even in death."

"You ass." Words full of petty triumph. "Bribed by gold. You named this body, and now it is mine."

"Do not talk with him," I told Arlen. "It is useless. He grows ever stronger as he talks."

"Kill me," Lonn taunted.

He was already dead. Kill the body of our own infant son, he meant, and we could not do that. There was the thought in us—we could not help that, but it anguished us, and Lonn knew it, and used our sorrow to feed his spite. Arlen stared at him, too sickened for anger.

"Do not upset Rae," he said finally, "or she will lose her milk." It was not a threat, for Arlen was not of the sort to threaten, but it was a level warning of a consequence, and Lonn knew it. We had tried him on cow's milk, to spare me the nursing, and it had made him painfully ill with colic; he knew that, too. He fell silent.

"The only thing for us to do," Arlen said to me softly, "is change the baby's name."

"Can we do that? And will it work? Lonn seems quite fully in possession."

"By ourselves, we might not be able to do it. The name was

sanctified at the shrine. But if it were changed with proper authority . . . ."

So it was that, in the brown and dreary days of late autumn, we set off on a journey to the oracle. We took some of our gold from one of our hiding places in the rocks, left the rest to the care of the logans, and departed with scarcely a glance at the home we left behind.

Back to the Sacred Catena, where Arlen had sworn he would never return. The Island of Passages, where the oracle gave the names, lay next below the cenotaph . . . . Rank has its privileges, or buys them, so I had never been there, but for the most part every youth and maiden of an age to make children or bear them had to journey there for the spring quarter day, the festival of names, make the last part of that pilgrimage alone, and spend the night on the island to undergo a secret ordeal. Then was received a true name from the oracle. His name was Ophid, I knew, Ophid the Seer or Ophid Dremided; he was also the oracle who gave the names to the sacred brides when they joined the Gwyneda. I felt sure he would have heard of us, of Arlen and me, and I was not at all certain whether he might not be inclined to betray us to the Gwyneda on their Sacred Isle, which lay only a day's journey away from his own. It could none of it be helped, and it was of no use to wonder what lay ahead. We had to take Lonn to the oracle.

Bucca was in fine fettle after a summer's good feeding. Well provisioned, we traveled rapidly, the more so because we knew exactly where we were going and took the shortest ways. Through the meadows where the aurochs and wisent roamed, through the Forever Forest, dark and boggy even though the mighty trees stood bare. Back to the moors and eskers, the northern fringes of the Secular Lands.

We did not turn aside from our path even to see Briony, though I urged that we should, to learn what we could of Ophid before we consulted him. But Arlen was in a fever to get us to the Naga before winter set in hard and cold. And, I suppose, to get us to the oracle, to put an end to our ordeal.

We rode late and long. I carried the baby in my arms, nestled within my mantle, close to my body for warmth and for feeding at the breast. It should have been a tender love's labor to carry him so, a sweet memory in the making, but it was quite otherwise, for Lonn's violet eyes were greedy on me, and his small hands ever more clever at the breast, and though he spoke little I knew what it was that I held. Hatred of him shook me and made me miserable.

Snow was falling when we came to the Naga, the white flakes melting into the black water.

"There it is," Arlen murmured.

The island lay long, low, and narrow, like a backbone in the rippling Naga, the upstream end of it swollen and thick with hazel. The river ran deep and fast by its flanks, and there was no way for us to get across: no bridge, no ford, no ferryman. I guessed there might be swan boats awaiting the initiates in the spring, but none awaited us. We had to risk the crossing in what way we could. Bucca sprang in and swam. The water swirled around the saddle, around our legs, icy cold, and I clung fast to Arlen and my babe, and he clung to Bucca, guiding him upstream against the current, chirruping to him, encouraging him onward, and the water washed about our waists, about Bucca's neck, the white mane lying like froth on the surface of the water. The strong Naga swept us down, down alongside the island, we could see the red ridgy nuts on the hazels that overhung the bank, we would soon pass the point and be gone down the serpentine—

"Bucca!" Arlen shouted.

The horse's churning hooves touched gravel, caught, found us purchase. Bucca took us onto the Island of Passages and stood with his head hanging nearly to the ground, panting as the water streamed off him and dripped from our clothing.

"By the holy whites," came a soft, sibilant voice, "what have we here?"

A person stood amidst the hazel twigs, leaning forward slightly as if to hearken at us or catch our scent, a slight, slim person in a robe the nameless color of tree trunks in winter, and that wintery voice like breath of wind hailed us. More we could not tell, for hands and feet were hidden in the folds of the robe, face completely covered by the hood so that the soft-spoken one, whoever it was, walked blind. Motioning me to stay where I was, Arlen slid down from Bucca and took three steps toward the one in the dark robe, and though he stood a head taller than the other, there could be no question but that he was the supplicant.

"Are you the oracle?" he asked. "Ophid Dremided?"

"Only the oracle lives on this island." The voice came out pale and muffled from under the dark robe. It is the way of seers to be riddlesome. Arlen pursued his query without anger.

"And do you live on this island?"

"Where the oracle lives, the oracle abides, and no one other—Arlen of the Sacred Isle!"

Startled, Arlen went to one knee before him, as if before his lord.

"And—Rae." The oracle turned toward me, questing with hidden senses. "And a babe who is no babe. My children, you have chosen the strangest of times to come here. Do you not know it is the eve of the festival of the winterking, your year-day?"

Arlen jumped up and stared at me, then past me, across the water, and with an odd prickling sensation I turned to look behind me. On the shore, a strong stone's throw away, my father and his retinue were riding by, bound upstream to the ceremonials.

"Be still," Arlen whispered.

"Do not fear." The oracle's soft voice sounded no longer vague, but serenely gentle. "They will not see you where they do not expect you. Most men are like that, not knowing the ways of seeing . . . . And least of all will they expect you here, so close, this day of all days. You could almost attend the feast with impunity."

"No, thank you," I murmured.

"Come here," he told me. "Let me look at that babe."

My father and his men had passed, leaving me shaken; the very sight of Rahv had set me aquiver with wrath and terror. Arlen came and helped me down from Bucca, as I was awkward, carrying Lonn. I held the baby out toward the oracle, and he leaned forward and bent toward the child for all the world as if he were somehow peering through the dark fabric of his swaddling hood.

"Can you truly see that way?" I asked.

"I can see most truly of all this way. More truly than most who use their eyes." He straightened. "But now that I have seen, I will look," he added, and he rolled up the front of his hood from neck to forehead.

A thin, sharp-featured face looked out at us, skin and hair very light of color, eyes sapphire blue, no beard, but on his lip a wispy blond mustache. Though he was beardless he did not appear young. He did not seem to mind that we were staring at him, for he was staring equally at us.

"Drenched, the pair of you, but the babe is warm and dry. You have not yet ceased to love him."

"Our own baby!" I protested.

"Yes, of course. Well, come within, before you take cold, you and your revenant." He led off without a backward look, as if it were nothing that he should know us and our secret grief, and we followed him meekly.

"Call me Ophid," he added, his voice a soft exhalation nearly lost in the winter wind.

It was a cave, of course, where he lived, a cave extending downward like a chasm into the rocky ridge of the island as well as backward under an overhang. A crude place, but warmed by a fire. There was no stabling for Bucca. We fastened blankets around him, hoping they would ward off the chill from his wet skin, and left him in the lee of a hazel grove,

then went within. Ophid had taken off his mantle, revealing
flaxen hair that floated untidily around his head, reaching and
clinging like cobweb. He wore a slate-gray robe, and centered
on his chest lay a blue pendant such as only seers and the great
bards could wear, for it was made of glain, the holy sea egg of
the glycon. I stood by his fire, not much comforted by the
warmth, for I was afraid to sit down. All the farther corners
and crevices of the cave writhed with snakes, knotted serpents
as yellow as Ophid's yellow hair, the chain markings of the
goddess brown on their yellow backs. Only around the fire
itself was the place clear of them.

"Sit," Ophid told me, not as an order but as a reassurance.
"They are not very active at this time of year, and they would
not harm you in any event; they have no fangs. The ordeal of
those who take passage here is nothing more than this: to
spend the night with me and my snakes." He grinned mis-
chievously. "And I have not lost a youngster yet. So sit down."

I sat, resigned; I was to undergo my initiation late, it
seemed. My fear turned to puzzlement. "How is it," I asked
him, "that you know my name? Rae, I mean." Since I had
taken it myself, or Arlen had given it to me.

"Why, it is your true name, that is all. The doe of the
mountaintops, the dear, the beloved one. You have given yourself the name that would have come from me."

He fed us grain and honey and hazelnuts, and for the span
of that meal we did not speak of the trouble that had driven us
to him.

"So," said Ophid when we were finished and dusk was
coming on, "Tell me about this revenant."

We told him, eagerly and at length, setting forth the tale in
counterpoint to each other, quite sure, and rightly so, that he
would understand all that we said without shock or demur.
And indeed his thin, taut face never changed; he simply
nodded at every frightful detail we told him, and his blue eyes
scarcely blinked. Lonn kept silence. He had learned, over the
course of the journey, that his distressing me would indeed

cause me to lose my milk, and that conversely my tenderness toward him increased if he did not speak, if he were less like his violet-eyed self and more like my lost babe whose body he had stolen. In the presence of the oracle he kept silence, to show us wrong in what we said of him. But Ophid knew him well enough; he had known him before we had ever spoken of him: Lonn, the dead hero who haunted us.

"Can you help us?" Arlen appealed when we were done.

Ophid stirred for the first time, looking vaguely out into the darkness beyond the fire. "Death is the greatest and most difficult of passages," he said to neither of us. "The spirit faced with death undergoes an ordeal as of those being initiated into the greatest of Mysteries. There are wanderings full of fear and hatred and every sort of terror and pain. But after that there are the wonderful lights and fountains and the halls and meadows where the crowned join in song and in the circle dance of the blessed."

Arlen and I looked at each other in dismay. During our days spent with Ophid we were to learn that he was the most gracious of hosts and a true friend, unless he was pressed in a professional way, when he would turn obscure and riddling to a maddening degree. To this day I cannot place finger on any one thing truly useful he ever told us—and yet his presence gave us a strong sense of comfort.

"If Lonn has not completed his passage," I murmured to Arlen, "perhaps Ophid can send him on his way."

Arlen decided to be very precise with the seer. "Ophid," he said, "we want you to give the baby a new name, so that Lonn will have to leave him."

"What is called for is not always what is wanted," said Ophid obliquely. "The goddess, her names are Meripen and Mestipen, death-in-life and fate-in-fortune. I will study the snakes." He got up, pulled a blazing fatwood stick out of his fire by way of a torch, and lifted it up into the vault of his cave. Its light revealed a design there, a circle carved in deep line and high relief into the stone, a sort of chart in the shape of a great wheel of twenty-eight segments. I saw the emblems for full moon and dark moon opposite each other, top and bottom, and within each segment was inscribed a runic figure, all loops and whorls, and other symbols I understood even less.

"The great mill wheel of the universe," Ophid murmured, and then, standing there with arms and torch raised, he seemed to go into a trance. The torch dropped from his slackened finders and lay yet burning on the stone floor. His hands came down, loosened his gray robe, drooped yet farther; the robe slipped from his narrow shoulders and fell about his feet. At the limits of the firelight the snakes stirred and slithered, rearranging themselves. Ophid turned slightly toward us, peering at them—

"But he is a woman!" I blurted.

Plainly, he had breasts. The sound of my voice startled him out of his trance, and he gazed at me blankly, not at all dismayed.

"I am both things," he said. "Like the glycon."

Indeed he was. The blue glain pendant that hung between his breasts nestled amidst thick curls of golden hair. And the forms of other organs showed through his linen loincloth; he tugged it tighter around his slender legs. "As an oracle, I have to be both," he said. "That is why there are not more seers." He smiled. "It would help if I were blind, but it is not required. Lady, I beg pardon for disrobing before you. I had forgotten you were here."

And I had thought he would be angry at me for startling him. "We will go outside," Arlen said.

"No need. I am done for the nonce." He put on his robe again, picked up his torch, and walked about to peer at his yellow serpents, glancing from their sleeping bodies to the wheel-like chart carved above us.

"Oh!" I exclaimed, then felt like a fool, always my mouth speaking out of turn. But Ophid merely nodded.

"Yes. I search for the runes in the twinings of the serpents." He studied them for a while longer, then gave it up with a shrug and a sigh. "The signs are very unclear," he said, coming back to sit by the fire with us.

Arlen got up and gifted him with a chain of rich gold that shone ruddily in the firelight.

"Thank you." Ophid took it placidly and wound it about one hand. "It is very handsome. Still, the signs are quite unclear. That was no hint for payment, but merest truth."

"So what are we to do?" Arlen asked.

"For the time, nothing. Sleep. Right where you are will do, by the fire. Never fear, the serpents will not pester you, for I am going to sit here and study your dreams. And here, let me hold that troublesome babe."

Arlen and I lay down at a seemly distance from each other. But even under the gaze of Ophid's bland and curious blue eyes we could not stay long apart. We inched toward each other until our faces lay side by side and our feet nudged against each other under the blankets, and then we slept. Twice during the night Lonn cried and I rose, unwillingly, to feed him.

# FOURTEEN

We stayed with Ophid for three days, and on each day he asked us different questions, and on each day he told us a different story. And although the stories said nothing to our hands, to tell us what we should do, they spoke to our hearts and comforted us, for we sensed that they made us part of a great circling pattern and a great wheeling dance.

On the first day he asked me questions about myself and Arlen, about our love. How had we come to be so much in league with each other, after such a short time, that we had conspired to run away together? In a confused fashion, I told him about that first night and my first sight of Arlen in the stable of the blessed on the Sacred Isle.

"There was a sort of—sheen of glory on him."

"The glamour of the goddess. Yes. But you stayed together once it was gone?"

"Well . . . ." I hestitated, faltering. "The bond . . . ."

"The golden chain of the goddess. Yes. But have you regretted it?"

I looked at him in astonishment. Times had some of them been hard for us, for Arlen and me, but how could I regret? "But I had never been loved before," I protested.

"Yes, you speak as one who knows the value of love." He looked away from me then and out across the mists of the Naga, as if finding something there. Arlen came and sat silently by us. When Ophid spoke again, it was very softly, his voice like a wind out of the caves of the departed and the departed times.

"Once before now, once very long ago, there were from the Sacred Isle a pair of legendary lovers. Rowan and Fionella were their names. He was one who was reared to be winter-king, and she was one who wore the white robe, not much older than he and her babe newborn. The child had been taken from her, as is the custom, and she knew nothing of it, but she felt an emptiness and an ache beneath her breasts. Seeking comfort, somehow her eyes came to rest on Rowan, and his on her, and they risked confidence in each other, and came to an agreement, and met, in secret, and met again, and again, and more often, their hunger for each other overcoming their fear. And though Rowan was pledged to chastity for the goddess, and though Fionella had sworn fidelity to a dead king as all Gwyneda must, and both knew the penalty should they break their vows, a love grew in them that could not be denied, and they consummated it.

"Rowan had a friend among the youths of his age who knew of this most harshly forbidden passion, who sometimes carried messages from lover to lover. And this friend betrayed them to the elders of the Gwyneda, so that one soft afternoon as they lay beneath the mayblossom they were surrounded and taken. The fury of the elders was without bounds, for these two youngsters had that which the others were never again to know: that is to say, love . . . . Rowan and Fionella were bidden to repudiate each other under oath, which they would not. They were tortured with fire and bidden to repudiate each other, which they would not, but only swore troth the more fiercely. Then Rowan was put to death much in the manner of sacred kings, except with reversals, so that he was castrated and flayed while yet alive and conscious, and Fionella was made to watch. Her heart broke, and she fell down in a swoon of death. But before they could touch her, her white-robed body underwent a change and arose, and she was a swan, a fair and lovely white swan, and she took wing. And the body of Rowan burst its bonds, and he was a swan as red as rubies, as red as his spilt blood on the mayblossom, and he took wing and soared to fly beside Fionella. And their necks entwined in embrace, and then they flew away together, down the Naga. And folk say that still they live on the ait that is called after them, Swans' Isle, the island where golden apples grow. It is said that the goddess gave them immortality in this way for the sake of their passion, and that they are yet lovers."

"So the Gwyneda and the goddess do not always agree," I murmured.

"I trust not."

We had taken the tale personally, Arlen and I, queasy at the mention of the tortures. "I trust you would not be inclined to turn us over to the gentle hands of the Gwyneda," Arlen said wryly.

"Why should I?" Ophid replied, and we took the question as he had intended it, as the simplest of reassurances. Why should he, indeed? He was not a cruel person, or one to lend hand to cruelty. If he provided an ordeal for the youngsters who came to him in the springtime, it was only the ordeal of his own strangeness.

We slept, and the snakes did not trouble us, and Ophid studied the runes. The second day he asked Arlen questions about himself and Lonn.

"He was my faithful friend since I can remember," Arlen explained. "How can I tell you—he was good to me in so many ways. When we were eight or ten, they would hang live animals from stakes, rabbits and such, and make us kill them with the spear, to prepare us for—the bound and living target someday to come. And I could never kill animals, still can't, or won't, so Lonn would kill mine on the sly, to save me from a beating. Yet I could be cruel in other ways, to humans, when he would not."

"It is an awkward world, always blundering through the dance," said Ophid quietly. "But how did you come to be such comrades?"

"It just happened. We were of much the same age—"

"How do you know? Can you tell me the dates of your births?"

Arlen scowled, for of course no one knew such things on the Sacred Isle. "No, but we must have been near the same age, for they said that already in our cradles we were comrades."

"How strange," Ophid murmured. "That they would say such a thing, I mean. Could it possibly be that you are brothers?"

Arlen merely blinked at this arrant nonsense. Gwyneda were allowed only one afternoon of joy in their lives, one child they could not even call their own. "How so?" he asked, as politely as he was able.

"Twins."

"But—" Arlen struggled with this—"We are—were—not so very much alike."

"Twins need not be alike."

"But how can we know such a thing?" Arlen shook his head violently. "It is not so odd that there were two babes much of the same age. Often there are three or more, for they bring them in from—somewhere—to make up the necessary numbers should a child die of disease, or the sacred king's bride bear a girl, which must be sent away, or, the goddess forbid, should she fail to bear at all—"

"What happens then?" I asked curiously.

Arlen would not answer me. "She is drowned," Ophid said briefly, "as one who lacks the goddess's favor. And it is true that they take boy babes from cradles all up and down the Naga. Which is one reason why few folk live here."

"So I might not even be the get of the Gwyneda," Arlen said.

"So much the better. A secular can have twins as well." Ophid leaned back and met Arlen's eyes levelly. "The signs are much in favor of it."

Arlen stared back with a face gone bleak. It was much to bear that he should have sacrificed not only a comrade but a brother, a twin. He licked his dry lips twice before he could speak. "What does it matter?" he whispered at last, and Ophid told the tale.

"In the beginning days lived the glycon, the great serpent, before it had been beaten down into the deep. And it lifted its long coils and embraced the goddess in her form as the moon, and of that union the first winterking was born. Son of the serpent was the winterking, and the serpent threatened to slay him. But the goddess wanted him for herself, and took form of the great copper-brown strong-necked mighty-breasted keen-hooved mare of war and trampled the glycon down and drove him into the deep, and she took form of the fierce undine with long, pointed teeth and she bound him there with chains of orichalc and iron. To this day he yearns for her and lifts his coils in the deep, and she beats him down with whips of wind.

"But before many months of his captivity had passed, the glycon gave forth the glain, the blue egg of stone, and the winterking found it lying on the strand and carried it to his mother moon, and she ate it and conceived. And out of that union the summerking was born. Within a few days' time he grew to be a man, the very brother and twin of the winterking, and the winterking looked on him and was enraged with jealous wrath, for he knew the goddess would love him. Therefore he took his spear of ice and slew him and put him in fire and burned him. And the goddess took the winterking in his stead to her black velvet bed of sky, and her hot love destroyed him, and he died. But from the ashes of the summerking arose the summerking again, as bright and beautiful as ever. But the get of the winterking was a serpent. And in the turning of the season the summerking lay with his mother, and the serpent stung him. But before he died he took sword and slew it. Then out of its severed body stepped his brother, whole and beautiful, and the two looked at each other, twins and rivals, and wept, for they knew there would be no end to their striving.

"And so on it goes, and winter vanquishes summer and summer vanquishes winter, and the goddess is mother and lover to them both, and so on it will go until the great mill wheel of sky ceases to turn on its chains."

Ophid stopped and looked at us as if he had told us something of importance.

"Are you saying," Arlen asked heavily, "that it is in the nature of sacred kings to betray each other?"

"I am saying that there is a pattern. Summer and winter, night and day, the turning of the wheel. You and Rae have stepped outside that pattern, with the help of Lonn you have shattered it, and now—"

"What Lonn did was valiant," Arlen interrupted, fire in his voice. "More than valiant—loving and mighty. He was a hero, the most courageous of heroes—"

"And now the pattern seeks to reassert itself," Ophid said.

We stared at him, not quite comprehending, and he tried most kindly to explain.

"It is not a punishment. It is in the nature of the world to cleave to the pattern, as it is in the nature of caterpillars to crawl or of birds to eat them . . . . A hero of Lonn's stature is quite outside the pattern. The wheel turns, and what is night to his day?"

"Villain," Arlen mumbled, reluctant to say the word.

We ate grain and honey and hazelnuts, and slept through another night, and Ophid studied his yellow snakes and the runes. On the third day he asked questions of Lonn.

"Why have you not taken your passage? What is your grudge?"

The little baby, lying in a nest of folded blankets amid a wreath of snakes, which did not offer to harm him. Lonn did not answer. He had not spoken for days, and my heart was melting for the sake of his infant body, his petal-pink skin and the soft, fragant hair of his small head. But his eyes looked hard and knowing out of that innocent face. What lay there was not really my baby son at all.

"Why have you not taken your passage? What is your grudge?"

Lonn would not answer. but Ophid persisted, gently but relentlessly, through the morning of the day, and as the day waned Lonn grew angry and spoke.

"Go away."

"But I live here," said Ophid with no sign of triumph. "Why are you here?"

"They brought me here, you know that!"

"But you should be dancing in the meadows of the blessed, you who were valiant and good. Why have you not taken your passage? What holds you here?"

Lonn grimaced and panted with rage, a terrible thing to see in a helpless babe. "She is mine!" he shouted hoarsely at last.

"Who is?"

"The lady, the bride. She is mine by right. I paid the price."

"But such was your gift of love to Arlen, freely given."

"Damn Arlen! Arlen be cursed! I would have let him die on the esker, the fool, but she saved him, and then I had to save her . . . . He would have died still, but she loved him back to life."

Arlen went rigid, trembling on an edge between rage and anguish. I put my arms around him, constraining him as much as comforting him. Lonn spoke on. He was well started now, and if he had heard the word "love," he seemed to remember only one meaning to it, and one beloved.

"She's mine! I loved her from the first time I beheld her," he declared in that dark, hoarse voice. "And if the winterking glamour had been on me to start with, she would have loved me instead of him."

Probably true. But it made no difference in my love for Arlen now. I held him more tightly, trying to shut out the pain.

"I have a body now again," said Lonn. "I will grow strong enough to take her from him."

Lonn ranted on, and after a time Ophid considered that he had heard enough and tried to hush him. Then, as Lonn would not hush, Ophid picked him up and glanced at me in surprise when the baby struggled against him.

"There is power already in these infant limbs," he said.

I nodded. I had noticed it as well, saying nothing.

"Unhand me, freak!" Lonn raged. "Morphodite! He-she!"

Expressionless, Ophid carried him off to the other end of the island so that we need no longer hear him. Later, by firelight, when the baby lay asleep, he told us the third tale.

"In the days of the high kingship, when all the wars were against the fierce folk from undersea, the fell folk out of the deep, there were two warriors of the sunlit kingdom who shone above all others in valor, in strength, and in loyalty to their lord, and their names were Elidir and Eladu. They were brothers—and more than brothers, blood brothers, and friends with a friendship forged in war, and comrades. When they fought side by side, as they always did, they were well nigh invincible, and only by sorcery did the undersea folk at all stand against them. And the king gifted them mightily with chains of gold and silver-gold for their valor, the chains that bind a warrior to his lord in love and loyalty.

"And as folk will make compare, even between their own children, so the castlefolk and even the countryfolk began to say to each other, 'Elidir is mightier than Eladu,' or 'Eladu is more courageous than Elidir,' or 'Elidir slew the more enemies in the recent battle,' or 'Eladu is the more honorable,' until coins and even landholdings were placed at stake, and all eyes looked to the king, as if for a decision. But the king dealt evenhandedly with the two heroes, and honored one as he honored the other.

"Then courtiers tried in subtle ways to set Elidir against Eladu, and in ways less subtle to set Eladu against Elidir, and finally quite openly they bribed and dared them to combat each other, and in all these attempts they failed. For Elidir and Eladu stood up together in scorn of those who would make them adversaries. And in defiance of all such scheming they made a pact with each other: that when they went into war thenceforth, they would chain themselves together each to the other, chain themselves together leg to leg and arm to arm with chains of gold and silver and glowing bronze, so that if one were to fall the other must fall also, and neither would be accounted mightier than the other. And they sealed this pact with their word and handbond and blood.

"In the course of time the forces of the glycon gathered and made ready once more to assault the land, and Elidir and Eladu met them with the others on the strand. Their helmets were of bronze, and their shields also, and their swords and greaves and breastplates were of orichalc, the glowing bronze, and they were chained together with chains of precious metal, arm to arm and leg to leg. They shone gloriously upon the field of battle. Then, seeing scorn and challenge and defiance in their splendor and their chains, the fierce undersea folk bent all their malice upon felling them, and as Eladu was the worse off, his sword arm being chained to his brother's shield brace, they focused their assault on him. In the long course of a bloody day, they succeeded in harrying him to his knees and then to the ground, and Elidir was staggering.

"Then Elidir felt the weight of his doomed brother dragging on him, his brother who was as good as dead, and he knew that chains were on him also to die in like wise. Chains were pulling him down to lie by his brother's side. But he wanted to live."

Ophid paused and merely glanced toward Arlen, who sat listening as if entranced.

"He cut the chains," Arlen whispered, and Ophid nodded.

"He cut the chains with his sword. But Eladu saw him do it, and with the last of his strength he reached up and caught at the dangling ends with his hand and pulled his brother down, and the sea folk swarmed over them both."

"Why?" Arlen breathed. There were tears in the word, and the ragged ends of dreams.

"Because the pattern tends always toward balance, and the wheel turns. Those who are born strangers to each other meet and cleave and become comrades or lovers; those who were born brothers must someday go their separate ways—or love turns to venom in them."

"But they were heroes," Arlen said.

Ophid pointed up at his great carved wheel, at the twenty-eight segments, the full moon and the dark. "Hero is all light," he said. "Villain is all dark. The one strives to overtake the other, and death attends them. We who live, we are more in the balance of the pattern. We are fools and churls and lechers and misers and madams and sluts; I could name you twenty more. We are dames, clerics, merchants, farmers, soldiers, maids. Some few of us are oracles who sit aside and talk." He grimaced, mocking himself. "We live. Are you a hero, Arlen?"

"No," said Arlen promptly, though his voice was low.

"Long life to you, then. And may you find the large joys and the small in all the days of it."

We lay down by the fire, but we did not sleep much that night, in spite of Ophid's warm words. We had sensed the weight of doom in his story, and we knew that in the morning he would tell us more of it.

He did, after we had eaten. "I have been lying to you," he admitted.

We stared at him, for of all things that was the last we would have thought of him, that he should mislead us.

"The signs have been plain," he explained, "all along, not obscure. But I had to be quite sure . . . ."

We sat silent and gazed at him, waiting.

"It is also in the pattern, the ancient pattern," Ophid said, "that the son of the winterking will wed his mother. And this is the pattern that seeks to conceive itself, the abomination against which the Gwyneda so carefully guard."

He looked at us, but we would not speak, and reluctantly he went on.

"I have searched and searched for a name for your babe, the boy babe who is truly yours, Arlen and Rae. And I find none except the one you have already given him—that is to say, Lonn—and one other, which is: Arlen. And whichever of those two you give him, his doom remains the same: that he should love you in the way of a consort, Rae."

# FIFTEEN

I sat like so much wood; I could not speak, and I did not dare to think. It was Arlen who spoke at last, wetting dry lips. "What are we to do?" he whispered.

"Send the babe away," said Ophid.

We looked at each other numbly, not willing to comprehend, and Ophid got up and walked back to some recess of his cave where the snakes lay. When he returned he was carrying a basket, and he laid it before us. It was a plain wicker basket, such as I had seen once before bumping against the shore of a certain crannog, and of a size and shape to accommodate a baby snugly. I looked at it with a chill, and in spite of myself I understood.

If the baby had been sleeping, the beloved little one, I think I could not have done it. But he was awake, Lonn was awake, peering at us with those unnatural violet eyes of his, and he saw the basket and yelled out loud. "You cannot!" he shouted. "Plotting to kill me, call it by no other name—"

That hated, husky voice. Arlen must have loathed it as I did. "What do you care?" he retorted, swiftly and savagely. "You are already dead."

But Lonn spoke only to me. "Lady, if you do this thing you will bear my curse," he cried, babbling in his haste to save himself. "Your breasts will sag forever full of milk, and they will pain you. Serpent dreams will harrow your sleep. Your face—"

I picked him up, leaving the blankets behind, and put him in the basket, and did not let my hands linger on him.

"Lines of sorrow will come on your face!" he shouted. "Your lovemaking will give you no joy—"

I picked up the basket, not touching the babe, and what more Lonn said I do not remember, for I shut my ears and my mind to it, though I know he shouted all the way down to the shore. I carried him to the water myself, and Arlen and Ophid came with me, and with my own hands I placed the basket in the Naga. It spun and eddied in the backwater by the island's shore. I remember that spinning, the turning and turning of Lonn's hard, hateful eyes in the baby's furious face, but I remember no sound. I think Arlen said something, and he went into the water and pushed the basket out so that the current took it, went into the water up to his knees. Then Lonn was gone, was only a speck floating down the Naga, into the mist and gone forever.

We walked back to Ophid's cave, and Arlen brought Bucca out of the hazel coppice and began to saddle him at once. We could not soon enough be gone from that place.

"Stay a minute," Ophid offered. "Sit by the fire, dry yourself."

Arlen wordlessly shook his head.

"Very well, if you must go . . . . Have you provision?"

"We have wherewithal," Arlen muttered. I brought our blankets, a few other possessions, and he tied and loaded them on Bucca.

"Be watchful," Ophid told us. "The lords will yet be riding homeward from the Sacred Isle."

We had forgotten. We stopped our preparations and looked at Ophid for a moment. His face had gone bleak, and we reached out of one accord and touched his shoulders, as if to say, It is not your fault. Then we mounted Bucca and departed as quickly as we could, sending him springing into the Naga and swimming across in the freezing cold.

We did not speak to each other. Ophid's warning concerning the lords gave us excuse enough to be silent. But in fact we met no one to fear. Arrow-straight and nearly as swift, we left the region of the Naga. We slept that night in an outlander's warm cottage, with no taint about us but not much cheer either, and we shivered beneath down comforters, not touching each other, and told ourselves the night was chill.

The first of Lonn's imprecations did not come to pass. My milk dried up within two days, and my breasts ceased to ache after three. On the fourth day a snowstorm whistled down from the north, a fierce winter storm as deadly as the one that had driven us to a cenotaph a year before. We took shelter with a homesteader this time, and I tried not to think of the baby out there, pelted by ice, somewhere on the Naga. He should have been dead before then even of the milder winter chill. I hoped he had not cried too much, my Spriggan. For my own part, I could not weep, could not grieve for the one I myself had cast away. I thought of him as floating, floating, forever floating, down the Long Lake and through the Wondermere and past the Isle of Promises and all the way down the Lake of the Lost City and out on to the great vastness of the sea, a speck, still floating. I myself felt as if I were floating, adrift in my world, lost, and I would not think of him in any other way, as aground in death, drowned, disintegrating, returning to earth; such thoughts hurt me. In my mind I kept him my pink-petal babe, forever rocked on the waves of the sea.

It took us a month and more to return home, in the snow, and in all that time we scarcely spoke to each other, Arlen and I, and the worst of it was, I did not care.

We reached our mountain haven on a gray day of deepest

winter, and all stood so silent, so still, so cold, that we sat on Bucca staring, reluctant to dismount and begin again. But there was nowhere else to journey to. Finally I slipped down, and Arlen went off to the village to fetch our chickens and our cow, and I began in a drifting way to lay a fire on the hearth.

We went through the motions of our days. Arlen tended to his animals, his friends. I cooked food, swept dirt, sat idle the rest of the time. I could have gone down to the village for companionship; there was no taint on me any more, no death dog. But I did not. Arlen tried harder than I did to find a way back to the contentment we had known before. He took up his calling as a healer again, went to the village every day, smiled at the folk he met. Sometimes he touched me on the shoulder or caressed my hair. I seldom responded. One day, as I sat by an empty cradle, he knelt beside me and placed gentle hands on mine, which lay twisting in my lap.

"We—could have another," he suggested, very softly, very diffidently. "Perhaps it might be a girl . . . ."

"And if it were not?" I snapped, as if the whole horror were somehow his fault. "What must I do with another boy? Drown it in the cistern?" So he got up and left me alone, as being alone was what I seemingly wanted.

What a quaint pattern life makes. When Lonn had been too much with us we had struggled, stolen moments to make love at times and in places safe from the spying of his angry eyes. And now that he was gone, now that we had all the world and time to spare, we scarcely looked at each other. We had not kissed since that last night beside Ophid's fire. Nor did I see how we ever could again.

"It will get better," Arlen said to me one evening during my long silence, helplessly. "Things will get better as time goes on. You must believe that, Rae."

I did not believe it, not in any measurable way. But time did go on. Signs of early spring appeared, the purple buds swelling, the tree frogs creaking in the night. Some sort of stirring took place in me also, within my numb endurance, and I began to think again. The small added pain of thinking did not matter to me any more. Snow melted, and something hard and frozen began to melt in me and pool, though I could not yet weep.

"I have been blaming you," I said quietly to Arlen one evening, in the midst of the silence, as he would sometimes speak to me. "And I have been blaming Ophid, and the goddess, and the world, and the Naga for being the way they are, anything to blame away my pain."

He looked at me with a sunrise of hope in his face, though he tried hard to suppress it, and he set down the pegs he was carving and came over to me.

"But now I see it is no use blaming anyone but myself," I told him. "What I did was wrong, deathly wrong, and all sense should have told me that."

Sunrise faded. "We had no choice, Rae," he said softly.

"I am not speaking of you. I am the mother, and I speak of me. I held a baby in my arms, and I cast it away. I was frightened, worn down by fear, but now I have suffered too much to be any longer afraid and I see that I was wrong. No mother can give up her child in such a way and be blameless. All nature is against it."

"Rae, give it over, let it go, turn away! Have you not grieved enough?" He had grasped me by the arms in his fervor, nearly shaking me, but I sat impassively in his hands. "Do not blame yourself," he begged. "It is just—something that happened. We have the authority of the oracle—"

"And I believed the oracle. And I still cannot think badly of Ophid; nor can I think badly, any longer, of you. But I have seen things in a new way, and I know now that what I did was wrong." I stood up, and he stood beside me, and suddenly he was angry at me.

"Very well," he flared. "You are a heartless, wicked woman. What are you going to do about it?" For he thought there was nothing to be done.

And I surprised him by smiling at him. I think it was an

unnerving smile. "But I have not said that I was wicked," I told him softly. "Only that what I did was wrong." And I went to bed and lay in the dark, half triumphant, for I had a plan. I had not, indeed, given up my child. And as for what had gone wrong, I hoped somehow to set it right.

I grew more cheerful over the next several days, and talked readily with Arlen about commonplace things, and he noticed it. This was all part of my plan, to comfort and reassure him. What I had not expected was that I felt my love for him again blooming in my heart. I would have to leave soon, or I would not be able to bear it.

For leave I must, to find the babe. And, as I felt certain that Arlen would not knowingly let me go, I would have to slip away in secret. In some other plight, perhaps, with nothing wrong between us, he might have let me go off on my own— but I felt sure he would hold desperately to me now, for he would be too afraid of losing me forever, too afraid that I would not come back. He would try to keep me by him, or, failing that, he would come with me. And I felt beyond all reason that this was a journey I had to make on my own. Only, how to leave him hopeful, comforted . . . ?

"Look, Arlen," I cried rather crazily one day, "the swallows."

The birds were coming back to their nests in the rocks. Back from the far reaches, as they did every spring.

"The swallows," I told him earnestly, "they are like us, Arlen, their fidelity. They return. They always return."

He peered at me strangely and merely nodded. Perhaps he thought I spoke of our returning to our home from the Naga. But I knew my eyes were wide, my color high, and I hoped he would remember afterward, and understand.

It was not difficult for me to make my way to one of our scattered hoards and take some gold for myself without being seen. Provision was more troublesome. I could not prepare anything of a quantity to see me through the wilderness without Arlen's noting it and wanting to know why. Nor, for that matter, could I prepare much for Arlen, either, to sustain him for a few days while I was gone. In the end I made a meat pie for each of us and put them aside, and that was all. And I kissed Arlen that evening before we went to sleep, and my heart ached for him, because I knew what happiness that made him hope for, and in the morning when he awoke I would be gone.

I waited until he was well asleep, and then I slipped out of our bed and took just a spare blanket and a few viands and a change of clothing, that was all, in haste, and I went to saddle Bucca. There was no question of my not taking Bucca, for unless I did so Arlen would himself ride and overtake me. On Bucca I could leave him well behind before morning. Arlen would have to borrow a horse to do the spring plowing . . . . When Bucca was standing at the ready, I went softly back inside the cottage for a moment and took a charred stick and drew the outline of a swallow on the flat, dressed stone of the hearth. I made it distinct, dark enough so that I could see it in the moonlight from the window. I wanted to kiss Arlen again, but I was afraid that I would wake him. I put his dinner on the table, and so I left him and rode toward the south and west, over the lip of the mountain.

We had found a way to ride down the terraces by then, a hard way but not impossible, and Bucca knew it as well as I did. Still, I must have been desperate or crazy to try that trail by moonlight, and half a dozen times I believe we nearly broke our necks, Bucca and I. And he wanted so badly to go back to his warm stall—I had to force him onward, kicking him and lashing him with a stick, weeping all the while because I longed for home as fervidly as he did.

When light of dawn began to show, I found the going easier, and by the time Arlen might have been stirring in our bed, I was well down past where we had found our hoard of treasure. For what treasure was worth.

I rode hard all day, and I rode late, and I ate little. No one pursued me or disturbed me, for no one lived in these parts except logans and the beasts of the wilderness. And the next day and the days that followed I rode early and late and as swiftly as I was able. My food was soon gone, and it was mushrooms and wild asparagus again to eat. I did not care, for I was not very hungry, as I had not been for months. I wanted only to get through the Forever Forest to the wild moorlands where the eskers were, and to a certain esker, and a soddy. I was on my way to see Briony. Mandrake that he was, speaker with spirits, he might be able to tell me a way to find my baby.

# SIXTEEN

The trees were fully in leaf when I reached the familiar soddy and stopped Bucca outside the door. I dismounted, but before I could knock, Briony opened it and came out to me.

"Rae," he said in a low voice, staring. "But—you are thin, your face is drawn down by sorrow. What has happened?"

His eyes were still as black as beads of onyx, his face expressionless. I found his blankness oddly comforting. We went in and sat facing each other, and I told him everything, told him things I would not have been able to tell anyone who would have cried out in shock or wept in pity. He had lit the lamp before I was done, and when I was finished he wordlessly prepared us some supper while I tended to Bucca. There was no question but that I would spend the night under his roof, nor did I think amiss of so doing.

We ate supper and cleaned away the leavings in a silence that troubled neither of us. After we were done, Briony spoke to my plaint as if I had only just voiced it.

"Wrong it may have been, as you feel it was wrong," he said. "But if wrong it was, then Ophid has erred gravely, and that would be unlike him, for he is a highly competent oracle."

"I was much impressed by Ophid," I said. "I do not think badly of him in any way. Nevertheless, and against all reason, I feel that I was terribly wrong to cast away the babe."

"And you wish to right the wrong."

"It is not just that." I swallowed. "I—I want my baby back."

He must have heard the pang in my voice, but his face did not change. "Yes," he murmured. "Of course."

"So will you tell me, Briony, where I might find him?"

"It seems reasonable to suppose," he said, "that the little one is in the realm of the dead."

He said that as another person might have said. "He is in Stanehold" or "She has gone to the marketplace"; he spoke as of a place he was familiar with. I sat up eagerly.

"But where is that, Briony? How do I reach it?"

"How does a serpent seek the underworld?" he questioned in return. I bristled, thinking he was trifling with me.

"Don't riddle me, Bri! I had quite enough of that with Ophid."

"But I speak of simple fact!" He raised his dark brows slightly. "One enters the Afterworld through the serpent's burrow."

"*What* serpent?"

"Why, the great serpent, to be sure."

Memory of an immense head, a forked tongue as long as a sword. "In the esker?" I hazarded.

"Nay, Rae. You'll have to go farther than that." He was not laughing at me after all. "The greatest of serpents. The Naga."

"Of course," I murmured.

"The adder's tongue feels the way."

It would be far to the north, at the source. "Is it a cave?" I asked. "A passage?"

"Yes. But you know, Rae, there are dangers. You may not be allowed to return, having once gone down there."

"I will have to risk it," I said, and my bravado was not all false; I cared for no danger, those days. I had even risked leaving Arlen.

"You will need gold," said Briony, "for the water crossing."

"I have gold enough."

"And do not eat in those nether regions, not so much as a crust of bread, and most especially not elderberries or any other of the foods of the dead."

The familiar prohibitions. "I will remember," I said, and I thought the conversation was done. But I was wrong.

"Rae . . . ."

What could he want of me?

"Has it gone wrong between you and Arlen?"

"I hope not," I told him. "I hope he will be waiting for me when I return. I hope there will be—love between us . . . ." My voice faltered as I wondered how, with the curse that seemed to be on us.

"If not," said Briony softly, "there is love for you here."

I stared at him, astonished beyond speaking, and he left his place at the table to come over and kneel on the dirt floor beside me. His hard brown face looked as blank as ever, except that maybe there was just a suggestion of pleading in it.

"I loved you from the first day I saw you," he said, "if what a mandrake conceives by way of devotion is to be called love. I am an unhearted thing, quiet; I can make no great show. But I am constant, Rae."

I found my tongue, and I am ashamed to say that all I had to offer him was annoyance.

"Half my childhood I wanted love," I exclaimed, "and now I have found all too much of it, it seems! Lonn, and now you—"

"I am sorry," he said, and he got up hastily. "I did not mean it to be an onus on you. I only told you because I thought, if you should ever want a shelter, a haven—I would ask nothing of you."

"I don't care," I shouted at him, because what he was saying frightened me. "I shall love Arlen forever. Even if we never touch each other again."

"I know that love," Briony said, his voice bleak, and I looked at him where he stood, then hung my head.

For some time there was silence. Finally he went to the hearth and sat down.

"It is a perplexity," he said in a dry, dispassionate voice, "how I, a mandrake and a dealer in philters for passion, could have let myself be surprised into such an entanglement." He spoke almost lightly, and I looked at him in growing amazement and something of compunction.

"You could have given me such a philter at any time while I was here, slipped it into my food or drink."

"What good would it have done?" He shrugged, waving away my reluctant gratitude. "I could only have inspired in you a passion equal to your love for Arlen, nothing more, for there is no greater devotion. You would have been torn, heart torn, between us."

He had refused to hurt me. "And you saved Arlen's life," I said in wonder, "when you could have let him die. You saved him for my sake."

"Of course."

"And you bear no grudge against him."

"Of course not." He peered at me as if to say, You humans are a skewed and twisted lot. "I like him very much," he added. "As much as a mandrake can like anyone."

"Might all men be as honorable as a certain mandrake." I got up uncertainly, no longer so willing to spend the night beneath his roof. "I should go."

"Why?" He got up also but did not offer to come near me. "I am, as you say, honorable. You have nothing to fear from me."

That was true, I felt sure. I could trust him; indeed, I would have trusted him with my very life. I wished I could somehow give him happiness. But I did not love him, could never love one whose eyes did not know how to smile, and I could not feel comfortable in the presence of his pain. Once I left him in the morning, I knew, I would not come near him again.

So I slept by his hearth, slept soundly, and he did not disturb me. And I ate with him in the morning with no fear, and took the provision he gave me with thanks and no thought of spells or entrapments.

"I should come with you," Briony said. "There will be dangers."

I am afraid I gave him a rather sharp glance. I wanted no man with me, not even a mandrake; I would not have wanted him before his declaration of devotion, and I wanted him all the less thereafter.

"This is a journey I must make alone," I told him.

"I dare say. May you survive it, Rae." He stood back and let me depart. I sent Bucca springing northward, and I did not look back or lift a hand in farewell.

"Remember what I have told you, Rae," he called after me. I did not respond.

But I thought on the things he had told me from time to time as I rode. Remember his declaration of love, he had meant—or had he meant his dour words of warning? Dangers. Might I survive. It was devoutly to be hoped. I assumed he spoke of the dangers of the passage to the Afterworld, as they were ones I had not faced before—and so perhaps he did. But I had not gone more than half a day's journey, with my mind far ahead, and never had I been thinking less of the old outworn ghosts of my childhood, when—hoofbeats, the leaves of a coppice stirred, shouts and the clash of weapons to both sides of me, and before I could urge Bucca past his first startled jump I was surrounded by armed men. My father's men.

And in a stately manner, Rahv himself rode up to confront me.

To my own fleeting bemusement, I did not feel afraid. I was all aflame with anger and chagrin that I had been so meekly taken, but—fear? Too much had happened since I had seen him last, and I had grown beyond fearing him. I considered briefly whether it might not be wise to tremble, cower, grovel, or produce a fit of timely tears, stratagems I had once used to survive with him. But there was no weeping of that sort left in me. I simply stared at him, hard-faced, as he stared at me, he an ill-humored man with a pointed beard, and if I was born of his loins my heart did not know it.

"Callous wench," he said coldly. "Ill favored, ill-begotten imp—"

"I am your daughter, or so I have been told," I retorted.

His thin face washed red, then white, with wrath. He forced his horse up to mine and went to thwack me across the face with the leather riding gloves he held in one hand. I eluded the blow, which enraged him, and two of his men reached out to hold me by the arms until he had beaten my cheeks to his satisfaction.

"Wicked!" he shouted, "Wanton!"

He was not satisfied, not really, because I had not wept or cried out. Then he spied a glint of precious metal at my neck.

"What is this? Gold?" he cried, and he seized the chain, twisting it until it snapped and came off my neck into his hand. Then he ripped my dress halfway down to my waist, searching for more, and he found them, found them all, and had them, and sat glaring at me with the golden chains dripping from his hand, his humor in no way improved. "Where has a slut like you come by gold?" he demanded.

I sat, wordless and smoldering as before, and in a moment he smiled at me, a parlous discomfiting smile.

"Never mind," he said. "In a few weeks I will hear you scream clear across the Naga."

My face must have changed, for his smile grew broader and yet more evil.

"Even so, my very own child. You seem not to fear me any more, brazen one, but you fear the Gwyneda, is it not so? Well, they want you, runaway bride."

"What—" The question escaped me before I could stop it entirely.

"What do they want you for? What are they going to do with you? Why, the goddess has need of vengeance, Cerilla." He was gloating, damn him. "On you, faithless one, and also on your precious Arlen. And you will tell the Gwyneda where he is, so that I and my men here may go to fetch him."

"No," I whispered.

"Ah, but yes, you will tell them. Believe me, most assuredly you will."

He had what he wanted. I was afraid now, trembling with fear. He sat for a while and watched me shaking, and then with a smug air he turned to his men.

"Let none of you touch her except to restrain her should she attempt to escape," he told them. "She belongs to the Gwyneda."

And in fact there was no opportunity for escape. He saw to that. Even as we rode I was always surrounded.

He himself did not touch me either, throughout that journey, to beat me or humiliate me. He preferred torments of a subtler sort. I was often aware that he watched me with a dark and subdued glee, apparently taking pleasure in the panic of my thoughts. And my thoughts grew more frantic with every rod we traveled toward the river. Who might rescue me? Arlen? Briony? I had left them both behind; I was on my own. Very well, then, how might I escape? A trick, a ruse, a lie? Nothing that I could think of seemed likely to work. My father was far more clever in that way than I.

My father. What sort of man was he, to do this? How could he be so cruel, and yet be kin to me? I was not cruel. Or was I?

The pace was wearing, for my father wanted to reach the Sacred Isle in time for the festival of the summerking. He wanted me to watch a sacred king die, he told me, knowing that it would sicken me. He wanted me to see how merciful the Gwyneda could be, compared to what they intended to do to Arlen. So we rode long, hard days, and as they went by I grew more weary than frightened any more, more weary than angry or hating, and I began to speak to this strange man, Rahv, my father, in merest curiosity.

"Why are you doing this?" I asked him levelly one day as we rode. "Taking me prisoner to the Gwyneda, I mean."

"So they will take their curse off my land and crops," he said. He was weary too.

"But there is more to it than that." There had to be. "It has been a year and a half, and you have not yet starved. Why have you followed me so long?"

He glanced over at me, blinking as if trying to focus his eyes, as if trying to see me clearly. Then he jerked his head up, recalling himself.

"Hold your tongue," he snapped. "It is not your place to ask me for reasons." I continued to look at him, and he shook his head as if the look goaded him. "If I ride a horse, shall it not obey me?" he shouted at me. "And if I have a hound, shall it not follow at heel or know the whip? Know your place, woman."

I had hurt his pride, it seemed, by my disobedience. I might as well have said to the Gwyneda, See, my father is no man, for he does not control me utterly. The ass. And injured pride had made him relentless. Well, let him be relentless.

"You killed my mother," I said to him. It was scarcely a question, though I had never spoken of her to him before.

He gave me a long stare filled with black hatred, but it was a measuring stare as well. "Why, yes," he said finally, "I did. She displeased me."

That last was said most ominously, but I grinned at him—or sneered, rather, showing my teeth in the hateful smile I had lately learned from him. As I was doomed to die anyway, I would displease him as much as I liked. I saw him go white with fury, but he did not lift fist to hit me. He merely spurred his horse away.

We were three days late for the ceremonials of the summer-king, to his vexation. All his lordly rivals had gone home, so he could not flaunt me in front of them as he would have liked to do. We merely stood in a cluster on the shore, and the five elders of the Gwyneda came across the dark waters of the Naga to us in five swan boats. In their midst swam a sixth boat of black.

"Very good, Rahv," said one of the elders to my father in a bored tone, and then to me, in tones quite venomous and not at all bored, "You will come to wish you had never heard of love, girl."

"I thought you did not speak to seculars," I replied. A foolish, childish retort, but I had to say something; I would not meekly stand and be threatened. She smiled, though, as if my words had given light to her wrath.

"Rules are for underlings," she told me. "We who are elders go where we will and speak to whom we like." Her face moved in soft folds as she spoke. It was wrinkled and graying, with a deadly pallor about it, so that almost she seemed of a piece with her hood and her robe. "Moreover, you are one of us, girl, remember? To your sorrow." She turned from me with a motion of dismissal and spoke to my lordly father again. "Very good, Rahv, we are well pleased. You may go until we summon you again."

"On the contrary, good priestess," he said courteously, "I propose to stay—and listen."

" As you will."

They seized me by the arms and put me into the black swan boat, wherein they fettered me by black chains of iron. Confound and curse them, how had they known I was planning to brave the dark waters of the Naga? As I had not been quite desperate enough to do on my first crossing . . . . Although it was summertime, I sat and shivered as the black swan swam me across to the Sacred Isle, the place of all places where I had wanted never to come again.

In their white robes the Gwyneda lined the shore, silent as snow, watching as I was taken in, still in my black chains. I wondered briefly which one was the youngest, the girl who had lately wed the summerking. Poor child, I could not tell, for they all looked the same . . . . Then I was brought down to the dungeon, and I had no time to wonder more.

# SEVENTEEN

Pain is partly subject to thinking, I discovered. In truth, the pain of what they were doing to me was no worse than the pain of childbirth, except perhaps that it gave less respite. No worse, and I had been glad enough to undergo the pain of childbirth for the sake of the babe—I would not think of the babe. No worse than the pain of childbirth. Only their hatred of me made the difference, the fact that the pain was not merely happening but was being inflicted on me by them, their white hands never soiled, their white robes never ruffled, five prim old women, for they had only to reach out now and then to turn a pin on one of their horrible machines . . . . Pain is only pain. So it made me scream, my body writhe; no matter. If a kind face had been at hand I would have smiled through my tears. Who cared for the hatred of the Gwyneda? Pain was of no significance.

"Let us have the boot," one of them said, "as she is a runaway."

I did not care. Whatever they did to my hands or feet or arms or legs or the muscles of my body did not matter to me. I avoided the thought that they were only just beginning.

"If you tell us where to find Arlen," said the eldest to me, "this will all stop—for the time." She had a mole on her face, and out of it grew two thick hairs like horns. I stared at it in blessed detachment as I shook my head.

"What, no longer so saucy?" she taunted. "You now obey the rule of silence, when it is least needed?"

"I have scarcely been silent," I told her, for I had screamed myself hoarse already. I had made my father happy, curse him. Curse old mole-face.

My insolence annoyed her, and she scowled. "Where is Arlen?" she cried sharply, as if to surprise an answer out of me.

"I'll die before I tell you that," I answered just as sharply. She hissed and spat like a snake, tightened a vise, and I shrieked as the great metal boot squeezed my foot. In a moment the small bones would crack, they would lame me—

A bell rang, a tolling sound, and the Gwyneda got up on the instant and filed out the door. It was dawn, time for them to see to the most high service of the goddess. The eldest of them went last, pausing for a moment at the door to speak to me.

"Pray do not run away," she said nastily, and she departed. I sat chained to a stone wall with a boot of iron on one foot. The pain of it gradually subsided to a dull ache, but I knew that it was squeezing the life out of a part of me. I wondered when they would return, then tried not to think of that. They would return only to do something worse.

Like the door of my chamber, a year and more before, the door of this torture chamber bore neither lock nor bar. Well, what need, with all the chains? And as I sat, thinking no farther than the next moment, it creaked and opened and a solitary woman in white slipped in. A familiar face, but changed, somehow, older . . . . Then I recognized her and found the name.

"Erta," I whispered.

By way of reply she crouched by my feet, unscrewed the vises of the boot and slipped it off. My foot came out of it chalk-white and wrinkled, then went purple and red, and I sat gasping in pain, but Erta took no time for sympathy. From some deep pocket of her robe she drew a tool, a rasp, and in greatest haste she began with it to cut the link that held my chains to the stone. For several moments there were no sounds but the scrape of metal on metal, my breathing, and the grunting noises she made as she labored.

"It's the best I could do," she panted, meaning the wood rasp, not meant for such a task. I ardently hoped it would not break. She was leaning on it with all her strength, but her strength was not great, and she was in a tumult, shaking and fumbling, her face running with sweat. She was terrified, and I wondered why she was helping me.

"I am grateful," I told her fervently.

"It's for Arl," she said, not unkindly. "They would have it out of you, sooner or later, where to find him, and I want one of my boys to live."

"Yours?" I exclaimed.

She sawed away all the harder, as if goaded by physical pain. "They should have both lived," she whispered. "If I'd been braver . . . ."

I sat without replying, letting her work.

"If I had taken them away early on, at any risk . . . . But they drug you, you know, in your food, for years, so you will be docile. Most of us remember nothing. But I wanted to remember, and I starved myself, and I do remember . . . the twins . . . ."

"Then it's true," I murmured.

"Pull on your chains," she said.

I pulled hard. They did not come loose. She sawed away again, frantically.

"You think I am a coward," she accused me suddenly.

"Hardly," I said. She was there, was she not?

"You say . . . I let my sons go . . . to the oak . . . ."

She gulped and shuddered, and tears trickled down with the sweat on her face. She stood still, and the file fell from her slackened fingers, fell with a clang to the stone floor.

"Erta," I urged her, "finish it. There is just a little more to do."

She did not move.

"Erta!" I pleaded. Then I looked at her face and saw that her mind had broken. I could hope for no more help from her.

I could not reach the rasp or the half-cut link. And the elder Gwyneda would be back at any moment, I felt sure of it. I stifled a sob of desperation, then rose as far as I was able and threw all the weight of my body against my bonds. I shoved against the wall with my legs, straining. My bruised foot hurt fiercely, and iron bracelets cut into my wrists. I jerked against them harder, I shrieked—and there was a snap, and I fell back on the stone floor.

Panic got me up within the moment, though I could scarcely see for pain. "Which way?" I muttered.

Erta was standing motionless, looking at me without comprehension. I grasped her by the arm and hurried her through the door, into the corridor. "Which way is out?" I demanded.

Vaguely she gestured to the left. Somewhere I heard the sound of footsteps. I ran, ignoring the throbbing of my bruised foot, and left her standing there.

It was not as difficult as I had feared to find my way out. The hold of the goddess was small enough when sorcery did not enlarge it, and it was merely a matter of going up the spiral stairs and out at a portal into morning light—I had spent but one long night there. River to either side, glimpsed through willows. My father's encampment on the eastern shore of the Naga. I turned toward the opposite side of the island and ran down toward the water. Heavy chains trailed from my wrists, burdening me, but I would swim if I had to, and in all likelihood drown. I would gladly have drowned rather than let them force me to betray Arlen. Thicket of willow and water's edge—

And something the color of a tree trunk moved. A figure in a robe of gray-green-brown came slowly toward me. The hood was drawn down completely over its face. I stood trembling with the thought of help but at the same time poised to flee, fearful of treachery. "Ophid?" I whispered. "Please, Ophid, let me see you."

"I can see you well enough." Nevertheless, he raised the hood, peered at me with pale blue eyes under brows the color of tow. "It is true," he muttered. "About the babe. But I don't understand how I can have been so wrong."

"*Ophid*," I said urgently, "what are you doing here? Can you help me get away? Please—"

A shriek sounded from the hold behind me, a chilling scream of anger, fearsome as a harpy's scream, and then another shriek, a long, gurgling cry of pain.

"They've found me gone already!" I cried.

"This way." He turned and led me swiftly, half running, through a band of willows and down into a small cove or inlet, and there floated his boat. It was in the shape of a cormorant, the snake bird, brown and, to my eyes, beautiful. We splashed through the shallows and blundered on board, and the boat pointed its sharp-beaked prow toward midstream and swam. More swiftly than the swan boats it swam, with head held high and alert, and I could have wept with relief as the Sacred Isle grew smaller behind me.

"I will take you to yon shore," said Ophid. "No farther."

The western shore, where no one but heroes trod, where my father and his minions could not reach me. It seemed fair enough, for the time. But Ophid went on as if I had reproached him.

"The Gwyneda allow me about and give me their good graces, as I am a harmless sort of half-woman creature," he said edgily, "and I have no wish to change that. I hope they have not seen me with you. The mist may have hidden us."

There was little mist that morning. I looked at him and wondered. "Ophid," I asked, "how did you come to be at hand when I was most sorely in need?"

"The Island of Passages has ears," he grumbled. "Now, listen!"—before I could speak again. "Go northward along the Naga until you come to the Island of Fugitives; it lies in the southern reaches of the Blackwater. If once you can come to that island and hang your chains on the holy ash that grows in the midst of the grove there, no one will ever again be able to pursue you to capture you. You will be under the protection of the Gwyneda themselves."

"The Island of Fugitives," I murmured. I had heard of it. Folk said the tree hung thick with chains.

With a small bump the cormorant brought us to shore. Ophid helped me out—or urged me, rather.

"I must be off," he said uneasily. "I am no hero, Rae. Fare well. The best of luck be with you."

I smiled my thanks and started off.

"Go speedily," he added, and then he went speedily himself, sending his cormorant skimming back downriver.

He need not have exhorted me. I wanted nothing more than to come to the Island of Fugitives before nightfall. I ran as far as I was able, limping, lifting my burden of chains, and then I walked until I had caught my breath, and then I ran again. But not too long, not too fast, not in panic; I ran as evenly as I was able. It would be of no use to exhaust myself, I reasoned. The way would lead through a long day—

And then I saw the swan boats coming up the Naga.

Instantly desperation seized me, and I ran as I would not have believed possible a moment before, my sore foot all but forgotten. I veered away from the riverbank, trying to put trees and thickets between me and those terrible white things, trying to hide—but I could not hide while I was moving, and I could not stray too far from the Naga, or I would never find the Island of Fugitives and the holy grove that grew on it. The going was harder father up the bank, in the thickets. Only when there were clearings could I run at speed, and then I was exposed to view. Two sorties they made and I crouched in the boskage and eluded them, but on the third try they spied me, and with cries like the blood-hungry cries of ravens they sent their swans sliding toward the shore.

I fled like a hunted deer, all the time trying to reason away my horror of them. Gently, I told myself, go more gently, keep a cool head. It was just the five of them, the five elders. Even lame, I ought to be able to outrun five old women—

And then a chill came upon me, a cold ghostly touch, and I knew most surely, knew to the marrow of my bones, that I stood upon sacred land.

White, white as milk and seemingly as dense, and larger than the tall oak trees, massive, larger even than mountain peaks—a presence. I knew presence by then. Presence not of death but of deity, rising from breast of earth, earth our mother, to meet me—or bar my way. Fog, some folk would have called it, but this was no mist such as that floating over the Naga. Enormous, opaque, shapeshifting—it seemed like a mighty ship, and then again like the old sow who eats her farrow, and then again like a huge mayblossom—moving, yet as solid of mien as a stronghold of ice, and as white. I stopped where I stood, glad that my feet were bare and my gown humble. I did not dare to venture near it.

Behind me, I heard the Gwyneda coming, and I turned to face them. Calm, I told myself, be calm. I would yet elude them somehow. They had no power of body; what could they do to me, to capture me?

No more than a short stone's throw away from me they stopped and formed a sort of arrowhead with the gray-faced eldest at its apex, nearest to me.

"Cerilla," she said.

Then I comprehended the power of the Gwyneda. Serpent

power, the power that tranfixes the bird before the eye of the snake, skewers the victim as firmly as if by a spear, rendering it helpless to flee. All my will was gone in horror; I could not move. They were no arrowhead, but the head of the adder, and they slithered toward me, shuffling along on slow old feet, and their leader held me in thrall with the unblinking stare of her eye.

"Cerilla," she repeated, the word an exhalation, a hiss. "Cerilla."

They drew closer. Indeed, they were almost on me. I could see the twin hairs on the old one's mole, hairs spread and seeking for all the world like an adder's black tongue . . . . Divinity to the back of me, white presence, I could feel it.

"Cerilla . . . ."

And as if by gift of that divinity, as if from some place beneath the soles of my bare feet, some hidden wellspring, a sudden insane glee bubbled up in me, and I threw back my head and laughed. It was not my true name! I yelled with laughter, and my movement broke the serpentine spell. As blithely as a teasing dog, I drew back.

"Come on, old women!" I cried, and lightly, forgetting my limp, I turned and ran. The white presence, the fog! But I was not afraid of it any longer. Heedlessly I ran into it, and it was warm, as warm as sunshine! I blinked in surprise. As warm as warm sleep, but I could not see much, not in the milky whiteness—but then it was gone as if it had never been, and I was running across a meadow, through a boggy glade, and up a small slope into a bramble thicket full of vine.

The thicket turned me aside. The Gwyneda had not followed me, nor were they in sight behind me. It would be some little while, I hoped, before they made their way back to their swan boats. I found the easier going, along the grassy bank of the Naga, and set myself to make the most of the time, starting off northward at my best speed. In the distance, on the far side of the river, I could see a troop of horsemen; that would be my father and his minions. Well, they could not harm me there. Nor would the Gwyneda harm me, ever again, I felt sure of it. I had bested them; the goddess had befriended me.

I should have known better. Within the hour the Gwyneda skimmed past me as I trotted along the riverbank, their faces full of fury and the looks they gave me nothing short of evil. I plunged away from the river, my chains falling from my upflung hands and catching on thorns. But they did not stop where they had seen me. They went on ahead of me somewhere. I understood. They knew I had to reach the Island of Fugitives, and they would stand ready to snare me.

Well, I thought, I am winded and in need of a rest.

Thickets were plentiful along the unsettled side of the Naga. I ran on until I found a lush boskage, and then I crept into the midst of it, sank down, and lay still, trying to quiet my breathing. Softly, softly, I told myself. My frock was not likely to betray me; it was old and drab, as ragged as dead leaves, and my skin from sun and weather was nearly as brown as the loam. I lay gratefully. As soon as I was able to breathe noiselessly, I listened. For what seemed like a parlous long time I lay watching and hearkening, and inwardly I began to fret and think of moving on—

When, forsooth, there at last they came, in line like so many beaters at a hunt, but drifting along as softly as swans, as clouds. I knew I would have to rush them to break through their line, and I felt once again the old horror of them. Stares that could transfix like so many lances, serpent power—but no power of body. I knew I could push aside their bodies, should I ever reach them. I would have to wait until they were quite close.

I eased myself up to my knees and tucked my feet under myself, preparing.

But the goddess must have been with me after all. I did not have to dare them. Some large animal, perhaps a deer, rustled the bracken a little distance behind me, and the Gwyneda hastened toward the sound, passing me by. In another mo-

ment I stole out of my thicket and started northward in silent
haste, and as soon as I passed their swan boats I ran for all I
was worth. I ran until my lungs ached, the pain of my bruised
foot became agony—and I ran still.

As the sun dipped westward I reached the southern tip of
the Blackwater.

It was a lake, but as smooth as a mere, shimmering like so
much black glass, motionless except that sometimes the small
black serpents who lived there made a delicate ripple, putting
their heads out to look. I did not mind them, for by then there
was very little that could have perturbed me. The island lay
out beyond a stretch of water, darkly shadowed in its smooth
surface, the trees on it, the sacred grove, soft and plumy with
leaves and perfectly still, like something in a dream. On the far
shore, beyond the island, stood my father and his minions, all
too real and watching me like the snakes.

They could not hurt me there. I could hide, wait until after
dark, make my attempt—

Far down the Naga white specks appeared: the swan boats.
And I knew without looking long that they were coming
closer.

There seemed nothing for it but to brave the black water at
once.

I waded in with no clear idea of what I was doing, only
determined to reach the Island of Fugitives or drown. Rather
than let the Gwyneda take me again, I would let my chains
sink me to the bottom, for Arlen's sake. I walked out as far as I
could, the snakes scattering before me, and when the lake's
surface lapped at my chin I hurled myself forward, thrashed,
and went under.

There followed a time I yet remember, some nights, in
horrible dreams. Blackwater: black water closing over me, a
blinding, strangling blackness with a touch seemingly like that
of scales, and the chains on my wrists like two cold and
clinging serpents, dragging me down. I gulped a breath, sometimes, by springing up from the bottom and breaking the

surface for a moment; then I would be swallowed up again at once. I do not know if I moved any closer to the island that was my goal; my heart pounded in mortal fear, and I saw only blackness. Wanderings full of fear and hatred and every sort of terror and pain . . . . I refused to realize that I was dying, even though my ears heard tolling bells and my eyes had gone blind. Then I felt movement. Something had seized my long, trailing hair and was tugging me upward.

The Gwyneda! I threw my head up wildly, striking out. At the surface of the water, I could breathe even though I could scarcely see, and I struggled frantically, pushing away from the touch of wood. I would not let them get me into the boat—

"Rae," said a sharp voice, sharp and frightened. "Stop that! Be of some use!"

I blinked. The boat was brown. It was Ophid! I lifted my hands to him, and he hauled in my chains, then me. I lay in the bottom of his cormorant, sodden and gasping. "I—thought you were no hero," I panted when I could speak.

"Briony is not the only one who thinks often of you," he snapped. He had the cormorant speeding, his fair hair lifted by the wind of its skimming, and he looked terrified. Sitting up, I could see why. The Gwyneda followed no more than a furlong behind us, and the savagery that showed in their faces sickened me with fear.

Splashings and shoutings sounded from another direction. Turning, I saw the Island of Fugitives close ahead of us, and beyond it the minions of Rahv in the water on their swimming steeds. They had been content to sit and watch, it seemed, as long as I was to drown or be taken by the Gwyneda. But when Ophid had saved me, my father had roared an order and leaped his charger into the Blackwater to deal with me himself.

All this I saw in a blurred glance before the cormorant struck the shore. We beached with a shock that sent me lurching forward, and almost before I had gathered myself Ophid had me up and hugging my burden of chains and headed toward the holy ash. "Run!" he cried, giving me a push, and he whirled to face the Gwyneda.

I ran, hearing my father's horse splash up on the opposite shore. I ran, knowing I had to prevail, not only for myself but for Ophid now, to gift his daring with victory. I ran, hearing a snake hiss from the white-robed ones he confronted . . . . The ash loomed ahead: graceful, lofty, pearl gray of bark, the many chains hanging in clusters, garlanding its spreading branches like some grim sort of festal ornaments. I saw nothing else. It seemed never to draw nearer. I ran, hearing a pounding sound, my heart, my own feet, the hooves of horses—no telling, through exhaustion and the roaring in my ears—

"Mother Meripen," I panted, "*please.*"

And I was there, and I flung my arms around her, holy, hard, and rough, and with a high, chiming sound the bracelets of captivity fell from my wrists.

My chains lay on the ground. With a barbaric yell, a word-less, uncouth whoop of triumph, I scooped them up and flung them skyward, and they caught in the boughs and hung there, swaying. I surveyed the world as if it belonged to me. At some small distance, near the island shore, my father stood glaring at me, and by him stood the five Gwyneda. Ophid came hastening up to me, his thin face alight with joy.

"Ten thousand thanks," I told him.

"My lady," he said, "the debt is mine. I have found that I need no longer be afraid of them."

"Why, what has happened?"

He shrugged dazedly. "I have outfaced them, that is all. Power I had not known I possessed . . . . I will be able to return to my island without fear."

I embraced him, but the embrace reminded me of some-thing. "How did you know," I asked slowly, "about Briony?"

"He told me, that is all. We see each other from time to time at the circling dance. Well, Rae, go claim what is yours."

"Ten thousand thanks," I told him again, and I strode down

to where my father and the Gwyneda waited, strode arrogantly, insanely certain that they would honor the custom that had brought me here. For surely there was no use in uncertainty, after all that had happened.

The eldest of the Gwyneda faced me first, her watery eyes unblinking in her gray face. "The goddess has smiled on you and taken you into the palm of her hand," she said to me. "You are highly favored, and free of the land forever, and whoever thinks to emperil you will bear our curse."

A murmur of accord sounded from the other Gwyneda, and with only small astonishment I realized that they willingly now embraced me and my cause, they who some few minutes earlier would just as willingly have killed me.

"Arlen?" I demanded.

"He is your consort. Your protection extends to him."

I nodded curtly, not wishing to speak overlong with them. "And Erta?"

"She died quickly," the eldest said, with no unease in her gaze. Killing Erta had been a minor matter at the time. Fervor grew in me to be gone from that place.

I wheeled on my father. He stood—if I had not felt such good reason to hate him I would have pitied him, his pallid face so mottled with emotion—he stood choking on wrath and frustration. One of his men was riding Bucca, I noted. "My horse," I told him.

He complied with a gesture that ordered the man to bring the steed to me, and his hands curled into white-knuckled fists.

"My gold," I said when I held Bucca's reins in my hand.

He drew the chains out of his pouch, fingered them a moment—and turned and flung them full force into the depths of the lake. "Go dive for them," he told me, with hatred grating in his voice.

"Thank you, but nay. I have had enough of swimming for today." I mounted Bucca. It would have been too much to expect, I suppose, that Rahv would have handed the gold to me or even hurled it at my feet. Indeed, if a horse could have been thrown so far, I think Bucca also would have been in the water.

"Slut," he muttered.

I said farewell only to Ophid, then swam Bucca across the lake to the eastern shore. The water lay quiet, very still; not even birds were calling. I remember that quiet. The sun was setting, dusk coming on, and thin wraiths of mist rising as I turned northward again toward the Adder's Head. I was on my own again, quite alone, with only the sodden frock on my back, no supplies or wherewithal either. I hoped the goddess who held me in the palm of her hand would somehow favor me with a bit of food.

# EIGHTEEN

Food was fish, mostly, as it turned out. Almost at once I found someone's lost net, snagged in the lakeside trees. I mended it with tough hairs plucked from Bucca's tail and netted fish in plenty, as well as a few snakes, which slithered away. Bucca's gear contained flint and steel for the making of a cooking fire and a knife for the gutting, so I was content. It was midsummer; there were strawberries growing in the meadow grass and currants coming ripe in the bogs. On fish and berries I could live.

And so I did, and I traveled northward along the Black-water, up the Naga past the Isle of Elders all in white bloom, past the four small linked tarns called the Lakes of the Winds, Lausta, Faris, Hirta, and Bora, four forms of the goddess. Then along the Naga again. The land had grown steep and high and rocky; presently I rode along the top of a gorge, and the water far below foamed and hissed between boulders with a sound as of a thousand serpents. There was a waterfall, and a rocky ait, and a waterfall again, and when I came to Adder's Head I looked down on it from far above, the water deepest greenish black, the eyot of rounded water-worn rock, wet and unblinking. No human had ever lived here, I could feel it, not since primal times. Only by hasty travelers like myself, uneasy in the stare of that shining eye, had this place been named. At the far end of the Adder's Head, at its blunt apex, the forked tongue of water came whitely down the surrounding rock, and between the cataracts I could see the dark entry, the passageway, the serpent's burrow.

I left Bucca in the best place I could find for him, a glade where the grass grew thick within a grove of alder, took off his gear and patted him, and went down the rocks afoot to seek the realm of the dead.

There were the guardians just within the entry, as I had expected. And they were black, the glossy black of lacquer, and sizable, their uplifted heads standing as high as mine, and their eyes amber gold, and on their backs patterns like chains of shining gold. How lovely they were, for all that they were serpents; I could not be very afraid of them. "May I pass?" I asked. "My name is Rae—"

Before I could tell them more they turned and flanked me, as if to assist me or provide me with a guard of honor, and as I walked they slipped along beside me, keeping me to the center of the way.

It was very dark at first, and damp-smelling, and rocky underfoot, another cave or a large tomb, the largest of tombs. I felt my way downward, shuffling along in the dark. Once one of the serpents put its head up to my outstretched hand—to guide me, I think. But the touch startled me badly, and I leaped back, stood and sweated until I gathered courage to go on again.

Soon, though, a dim light began to show, and it grew, a white and spectral light. Then the stony passage leveled off into a floor of polished marble, and I saw that I was in a place such as had never been on earth, a place a world and a life apart from the river and trees I had just left behind.

Jeweled pillars and, spiraled around them, great serpents of fire. It was from them that the light glowed; they shone white with the soundless, motionless fire that is hotter than any flame, fire as of white embers, fine as thistledown. The jewels beneath their coils took their light and splintered it into shards, sent it darting off the water—for there was water, snake-loop meanders of water as smooth as the marble floor; I scarcely could tell where stone stopped and water began save for milky lilies floating and the white fish beneath them. The water formed still black pools, and amidst the pools a silver serpent the girth of a man lifted its head and sang. Nor have I ever been able to remember what melody the serpent sang, or whether there were words. But the feeling that song gave me haunts my dreams.

On the waterways floated a boat shaped like a silver harp, and an old hunchbacked boatman poled it toward me. His robes were of velvet twinkling with brooches and clasps of precious gold. I remembered that I had not gold to pay him with, and the black serpents, my retinue, had left me.

I spread wide my hands as he came up to me. "I have nothing," I told him. "They have taken it all from me."

He gestured me on board, and by the merry glance of his old eye I saw that he was not at all perturbed.

I seated myself. "Thank you," I said. "They told me I would have to pay you."

He said nothing, but poled us smoothly to the far marble shore, and with one hand he helped me out. A cluster of maidens awaited me there, lovely maidens but strange, and in a moment I saw that they were elementals. Sylphs, clad in airy, floating garments, themselves so pale as to seem nearly transparent; and the nagini, the snake women, very slender, very beautiful; and nymphs—I was wary of the nymphs, though perhaps they did not, like undines, have razor-sharp teeth. The brown earth maidens were most like me, they in their peasant frocks, though there was a glow about them as of polished wood, whereas I—

"But she cannot go before the Presence like that!" one of them exclaimed.

"My baby," I started to ask them. "Lonn—"

They hushed me gently and hurried me off. I was to have audience, they told me. Ask it of the mighty one at that time. We walked through splendor. Past gardens walled with chalcedony, where fountains bloomed into motes of gold and trees stood leafed in jade, where birds bright as jewels flew—I blinked. They spread feathered wings, but they were small plump serpents flitting past me, red as rubies or lapis blue, as lovely as any songbird of the world I had left behind.

I do not know when we came inside. Perhaps we had always been inside. But presently there were chambers filled with the rustle of silk, a bedchamber and antechamber with walls draped in spiral-patterned silk and cloth of gold. I was seated on a couch, and a basin of water for washing was brought to me, and a white linen towel, and when I had cleaned my hands the cup of the house was presented to me by a nagini on bended knee. And when I had drunk it down, a meal was set before me. Three sorts of meats, and more sauces and pastries and sweets than I can remember or tell. Long-starved as I was, I ate without thought, immediately. Only when I came to a small bowl of fresh elderberries—and it was not yet the season for elderberries—did I remember Briony's warning. I pushed it aside and sat, my hunger and my pleasure abruptly gone.

"It will not hurt you," said one of the sylphs, and she laughed at me softly, not unkindly. "Go ahead, eat! The dead do not eat nearly so heartily."

"I might as well be dead," I muttered.

"Indeed, my lady, no! When you are dead, you will need gold for the boatman. Now you come and go as you please." She laughed again, a wafting, summery sound. "Are you truly finished eating?"

I looked at her, feeling the birthing of an unreasonable hope, but indeed I was no longer hungry. "I am done," I said.

"Then you should bathe."

In the antechamber a great silver basin of warm water awaited me, attended by the nymphs. I reclined in it and was bathed, and afterward they wrapped me in furs to dry, and when that was done they lightly rubbed me with scented oil, so that I glowed as they did and could not help but feel my own well-being.

"Now," said one of the earth maidens, "we must properly attire you if you are to speak with the goddess. Or would you rather sleep first?"

Nervousness took hold of me at the mention of the goddess, and though I was tired, I knew I could not have slept. Best to brave the goddess and have it over with. "I am not sleepy," I said.

"I thought those who lived were always sleepy after they had eaten heartily," said my sylph, puzzled.

"Not always," I told her.

So they clothed me in the colors most sacred to the goddess, in a gown of green samite, as green as new leaves, and over it a tabard of white trimmed with fringe of gold, and a girdle of linked gold around my waist, and on my feet slippers of red leather, and on my shoulders a cloak of red wool, as red as oxblood, lined with red satin and edged in ermine. My hair was braided and dressed with emeralds, rubies, and pearls.

"Green for birthing, growth, and dying," the maidens chanted as they arrayed me.

"Green for birthing, growth, and dying,
    Green for grass and red for blood,
    White for the mystic moon."

And they fastened my cloak with a silver brooch, the wheel brooch of twenty-eight spokes. Then, under golden archways molded in links as of chain, they escorted me into the great hall of that afterworld place.

A hall, with a smooth floor that shone like black water. But so vast I could see no walls—and above, where there must have been a roof of stone. . . .I shut my eyes for a moment, dazzled, then looked again at a sun and several moons. But the sun was a golden serpent of flame floating far above me, slowly wheeling, his mouth clinging to his tail. And the moons were serpents of silver fire, some of them biting their tails, some curved into crescents. And between them arched the serpent of seven colors, the rainbow.

There was no time for gazing. Many presences filled that place; I sensed them. But I saw only one Presence, the mighty one beneath a canopy of gems and golden chains resplendent in snakelight. The elementals led me before her, and it was she, deity, the goddess.

Her Presence needed no throne. She lay on the dais, on lavishings of fur, coverlets and pillows of fur. Naked she lay there, brown, deep-breasted as earth, and all about her on the dais or beside it the most regal of beasts crouched or sat or lay, wolves and leopards and golden-maned yaels and suckling bears, and by her right hand rested a whip as she reclined, a whip of nine black strands, and knotted on the strands were white knucklebones from human hands.

"Little daughter," she said to me, "welcome. It has been a long time since one of my children came so boldly to visit me."

She was larger than any mortal woman, thewed mightily and yet billowing with softness like brown hillsides, clad only in her own lush hair of head and elsewhere, and there was a golden chain around her loins which covered nothing. Left hand and forearm steadied her head, and she regarded me levelly out of wide-set dark eyes, a handsome and frightening face. On her brow lay a golden fillet in the shape of a snake, a small and delicate serpent—or at least I thought it to be made of gold until it lazily lifted its head and flickered its tongue at me.

"Kneel," someone hissed in my ear.

"She need not kneel," the goddess said. "Leave us, all of you."

I heard rather than saw my retinue withdraw. I stood

speechless, my eyes caught by the Great Mother's eyes, my thoughts empty of everything except holy dread.

"So you have been unhappy, daughter," she said in a voice that might have been intended to be soft, gentle; coming out of her it yet filled me with fear. "I had not meant it to be so for you."

I moved my mouth with a great effort, wet my dry lips. "Lonn," I whispered.

"Yes," she agreed, "he is troublesome."

"No. . . . Yes, but I mean Lonn, my baby."

"You named him that?" Her head came up somewhat, and her brow creased in a puzzled frown. I quailed before that frown. But I had to ask her.

"Yes. I—we—I thought he might be here."

"But why?" Her strong left hand came down, and she sat almost upright in her astonishment. "I know nothing of this."

"I—we—that is, the oracle said—" It seemed more horrible, more wrong than ever, and I could no longer meet her eyes. I felt myself shrinking into an earthen lump of shame.

"Speak," she told me sharply.

"We cast him away upon the Naga."

Her breath hissed between her teeth, she tore off the serpent from her brow and flung it away, and in one horrible moment I saw her crouched like an animal among her animals, her gruesome whip raised in her hand, and I thought she would use it on me. I shut my eyes and stood still for it; I felt I deserved it. But she did not.

"There must be at worst a mistake, at best a reason," she said roughly. "Foolish child, I gave you everything, and you have thrown it away, cast it away, your blessedness! Tell me why."

So I told her, not daring to look at her again, told her the tale of Lonn's interference and our journeying in search of a remedy, and when I had finished she remained as angry as ever.

"Rae Cerilla Runaway of the Gwyneda!" So she really did know me, fully know me, my name and all about me. "Little fool, did you not know—could you not tell—look at me!"

I looked up, compelled by her command, and gasped: she
was a skeletal serpent, huge, crawling toward me on the ends
of her bleached ribs. But even as I gasped she was a hag, a
wizened mandrake woman, hard and knotty as old roots in
winter; and then the fierce mare, beast among beasts, rearing
up with a mighty neigh; and the breasted serpent rising and
swaying far above my head; and the wicca, the old wise
woman of the woods, dressed as a peasant and laughing at me.
And then she was standing naked as before, but her breasts
were many, they hung like clustered fruit all around her. And
she raised her whip, and she was the black aurochs with long
white horns, and she was a raven stooping at me with a
croaking scream. But before I could wince she was herself
again in naked and motherly form, and she laid her whip aside
and looked at me.

"You are brave," she said.

Indeed, I was merely too stunned and miserable to run. I
said nothing.

"And I know you are not stupid," she went on, somewhat
bitter but no longer angry. "You have all your father's
shrewdness, and none of his spleen. . . .I thought it was all so
plain. Could you not tell that my special favor went with you?
That I suspended the requirements of the ceremonial for your
sake? That none of the usual strictures apply to you? You
could leave the Sacred Isle by my good grace, find shelter, eat
the elderberries, receive the aid of the most puissant of man-
drakes when you needed it, eat the food of the oak elves
without harm, pass the many guardians of the forbidden
places, be they serpents, wolves, bears or wild bulls, or the
odd folk who live under the swaying stones . . . . You should
have known you bore my blessing. Ophid should have known
as well. You could have named the babe whatever you
wanted."

Utter astonishment made me bold. "But why?" I cried.
"Why have you so favored us?"

She shrugged one vast bare shoulder, whimsical. "Who

knows? Arlen, his love for my creatures, his wonder—I have always held a special affection for him. And you, your yearnings, your daring—"

Heart broke into anger at the thought of the gift that had availed us naught. "But how were we to know?" I shouted, stamping. "Whatever your—gracious intentions for us, our way was hard enough!"

"Daring," said the goddess coldly, "can be overdone."

I froze, eyes lowered.

"That was Lonn's doing," she added more softly.

I ventured to glance at her again; she looked merely thoughtful. "But why?" I asked again, quietly this time.

"His reasons are his own." She sounded mildly amused. "I am not privy to them."

"Is he here, that I might ask him?"

"I think not. He is one who skulks about on the far side of the bourne, in the shadows, one who comes and goes. I have not heard of him lately, and I think he has not yet found the wherewithal to pay the boatman." By my life, but she was callous, she! "But we shall see, if you like. Come here, sit."

Warily I obeyed her, sitting at the feet of a leopard, on the edge of the dais. She still loomed above me; I did not dare turn my head to look at her, so close. Idly she clapped her hands, and tiny lights grew in the depths of the hall, as if stars somehow floated there, or white fireflies, reflecting faintly on the smooth, gleaming floor.

"Dance," the goddess said.

The lights grew larger, yet softer, until they formed pale, human semblances, head and shoulders and a hint of trailing limbs. A vast crowd of them, a sea, a flood, spread into the reaches of that great hall, and they arranged themselves into serpentine lines such as the waves of the sea must be. At once, swaying, they started to move.

"You will see that your babe is not here either," the goddess told me.

I became aware that there was music, a voiceless music

coursing through me, my body, my heartbeat, my breathing. Such a silent dance, no scrape of feet, no talk, and yet all moved in perfect accord with that swelling rhythm, the rhythm of tides and days and seasons. The white lines rippled into spirals, flowed into interlocking circles that turned through each other, and after a while I dimly saw that the whole swirled in form of a great, circling wheel that slowly spun on darkness—the goddess, she the hub. The shifting vortex floated past me where I sat on the dais, and within the wheel the smaller circles ebbed and flowed, blooming like flowers, melting into each other, until I grew aware of a pattern I scarcely could grasp and knew that every luminous spirit of that whole vast throng had, for a moment at least, his place before me. And there were many whom I knew: my mother, my earthly mother, a white spiritous stranger; and Erta, and others who had gone beyond. And there were babies aplenty, but not my baby. And comely youths, but not Lonn. It must have been a long time that I sat there, but I think I went into a kindly trance, for I do not remember it so. I remember only the dance turning, turning, turning—

"Be done," said the goddess, and the lights dimmed away.

"So you see," she told me in tones of patience, "they are not here."

"Is there not another place—" I hesitated, but I had to ask her. "—even more pleasant than this, a sort of meadow. . . ?"

"Yes indeed. But Lonn is not there, I assure you."

I looked up at her, letting her see my perplexity. "But he was a hero."

"A hero without wisdom is only another sort of fool. Lonn was the usual sort of young ass, knowing only how to be loyal and brave. The shadow within self he could not deal with. The human way is not often the hero's way." She stood up, waving me off the dais with one hand, and I went down to stand before her again.

"Go eat again, Rae," she told me, "and sleep. I will consult the deep pools, to see what has become of your child."

I stood blinking up at her. I must have been more weary than I knew, for I spoke as a child myself. "So you do not hate me, Mother," I blurted. I dared to call her that to her face.

"Indeed, no!" She sounded shocked, amused, even tender— she who demanded twice yearly the sacrifice of youthful blood. "Where I have once given my favor, even on a whim, I will not lightly withdraw it, Rae. Your faithfulness is a mirror of my own." She gestured softly, vaguely, in my direction. "Go, eat, sleep."

I gave an awkward bow by way of courtesy, turned, and went blindly. Soon I was flanked by the elementals again. They led me back to my sumptuous chamber, and I slept for many hours.

I had one more audience with the goddess before I left that place. This time the hall glowed with the light of nine serpent suns, and the animals lay sleeping, even the serpent on her forehead. The goddess wore a full-skirted gown of a golden cloth that swirled about her hips; her bodice was studded with gems, and her breasts stood bare except for the nipples, which were gilded. I felt more uncomfortable in the presence of that finery than I had before her nakedness.

"I have seen the babe floating in the basket down the Naga," she told me, and instantly I forgot her deep-clefted breasts. "He was struggling," she added.

"Crying," I murmured, aching with the old pang.

"No, not so much crying in the manner of babes; struggling. The tiny ones do not struggle against death, for they do not understand. This was Lonn struggling against loss of the body he had taken for himself. And he found strength in it somehow to tip himself into the shallows, and he crawled ashore."

I listened with breathless hope. "Yes," I said eagerly, "yes, he was growing very strong even before I—"

"Abandoned him. Say it candidly. So he had to grow rapidly, and he has grown more rapidly since. He learned to walk that first day, the pool tells me, toddled away from the

river until some few days later he found shelter in a homestead."

"Before—before the storm came down?"

"It must have been. At any rate he was fed, and the folk
there think they were visited by a god, for within a few weeks
he had grown to the size and skill of a boy of seven years, and
within a few months he had grown to the likeness of a stripling
of the age of passage, and a churlish one at that. And by the
time the whitethorn bloomed he had attained the strength of a
youth. And at the time of the ceremonial of the summerking
he left them."

"Bound where?" I cried.

"He did not say. But I think you know where."

I did indeed know, and I fervently hoped I would return to
Arlen before Lonn did. I took a few hasty steps before I
recalled my manners. "Good my Mother," I requested, "may I
leave you now?"

"Certainly. The clothes you wear are yours to keep. And
you know you need no gold for the boatman. Go with all
blessing."

"Thank you, Mother," I told her, bowing, and I turned and
ran, my red cloak flying behind me.

"And may yours be the victory," she added, and though her
words were quiet I heard them. But I gave no sign, for I was in
haste.

Back under golden archways. Back past jade gardens, over
marble floors; back past black pools where white swans floated
amid waterlilies, past the singing serpent. It did not occur to
me that I should ever muse on those things or remember them
with wonder. I thought only of reaching the passage and
Bucca. Should he still be there in his glade, should he not have
strayed too far—

He was standing just at the rim of the rock, close by the
passage entry, already saddled and bridled and awaiting me,
and on him were loaded blankets and bags full of provision; I
noticed the aroma of meats and freshly baked bread. And laid

across his saddle was a single gold chain. I slipped it around
my neck, hid it under my gown of green.

"Thank you, Mother," I shouted to the forest, the rocks, the
Adder's Head far below, glinting in the sunlight. Then I
sprang onto Bucca and started with all speed back toward
home.

# NINETEEN

The season had advanced since I had ventured into the Afterworld. The early trees were starting to yellow. All my thoughts turned to hurry, the more so when I thought of Arlen; I tried not to do so. I hurt with yearning for him.

Down, down, we went, along the Naga as far as the Black-water, for a rocky wilderness barred any other way, forcing me southward. And then, at last, moorland, and I turned sharply northward and eastward. The goddess had provisioned me well, and Bucca was well rested; we went relentlessly, the horse and I, dawn and day and twilight. I let Bucca gulp the tall grasses on the move. And although the Naga and the moorlands seemed to crawl snailishly away behind us, I am sure we traveled swiftly, more swiftly than heroes in legends of old. If Lonn went afoot, I reasoned, we might yet reach Arlen before him, or even overtake him.

I skirted Briony's soddy, passed it a day's journey away, for I wanted no sight of it or of him. At the last homesteads before the Forever Forest I stopped, trading links of gold for food, and the folk spoke of a strange shining youth who had passed that way some few days before, spoke of him with awe though they could scarcely describe him. I pressed on all the more quickly. When I reached the forest, the great trees loomed ablaze in red and orange leaf, bright as flame.

Passion's flame, I said to myself, and my heart ached for Arlen.

Thinking of flame and passion, I knew what to do about Lonn. I wanted to confront him—for reasons of my own, without hope of gain—and I felt that he should be nearby, but how to find him amidst the thickets and vines of the wilderness? The ancient, crowding trees closed off all sight within a furlong of the seeker. But that way lay home, so I sent Bucca into the shadows under those huge boles, the ivy twining them as red as blood above the green of moss. And when I camped that night, I gathered a great mound of wood and made a fire, and not just to ward off the autumn chill or the oak elves, either. I built it far larger than I customarily would have, and I sat beside it late into the night.

Lonn did not come to me that night, or the next, or the next. I traveled a week more without a sign of him, and I had long since decided I was mistaken. I built my fires each night out of habit and to cook the meat that the wolves, the bears, the goddess gave me. But on a night when I estimated I must soon reach the northern limit of the forest and come out again within sight of the mountains, my home, on a night when the moon shone full and golden, I heard a small stirring as of golden leaves and looked up, and there beyond the fire he stood.

Lonn. Lord of all lords, but he was magnificent! The glow

could not have been only moonlight or firelight—all the glory of his last living day lay on him yet, glory given by the goddess, serpent power. His hair moved and shone like the flames, as if he were crowned with fire. And the splendor of his broad glistening brow, his broad bare shoulders—for bare they were, as if he were a slave or a felon, but I did not think of it so at the time, but saw only how they rippled and shone, how the light played upon him, golden hair of his bare chest, even his breathing visible and full of a mystic energy—and his eyes, holding me with their shadowed gaze, dark and full of meaning. I could have fallen in love with him for the mere gaze of those eyes. Everything I had in mind to say to him left me, vanished, and I sat wordless and openmouthed, staring at him in hunger for his beauty . . . and then I hated myself. For all that Arlen might be but a memory—

"Rae," Lonn murmured, the word vibrant with meaning, and he came around the fire to me. He sat by me and reached toward me to touch me, and I drew back, still shamed by my own weakness, that I should have been for a moment so ensnared by his glamour. Battle, victory, they were to be with self, it seemed, as much as anything. And still I found nothing to say to him.

"You have wanted me to come to you," he declared. "I know you have. Why else these great fires. . . ?"

Eyes the color of wood violets, of some nameless gem bluer than amethyst, darker than sapphire, eyes fixed on me ardently, nearly glowing—duskier now than violets, in firelight, the color of purple oak leaves in autumn.

"But you are lovely," he said softly, "so lovely, in your cloak of red with the black hair all in a torrent down your back, a cataract—"

"All in a tangle," I said sourly, the first words I had spoken to him.

"A falling flow, like the black water. And your face, your hands, brown as earth but fairer than rosewood against that white silk. And gown of green—you look like a queen of the earth maidens sitting there so darkly. Nay, more: like spirit of summer night, fecund. Like the goddess herself."

"Speak more kindly of the goddess," I said sharply.

"She has done nothing for me." He shrugged, the movement setting his glorious hair a-shimmer. "But you might. . . ."

I saw that there was going to be no sleep for me that night.

"Love me, Rae," he whispered.

"I love Arlen," I told him, nearly as softly.

"But Arlen is not here; I am here! Rae, lady, I want your love, I long for it, and I know you have felt that pang; love me too."

"And never again look on my beloved without guilt? Thank you, but no."

"You need never look at him again," said Lonn eagerly, far too eagerly. "Come away with me. We shall travel together; I will show you places you have scarcely dreamed of. The strand where the blue glain lies, and the burning sea where the sun goes down, and the white castles of ice beyond the snow mountains—"

I thought of my own small home with sudden fierce longing, my humble stone house in the mountains. "No," I said.

"Love me," he begged.

He went on in this way for some time, declaring to me his eternal devotion, asking me to cleave to him, or at the very least to lie with him that night. Oddly, the longer he pleaded the less his entreaties moved me. That he desired me I could not doubt, but that he loved me—I wondered. That passion in him, that energy; not love, forsooth. Love would not so urge me toward a tearing injury, a sundering of self.

I sat stolidly. "No," I told him for the hundredth time.

"Rae," he said, a darker tone to his voice, a hint of threat, "I will have you."

So. It was a matter of possession, then. Passion for possession. I was a prize to him, a trophy, little more, as I had once been but a possession to a man called Rahv.

"Yield to me. I can take you, you know, perforce and forthwith. Immense power is in me."

"I do not doubt it," I flared at him, feeling the hot rush of an old anger, very old. "But do not call me Rae then, if you think to force me. A good, gentle man gave me that name."

The allusion to Arlen infuriated him. "Proud piece," he breathed. I heard rage in his voice to answer my own, and I looked at him, intending to stare him down—and he had no eyes.

Horrible, empty sockets with the blood oozing—startled beyond screaming, I gave a dry gasp and scrambled up from where I had been sitting.

"So," he said grimly, "at last I have moved you." And he stood up as well, to face me. "You would not have me fair," he said, "so you shall have me foul."

Whip weals sprang up across the flesh of his shoulders, raw red lines with trickles of blood starting down. More of them came upon more of them by the moment, until all I saw was cruel red of blood, and I winced and looked away. Lonn brought his hands up to his waist, loosened the ties of his trousers.

"Yield to me," he said, "or you will see what you could not bear to watch the first time."

*Run from him*, I thought. *If he is blind, he will be hard put to pursue me.* But something stubborn in me would not run from him, wanted only to face him down.

"It was your pain I could not bear to watch!" I cried at him. "But there's no pain in you any longer, only anger."

Indeed, his face was so contorted in anger that even his eyeless stare did not look very much amiss in it. He pulled off his breeches with a jerk, tearing them, and the wound beneath—a horrible wound, a ragged, empty place, bereft. I felt faint at the sight of it. But the wound was not as ugly as the look of his face.

"Yield," he warned.

"Stay that way, and you'll take small pleasure in forcing me," I retorted. My voice shook, and tears were running down my face. I was glad he could not see them.

"Yield to me, or there will be more than weeping."

The sorcerer, he could see me well enough! His wounds were all illusion, no agony; I could have choked with anger. But just as suddenly anger faded. It did not matter. I knew what his pain had been the first time, the true time that had bought my happiness. Better truth lay beyond anger.

"I pity you," I told him, weeping aloud; let him hear and see. "You have suffered, and suffering has bested you, and I pity you terribly."

Pity was not what he wanted of me. Terror would have been more to his liking. With a wordless roar he strode toward me, and he was all red, entirely horrible, the flayed man. I gasped, and for the first time I hid my face.

"Yield!" he shouted at me.

"No." I did not shout; I am not even sure he heard me. "Take your head off," I mumbled, "take your bones apart, turn yourself into meat and stew it. I don't care."

He grasped my wrists and shook my hands loose of my face, and I opened my eyes to look at him, there, so close to me, knowing that my nightmares would all be bested. But he was himself again in his fairest form, winterking come to bed his bride, sheen of glamour on him.

"You are still ugly," I told him.

It was true. That golden glow shone red as blood to me, baleful, hair a living fire that would hurt me, eyes no better than knives—

He hit me, hard, on the side of my face.

There was truly no use in fighting him. That alone would not have stopped me—I had fought Eachan at the esker when all hope was gone. But Lonn was not Eachan, not my enemy; he had been a friend, the friend beyond friendship, giver of a supreme gift. . . .

He struck me again, with his fist. For a moment I could not

see. But I stood as firmly as I was able, not resisting him, not yielding to him either, and I met the fury in his eyes with love in my own—a friend's love, not the sort he wanted.

"You will be mine!" he cried.

"Never," I told him, softly, warmly. "Never, not really, do to my body what you will."

He hit me a third time, knocking me sideways; I would have fallen if it were not that he still grasped my wrists. *He will push me down now,* I thought. But he pulled me upright and stood glaring wildly at me, and I stood gazing back at him, not afraid, not hoping, no longer angry, meeting his stare with no hatred in my own, thinking, *I have changed, I will never be afraid again.* No shrewdness, no bravado, only truth—and his eyes closed in anguish and he gave a terrible cry, a cry of agony such as his torture and death had never wrung from him, and he released me and flung himself away from me, flung himself face down on the earth by the embers of the fire.

I did not move, could not move. I only stood looking at him by moonlight and faint firelight, looked at his shoulders, taut and shuddering with the spasms of pain that had hold of him, and when he turned to face me I was sure. It was Lonn who lay there, no winterking but, beyond all expectation, the true Lonn, he the hero and supreme friend, he of the brown hair, the gentle rugged face, the gentle eyes. Misery in them. He winced, facing me, reached for the huddled mound that was his trousers.

"Rae—" He stopped, his voice breaking. "Cerilla, my lady, I will never trouble you again." Sobs shook him. "I—give you—my most solemn promise. . . ."

And with scrambling quickness he was gone, off at the run into the shadows of the forest. Numb as I was, I had not even spoken to stop him.

My baby!

Panic stirred me out of my stupor. Bucca stood browsing just beyond the fire, and I ran to him, undid his tether with fumbling haste, scrambled onto him. Without saddle or bridle, my skirts above my knees, I straddled the horse and with a kick and a yell I sent him springing into the darkness beneath the giant trees.

I guided him by a yank at the crest of his mane, by the pressure of my hands against his neck, by the pressure of my heels in his sides. It was an awkward business, and dangerous. If Lonn had been thinking, I am sure he could have escaped us quickly, for there were thickets and shadows aplenty to hide in. But he was too stricken for thinking. He ran at random, blindly, crashing through bracken, and I soon found him by his noise and by moonlight. Then it was but a matter of following him at trot and easy canter. Even so, he could have eluded us, for there were places Bucca could not pass, giant boles we had to circle around, fallen trunks so immense they could not be leaped, boggy places and tangles of every kind. It was far from easy for me to follow him in the dark and on horseback with branches striking my bruised face—often I lost him. But I found him again each time, for his pace had slowed; he was panting, and it seemed he could not stop sobbing.

"Cerilla, let me be!" he cried at me once, desperate words flung over his shoulder. But of course I could not let him be. He had something of mine.

He turned at bay finally in a marshy clearing where the tall grass grew in yellow hummocks, sank down amidst the tussocks and pleaded with me.

"My lady, I beg you, do not come near me. By the great goddess, mother of us both, I want only to leave and never look on you again. I cannot face you, I cannot bear it. All powers help me, what have I done, what have I become? Any beast is better. To beat a woman, betray a friend—"

I sat on Bucca at a small distance, letting Lonn rant. I could see him by more than aureate moonlight, I realized. Dawn was breaking.

"—crawl into a hole somewhere, like the worm that I am. How have I become so debased? I wish I were dead." He was not looking at me, but he choked and shuddered at that. Death had not been peaceful for him. "If I have to find a cave in the snow mountains and chain myself inside. . . . Lady, I have given you my promise. Why are you following me? What do you want of me?"

"My baby," I said, and though I had meant them to be firm and quiet, the words came out with a quaver.

"What?" He looked at me then, his tumult for the moment stilled. "But—you cast it away."

My face must have changed when he said that, for his changed piteously; he bit his lip. "I—I am sorry," he stammered.

"I cast you away," I said, meaning no hurt by the words; it was simple truth. "My baby I never cast away—" I could say no more; pain of longing filled me as if it had been but yesterday, that baneful day on the Island of Passages. I lowered my head, and Lonn stood up and took a few steps closer, staring at me.

"This, too, I have done to you," he said in a faltering voice.

My silence spoke to him.

"I—do not know how to make it right."

"There must be some way," I whispered.

"As earth is my witness," he said painfully, "I do not know what way."

"Come with me," I told him. "Come with me to Arlen. Together perhaps we will think of a way."

"But I—Rae, I do not dare." He shook his head wildly. "It—I am free of it for the time, all powers be praised, but at any moment it might return, and I—I may not be strong enough—"

"I think it will never again be as severe. You will conquer it more quickly each time." I held out a hand to him. "Come. You have seen I am not afraid."

"Rae, I must be away from you!"

"You have not hurt me. It hurts you the more."

"Those marks on your face, no hurt?" he muttered.

"Bruises. They will soon fade. Lonn, I know it is hard,

but—be brave for me, just this one more time, for Arlen and me. Please."

All the raving and weeping had left him; he stood calm and terribly pale. "I will make my own way," he said at last. "I will walk."

"No. The horse is faster, and it has been long enough, Lonn; please!"

It must be hapless, being a hero, a grievous curse, thinking of oneself in that way. He had to do it for me, and I knew it as well as he did.

Slowly, step by reluctant step, he came over to me, took my proffered hand, and let himself be helped up to sit on the horse behind me.

# TWENTY

He would not touch me. Even that first day, when we rode bareback—and it took us half the day to find our way back to my camp, my gear, the saddle—he would not hold onto my waist but balanced himself edgily behind me, and days to follow he clung to the cantle of the saddle, not to me. We rode fast, taking the straight way across the open grassland where the herding beasts roamed. I was filled with urgency.

"Do you think Arlen will be there?" Lonn asked on the day the mountains came in view. He spoke in a tone so low, so diffident, that I could not hate him for echoing my own fear.

"I dare not think differently," I answered. But yet, I had been gone so long. Autumn leaves were falling.

"If he is angry," Lonn added after a while, "it will quickly pass. He is like that."

It was unwonted that he should have said so much. For the most part he would not speak. When we faced each other to eat he would not look at me, or if he did he would wince and glance away. The sight of my bruises hurt him, the purple marks on my face, but it seemed they excited him too, for sometimes he would get up abruptly and go off by himself. I sometimes saw a hint of that winterking splendor about him as he left. But it was never on him when he returned.

It came on him in earnest and without warning one day as we made our way across the meadowland to the mountains' feet. The sun was warm, for a blessing, and I sat drowsily in it, swaying to the gait of the horse, and did not at first pay attention when he spoke. Nor do I know what he had been thinking, that brought it on him.

"Rae—" He spoke but the single word, over my shoulder.

"What?" I murmured. Then I thought how hoarse he had sounded, how struggling, like a drowning person, and I turned in the saddle and looked. And there he sat, all afire with glory and only inches from me. I pulled Bucca to a plunging stop, and Lonn got off, fell off as if he had no strength, as if in the grip of an adversary. That passed quickly. On the instant he sprang up and rushed me.

"Rae, you will be mine!" he roared, and I eluded him easily, cantering Bucca away.

"Don't leave me!" he shouted in fright.

I stopped the horse at a safe distance and turned to watch him. Splendor—it no longer appealed to me. When he came stumbling after me I sent the horse trotting forward again as Lonn cursed me every step of his way with curses I do not care to remember. Finally his noise stopped and I looked at him again. There he stood, still and ordinary, with tears on his face, and I went back to him and offered him my hand.

"That was very well done," I said when he sat behind me once more. I should not have spoken; he swung his head as if the words hurt him. How I pitied him, for all he was a dead hero gone sinister. He was but a youth, after all, a comely youth with freckles on his cheekbones and brown unruly hair, and he bore a heavy burden.

The burden grew lighter as we went on, for when we

reached the terraces beneath the rocking stones he walked, and he no longer had to be so close to me. Sturdy though Bucca was, he could hardly be expected to carry the two of us on that terrain. . . . I did not entirely trust Lonn and would not let him take the horse alone or lag too far behind me. His steps slowed, and my heart clamored with impatience as we grew closer.

Some few golden leaves still hung on our small trees at the entry of the haven. The day stood at noon, the sun suspended in blue-gray sky, and I stopped Bucca, sat as breathless as the sun, looking at the few golden leaves.

"Go on," Lonn said. "Take your horse and go. I will follow."

"Lonn. . . ." I shifted my stare to him, studied him warily.

"I will, you know I will! I will be after you within a few minutes. I cannot do otherwise."

So I rode forward, fearing that Lonn would turn back and knowing in a deeper way that he would follow for the sake of his honor. Just as I feared that Arlen would not be awaiting me, and knew in a deeper way that he would, for the sake of his love. . . .

Soft grass, tilled fields fallow for winter. Smoke wisping from the chimney of the small stone cot—and a man splitting kindling near the door. . . .

He looked so strange, almost as if I had never seen him before, and yet he had not changed, he was Arlen still, russet hair, broad shoulders, deft and gentle hands, and—turning, staring at me as if I were a stranger.

I stopped Bucca, suddenly shy, awkward, unsure of my welcome. If he were angry with me—but he dropped his ax with a clatter and came running toward me, and all doubts left me at the sight of his beloved face. I slipped down from Bucca, took one step to meet him—and I was in his arms.

"Rae," he whispered. "Ai, my Rae—" and I was crying. "Are you all right?" he was asking, but of course I was all right, and for a moment we babbled at each other, neither answering the other's questions.

"You've managed?" I said anxiously. "You've eaten, tended the animals, the garden—"

But of course he had managed. He loosened his clasp on me somewhat, studied me at arm's length. "So my swallow has returned," he murmured, smiling, lifting a sleeve to brush away tears.

"Goddess be willing, I shall never have to leave you again."

"That is as it comes," he said soberly. "Did you find what you were searching for?"

"I—am not sure." I turned to look behind me. Lonn should be coming soon.

"You found something, I can see that. There is a newness about you, a—sureness."

I gazed at him, at his quiet, open face. "I have found a true love," I told him, "awaiting me here."

He moved his mouth wordlessly.

"If you are no hero, Arlen," I told him, "then there ought to be a title of higher honor."

Behind me Lonn came walking into view.

I saw Arlen staring past me, then turned to look myself. Lonn walked slowly, very slowly, as if every step were weighted with felon's chains, but steadily onward, toward us. I could only begin to imagine what courage that march was costing him.

"Lonn?" Arlen breathed, incredulous. "But how can that be?"

Lonn forced himself closer, forced himself to raise eyes filled with shame, to meet Arlen's astonished gaze.

"You are dead. I—slew you. I saw your severed head."

Lonn reached us, and with a groan he sank to the ground at Arlen's feet in posture of supplication. "I have wronged you," he said. His voice came out as hollowly as if it sounded from a grave.

"Lonn! I—get up." Arlen grasped Lonn's left arm and tugged him bodily to his feet, lifted Lonn's chin with one hand; there was about Arl that air of reckless daring, abandonment of reason, that he had worn once at an esker. "I don't care," he said fiercely, staring into Lonn's anguished eyes. "I don't understand, and I don't care what you have done; there is nothing that can stop me from being your friend. Not even death, it seems. Nothing." And he kissed him on the cheek and embraced him.

"He looks faint," I said. "Take him inside. I will tend to Bucca."

Brothers, I thought, taking the horse to the barn. There was another horse in there, a bay. Arlen must have bought it for want of Bucca while I was gone. Brothers, not merely friends, but brothers, twins. I had told Lonn nothing of Erta, nor would I tell him now, nor would I tell Arlen. The two of them bore trouble enough.

I went inside, and there was honey and porridge to eat, and the three of us talked for a fortnight.

Understanding always comes about piecemeal after long separations. It was well into the evening before Arlen understood what had happened to bring Lonn before him in living flesh, and farther into the night before I learned what he had done when I left.

"I didn't think at first that you could be gone more than a day," he explained with a wry look. "Where I believed you were to go in that time, I am sure I do not know, but I felt certain you would be back by suppertime."

"She went to the Afterworld," Lonn put in.

Arlen stared blankly, for he could not yet encompass that. "And then," he continued, "I thought you would be back the next day, and the next. And when a week had passed in that way, it was too late for me to try to follow, even if I had known which way you had gone. And there were the crops to be tended to, if we were not to starve in the winter. I could only trust you would be back before winter."

"As I am," I remarked.

"Yes. Well, but I was not always reasonable. There came a time near midsummer when I cared nothing for crops or the

care of animals and not much for you, either, should you
return while I was gone, and I took Teague—"

I raised my brows at him.

"The new horse. He is hard-mouthed and obstinate, but
steady."

"You took Teague," I prompted.

"And went in haste to see Briony. I hoped you had perhaps
had the sense to go to him. He loves you, and he would help
you in any way he could."

I gaped at him. "He told you that?" I gasped.

"No indeed. But one could always see it when he was near
you. He even cherished you so far as to save me." Arlen smiled
crookedly. "A most remarkable mandrake. And when I
reached him and talked of searching for you, he told me not to
be a fool, to go back home and await you or I would destroy
your faith in me."

"And that was all?"

"Yes. So I did. And when I returned, the beans were still
hanging on the vine as tender and green as when I had left
them." Arlen gave a bemused shrug. "So I took that as a sign
of the blessing of the goddess and went back to work."

It was very late. Lonn got up. "I will go sleep in the barn,"
he said, "on the hay, with the horses."

"No need," Arlen protested. "We can spread a pallet for you
here, before the fire."

"I have no wish to lie so near your bed. Arlen, have mercy
on a poor stray from the beyond, and loan me a blanket."

I found him two, and he went out. And presently Arlen and
I celebrated our love.

Even so, it was the next day before Arlen understood fully
where I had been, the dangers I had faced and why, and that
indeed, yes, it had truly been necessary, or at least so it had
seemed at the time. His mind balked at the thought that he
could have lost me to Rahv or the Gwyneda or the Naga.

"If only that fool Briony had told me," he said hotly, "I
could have come after you, saved you—"

"I had to save myself," I said. Though admittedly Ophid had been there. And I had been a dolt to let Rahv take me to start with.

Perhaps Arlen still did not understand, but he accepted. "Well," he said ruefully, "I should have known or guessed that you had gone after your babe."

"How were you to comprehend, you or Lonn either? You two were reared in a place where each woman sacrificed her child."

I had glossed over the matter of Erta, her reason for freeing me, and there was so much to think about they had not remarked it.

"For all I know," Lonn added softly, "my own mother helped to kill me."

I said nothing. She had. But he had her courage, he to think it and she to acknowledge it. Now she lay dead and gone beyond.

"I thought of that, there on the tree," Lonn added with difficulty. "I wondered which one of those white ghouls might be my mother. It makes it hard, the anger . . . ."

It was a week and more before we heard most of the story from him, the tale of his own experience of death: wanderings full of fear and hatred, terror and pain. He would not speak much in front of me, for my presence made him taut and unhappy; indeed, he was plainly unhappy most of the time he was with us. But sometimes, as I hummed and puttered about the hearth and scullery, cooking or clearing away the summer's worth of mess Arlen had left me, he would forget me for a while, and he would talk more freely to Arlen as they sat at the table.

"I hated you," he said to Arlen once, painfully. "I wanted you to die, there at the esker, and I made no move to save you, only Rae. And I wanted you to die at the soddy."

Arlen sat staring at him, surprised but not angry. "I must have known, in a way," he said finally. "I bade you go."

"And I went because I felt miserable, even then."

"I had been near to death myself, so I knew. But then I forgot."

"Yes, you generous fool. . . . All that I did, the food, the treasure, all for Rae, and you were merely with her—and then, you dolt, you had to go and name your firstborn after me."

Arlen's eyes widened with astonishment, and then his sense of the ludicrous got the better of him and he put his head back and shouted with laughter. Even Lonn had to smile.

"But that must have galled you!" Arlen cried.

Lonn said nothing, but got up to go outside for a while, and Arlen sobered and went after him, stopping him at the door.

"But all that is past," he said to Lonn gently. "You do not hate me any longer?"

"No. How could I?" Lonn spoke with lowered head, like a penitent. "I hated myself for it, even then. . . . I am better now, but any time it could return."

"I think not."

"You don't know—how cruel—Arl, we must do something."

"But what? I can scarcely slay you again."

Lonn's head came up and he stared, wide-eyed and frightened, then ran out the door, making toward a copse of alders. Arlen stood looking dismayed.

"Me and my stupid tongue!" he said forcefully, and he would have gone after Lonn, but I took hold of him.

"He will not want you right now. He has to fight it off again."

And Arlen also went away in another direction, to brood.

He would have liked to have kept Lonn with us, I knew he would. It was as if an unspoken wish had been granted to him, an impossible wish, to have his friend with him, returned from the dead, his brother, his rival—Lonn, in mortal flesh. It was going to grieve Arlen anew to part from him again. But I knew that Lonn's unhappiness would not let it be otherwise. Once they had talked. . . .

"You slew me," Lonn said to him another day, as if it were a new thought, a discovery. There was nothing of accusation in his tone, but all the same Arlen's head came up in protest.

"I had to! You told me to."

"I know it! Do I have to make sense? There is no sense in any of this."

"And the thought of it has nearly killed me since," Arlen added in a low voice.

They sat as if each were in a separate trance, speaking out of different circles in the same circling dance. They did not look at each other.

"Hanging there on that horrible tree, my blood feeding the roots, my life draining away—"

"I danced, I danced around the fires, I leaped high and lashed the frenzy. Else I could not have borne it."

"I could not remember why I was there, what I had done to deserve such punishment."

"I threw the spear with all my force—"

"I could not see, but I knew it was you. Wild-eyed—"

"For your sake, straight and true, so that you would go quickly."

"First the pain, the horrible pain, and then the sickness, weak, pitiful. Long, it all lasted so long—"

"You had given me my life, my love, my bride, everything."

"Why? Why were they killing me? The death blow, and I knew they expected me to go away, but I stayed, watching."

"The steed, saddled for us and waiting—"

"They had even taken my horse. How was I to go?"

"That also was your gift. Heroes would welcome you into the blessed realm—"

"They expected me to take passage to the land of the dead. They were mistaken."

"Heroes would welcome you as the greatest of heroes."

"No one wept for me."

"I wept."

"No one wept for me. They—"

Lonn's voice stopped as if choked off by a giant grip at his throat. He got up so hastily that he knocked over his stool, ran outside and away. Arlen sat numbly, watching him go. After a while I went and touched Arl, and he looked at me, put his arms around my waist, and buried his face in the cloth of my skirt. There was no need for words; we both knew I was a prize hard won.

"Bucca was for him," I said after a long moment.

"The dead need horses?" Arlen muttered, his voice thickened by cloth.

"No, Arl, think." I sat beside him. "There was no time after you two exchanged places—no time for him to ready a horse for us. It had been done earlier. His horse, not yours."

Arlen looked at me, then at his hands.

"He meant it for himself, to escape the ceremonials. So that he would not have to see you die, or strike you."

Arl sat silent for a while. "Now this time," he said finally, "I am going to him." And he strode out in search of Lonn, and the two of them did not return until after nightfall.

What they talked about I do not know. But it must have cleared a way, somehow, for the next day Lonn's rage came plain, with him in control and in ordinary form it came out, and our answer with it.

"I was willing enough to die," Lonn said abruptly after the noonday meal. "I wanted to die rather than let them kill you— I thought. Only—"

"Only what?" Arlen prompted.

"No one wept for me."

"I wept."

"I did not see it. You were gone. There was no—"

"No what?"

"No honor. No mourning." Lonn got up as if to leave. "I sound so petty."

"It does not matter." Arlen took him by the arm and urged him back to his stool again. "Go on," he coaxed with that irreverent perverseness of his. "Tell me what it is like to be dead and cut in pieces."

Lonn went rigid, and Arlen looked up in instant remorse, wanting to swallow his words. But Lonn did not flee this time, or turn into a shining horror.

"It is—it was—they feasted! They laughed and made merry." Anger edging out of those words. "And when they were done—"

He could not speak, sat gasping for breath as if he were strangling, but he did not again offer to leave. I stood watching, waiting, and Arlen leaned forward, waiting, gazing at Lonn. And then the hurtful secret burst from him.

"They threw me in the river like so much offal!"

He sprang up, but not to run, only to stand there with fists curled in wrath, and he shouted at us as if it were somehow our fault.

"No honor, mine, no marker, no tomb. They did not even give me burial. What remained of me, they—they threw it in the river! Like filth! Do you know what folk send to death on the Naga? Suicides, and corpses of the murdered and of murderers, and women who have died screaming in childbirth. All those who have gone to a bad death. All whom they want rid of, far, far rid of, whom they want not to think of after they are gone. . . ."

He stood panting, an ordinary mortal in a godlike rage, and then the fury left him, his body sagged, and he wept. Arlen went to him and took him into a tight embrace, clasping him and rocking him as if he were a babe. "You deserved better," he said softly, "far better. You were a hero, a sacrifice, the most generous—"

"Stop it." Lonn freed himself gently, wiped the tears from his face with a grimace. "I felt very sorry for myself," he said in wry tones. "As I still do."

"Yours was a winterking's suffering without the reward," I put in.

He turned to me; they both turned to me as if they had forgotten I was there, staring at me.

"Yes. The bride." Lonn said it with some small struggle, but he said it. "I felt that I should at least have had the bride. Rae, I am sorry."

"No need." I went and sat down at the table, and they sat across from me.

"But—I had given the gift freely, and I should not have thought of—taking it back."

"The gift you gave was so great, you could not encompass it, being only flesh, after all, and no god. Lonn, it was well thought of and well done. Say no more of it."

Indeed, there was no more to be said. He was emptied, and he sighed in assent.

"I think," I told the two of them, "that I know what we must do."

# TWENTY-ONE

Within a few days we set out, well provisioned, with Lonn
on Bucca and me on Teague behind Arlen. I wished we had
yet another horse, for there was a great deal of baggage, but as
we did not, we managed. We rode steadily but not overly
hard, for we had time enough before the solstice day of the
ceremonials. And we journeyed for the most part in silence,
and Lonn in particular was silent.

"I only hope that I can do it," he muttered once, as we
wended our way through the Forever Forest.

"Are you determined to do it?" Arlen asked. "Bound?"

"Mighty Mother, yes. Bound as by chains of gold. I have
brought you and Rae nothing but misery by cleaving to you. I
will take the passage this time; I have sworn it."

"Then you will do it," Arlen said.

After we came out on the moorlands, Lonn left us for two
days. He wanted to see Briony and beg his advice. I would not
go to the soddy, for my going there would only cause Briony

pain and make me uneasy on his account. I said as much, and
Arlen and I passed the place a day's journey away. We were to
wait for Lonn at the next bend of the esker. We spent the night
in warmth and comfort at a friendly homestead and found that
the folk had made great fires and were burning beans and
elderberries; it was the eve of the festival of the dead. A year, a
full year since the babe had been named.

The next day, as we rode, hoofbeats sounded and Lonn rode
up behind us.

"So," Arlen greeted him, "did you see Briony?"

"He was not there, nor had he been there for some time.
The soddy was all shut up and deserted."

"How can that be?" Arlen scowled, puzzled. "Are you sure
you found the right place?"

"Quite sure," Lonn retorted with more spirit than he had
shown of late. "I have been there before, might I remind you."

"Oh." Arlen mused on that. "So you were."

"Also, I went to inquire of the neighbors."

"Oh?" Arlen turned to face him more attentively.

"And they said the witch has gone away for good. He told
them he was going to apprentice with the masters beyond the
burning sea."

Arlen gave me a searching glance. I said nothing.

"I spent the night by a small campfire on the open moor,"
Lonn said.

In the open, on that night of all nights. It was a deed to be
accounted brave, or foolish, or perhaps insane.

"Did you not know—" Arlen started.

"Not until the dance crowded round. But then, there ought
to be no reason for a dead man to fear the dead." He wore an
air of satisfaction, of mischief even, which I had not seen in
him before. "I think I gave a good accounting of myself," he
added.

He did not tell us the whole tale of that night. But he held
his head higher thereafter, and rode with more command, and
Arlen watched him with pleasure tinged with sadness.

"This is the Lonn I remember," he told me privately.

When we came to the Naga the cavalcades were riding along the bank, upstream toward the Sacred Isle to attend the sacral rites of the winterking. My father and his retinue rode close by us; he glared at us and passed on.

At the edge of the mist, beyond the dark water, lay the Island of Passages. We stopped at the closest point of the shore, looking over.

"Is that Ophid?" Arlen muttered.

I thought I could see a dark stumpy shape, like a leafless pollard, a figure the same color as the winter tree trunks around it. If we had not known what to look for we would never have noted it, and even so we could not be sure, it stood so still.

"Ophid!" Arlen shouted, and he signaled it.

The dark shape stirred and moved to the island shore. Presently another dark shape appeared around the downstream point, a swimming shape, long-necked and graceful, a cormorant boat. In it Ophid came over the water to speak with us.

"It goes well for you?" I asked him.

"It goes well." He nodded gravely to me, and though he wore his all-masking mantle I could tell that fear had indeed left him, for he carried himself as erect as the sacral ash on the Island of Fugitives.

He and Arlen went aside to talk. They spoke for a long while, their voices a low murmur, and I saw Ophid nod; he had agreed to help us. Presently he rode his cormorant back to his island again, and Lonn and Arlen and I went on.

The Sacred Isle. Low and dark it lay on the dark water in the dusk. Odd, very odd and unnatural, it felt, to be camped on the river shore looking across at it, just three more seculars among the crowd of those come to honor the morrow's rites. Arlen hardly spoke that eve at all, and as for Lonn, he looked taut, as if he were gathering himself. An ordeal lay ahead of him, a passage, the greatest and most final of all passages.

We slept only lightly, uneasily, and by turns. Before dawn, when only the stirrings of the winter birds spoke of dawn, before anyone else of the vast encampment was about, we got up and slipped down to the shore, waiting, watching the faint sheen of starlight on the black water. Presently there came a shadow and a lapping sound, and the cormorant slid up to us. By the time the sky had turned from velvet black to a dark silken gray, Ophid had ferried us all across to the island, to the southern tip of it where the willows grew most thickly. Then he went away to tend our horses and gear for us. Arlen and Lonn and I settled ourselves amongst the willows and waited.

There was all to be said and nothing to say, and we did not speak, all the long day through. And though we had brought food with us, none of us could eat it, and though we had brought blankets and sat or lay on them and wrapped ourselves in them, we shivered. The day crept slowly, terribly slowly, from dawn to morning, from morning to a noon undiscerned in the white winter sky, from noon to afternoon and early evening. Lonn stirred restlessly, threw off his blanket, and came over to sit closer to Arlen and me. Dusk deepened—

Sound of a scream, distant, chill on the chill air.

Lonn shuddered; we all huddled together. "Poor devil," Lonn muttered. "They have built the fires and tied him in the fivefold bond, and the scourging has begun."

Praise be, we could not hear much, neither the grim song of the whips nor the chanting of the dancers. But we knew, all too well we knew what was happening. And the winterking screamed again. Lonn winced.

"Did I scream?" he asked, a wild light beginning in his eyes, edge of panic. "I—don't remember screaming."

"No," I told him, "you did not." This youth, this winterking, whoever he was, did not bear it as silently as Lonn had.

"I should have screamed. I should have screamed." Lonn was panting. "Perhaps it would have let some of the venom out. Aaah!" He twisted as if caught by a long lash. "Mother, it hurts!"

He crouched with his whole borrowed body clenched against agony, every muscle twitching, tensed to flee, but he could not flee. He stayed as still as if bound by invisible chains.

"Mother of us all, the pain!" he burst out. "You are cruel, cruel—" He closed his eyes hard against her, against torment. "Did I disgrace myself?" he asked, gulping, "Befoul myself?"

"I do not recall that you did," I told him, quite truthfully. Perhaps he would not remember how I had stood with eyes tightly shut.

"I hope not. . . ."

Arlen was biting his lip, face aquiver, reaching out toward Lonn but afraid to touch him. I took Arlen's hand to comfort him—and Lonn gasped and writhed as if the full force of agony had only just then struck him.

"Rae!" The words slipped out between sobs. "Arl. Help—me. Hold me."

We put our arms around him, and around each other as well, and we drew him to us, close, gathered him against us so that the three of us made a sort of flower of three petals, or a pod, a cluster, huddled against harm. We embraced him, murmuring to him, soothing him as if he were our child. I kissed his face, laid my head for a moment on Arlen's shoulder. Then the distant winterking shrieked again, and Lonn groaned aloud in anguish.

"Courage," Arlen whispered to him. "It must soon be over."

It was not. How could the evening seem longer than the day had been? The three of us cowered in the darkness beneath the willows, clasped tight each to each, hearing the sounds of pain, feeling the hot breath of cruel hatred; it was alive in that night on that island; it prowled. We all shook in terror of it, and Lonn trembled in agony of another sort, and strained and moaned in our arms. Toward the end he screamed at last, scream after long desperate scream, wild screams that echoed across the black water. His whole body quivered, his soul seemed torn out with those screams. But the Gwyneda would not have heard him, for they were far gone in their frenzy by then—and then in the distance the death roar sounded, and Lonn slumped limp against us.

"It is over," Arlen breathed.

He got up shakily. I sat and held Lonn's head and upper body on my lap, weeping; we were both weeping, Arl and I. But Lonn did not move or weep. Arlen built a small fire, just fire enough for us to see by, and he knelt beside me and started gently, ever so gently, to strip the body.

Not a corpse, exactly. Lonn still softly breathed. But he lay pale and still with lidded eyes—I smoothed the lids with my fingertips and let my tears fall on the face. Our sorrow was keen and real, for we were sending Lonn away. He was our friend, the winterking who had died. We would never see him again.

"He bore it nobly," Arlen said, his voice far from steady. "No draught of mead to soften it, no glamour, serpent power of the goddess. Only poor human comfort. . . ." His voice caught, the words faded.

We had with us what we needed, the towels of linen, the soft fleeces, new napkins for washing, and some things Ophid had provided, basins of silver, a richly embroidered mantle. We laid the body on the soft fleeces and washed it tenderly with wine, three times, until the wine was all gone. And then we washed it in like wise with milk. Lonn still breathed, but he seemed quite unaware of us, and I felt a pang of pride for him. This was his choice, his going: his the struggle and his the victory.

"I loved him like a brother," Arlen said, tears finally stilled, and I hoped that in some sense Lonn had heard.

The third time we washed him with the milk, until it was all gone, and then we washed him with river water warmed over the fire. And then I gathered him up and held him to my bosom as I dried him with the linen towels, held him to my bosom and warmed him and gathered him close and rocked him as if he were a child. He lay limp, he never stirred, but the holding of him set me to weeping again. I cried softly, easily, and I noticed light amidst the looping branches of the willows. We had done our vigil, and it was dawn.

New clothing for Lonn, tunic of soft velvet and breeches of doeskin, fit for a king's son; there had been time enough to stitch them on our journey. Arlen slipped the things on him. A lapping sounded at the shore beyond the willows, and in a moment Ophid walked up to us.

"Look," he said. "I have borrowed you a worthy bier."

We looked, and gasped. It was a great swan boat, larger than the others we had seen, grand and high-headed, and the swan swam as red as blood, a shining lacquer red, and its beak and eyes were gilded.

"All the dead of the Sacred Isle go down the river," Ophid said, "one way or another. This is the bird that carries them in state."

"Let us make of it the softest couch we can," said Arlen.

He took the fleeces and all the blankets he could gather, blankets of finest wool, and he and Ophid piled them high while I held Lonn in my arms. Then they came and wrapped him in the rich red mantle emblazoned with thread of gold, slipped it around his shoulders and fastened it at his throat with a serpent clasp. Then Arlen took him from me and carried him to the swan boat, laid him there straight and stately with the mantle spread and trailing like wings about him, and the waist of his green tunic was bound by a golden chain.

The swan sailed away. We followed in the cormorant. In slow and silent progression we swam down the Naga, seeming at times to hardly more than drift, and all the noble folk along the bank stared at us, stared at Lonn lying so still in the great red swan, and some of them knelt, and some averted their eyes as if they had seen an omen.

We came to the crannog that bore the cenotaph.

"There are bundles of sweet reeds for strewing," Ophid told us, "and three beeswax candles for light. I will leave you."

"Thank you," Arlen murmured to him. He stepped into the shallows and lifted Lonn from his couch, carrying him cradled against his shoulder. I gathered up the bedding. The swan gravely bowed its head in salute, lowering its gilded beak to the surface of the water. Then it turned and sailed away upstream to its home, leaving us.

I spread blankets on the grass above the stone of the shore, and we laid Lonn there. I stayed with him while Arlen prepared the tomb. They sky had darkened, purple-gray clouds scudding, and the yew trees by the cenotaph were turning up the pale undersides of their small evergreen leaves. As Arlen came and stood beside me, a rumbling sounded in the sky.

"Thunder?" he exclaimed. "In winter?"

We stared at each other for a moment. We had not thought such great events were afoot.

"Well," said Arl at last, "we had better get Lonn within before it storms."

We placed him on our stoutest blanket and tugged him gently through the passageway, Arlen before, pulling, and I behind to guide. Candlelight made a great difference; the place seemed not dark and frightening, as I remembered it, but hushed, dim, awesome and silent under great stones. And quite empty, no bones, not even those of birds or vermin. And the air within was as sweet as that without. Under the vault of the corbeled main chamber lay a great stone slab draped with woolens and fleeces. Fragrant rushes were strewn about, and by the stone the three candles burned with a serene, unwavering light.

From outside, distant, came the sound of rain, as if the goddess softly wept.

"Sleep in peace, Lonn," Arlen murmured as if Lonn could hear him. As perhaps he could.

We laid him straight and regal on the slab, arranged his rich cloak in folds about him, crossed his hands on his chest. Then from under our own tunics we brought forth satin bags, opened them, and spilled forth treasure with a soft rustle as of serpents: clasps and jeweled brooches and armbands and the chains, ever the golden chains. All around Lonn and on him, by his head, his hands, his feet, in the folds of his tunic and mantle we placed our gifts of treasure, the red gold and the white gold and the gold as yellow as the sun, and on his chest the golden chains; we held nothing back. I even took off the golden chain from around my neck, the one the goddess my mother had given me, and placed it around his own. We upended the bags to make sure that not so much as a single small and shining jewel remained within them.

"These things are yours to keep forever, Lonn," Arlen told him. "Our gifts of love, freely bestowed. Unasked for."

Lonn's quiet breathing shuddered slightly and then softened into a sigh, as if he had only just then ceased to weep.

"Go with—all love. . . ."

Arlen's voice broke on the words, and tears slid down his face, the very quiet, easy tears of an old sorrow. It was time for Lonn to take passage, he who had died two years before.

"Go decked in glory to the dance," I murmured.

We were both weary, very weary, too weary to wonder very much what might happen next. Soft wash of rain outside seemed very far away. Arlen sat down on the ground amidst the sweet rushes as if to keep a vigil, and I sank down and rested my head against the stone of the slab near Lonn's feet. For no reason I was humming to myself, a lulling hum such as one might use to send an infant off to sleep. And after a hazy time I became aware that Arlen had risen to his knees, head up like that of a questing stag, gazing with open mouth and caught breath. And I also sat up and looked.

Lonn was fading. I could yet see his face, so still, his lidded eyes, but he looked somehow—insubstantial, as if a touch would have gone through him, and I inched away from him lest I should touch him by chance. Then I could no longer clearly see his face. He looked wavering, hovering, a shadow on the slab, and within that shadow—a smaller form—

"Wait," Arlen whispered to me, seeing my arms rise, my

hands reach out, and I stopped them in midair, and I stopped breathing.

Lonn had not yet finished his passing. His presence yet lingered, a watery sheen in the candlelight, nothing more—and then I sensed or felt a gentle exhalation, sigh of earth, breath of the goddess, and he was gone, truly gone. One short candle guttered and went out.

And there on the slab lay treasure and shapeless cloth, and amidst the velvet and the chains of gold lay—the babe, a sturdy boy baby of a year and more, naked and sleeping peacefully, and on his small left shoulder was the serpentine mark I remembered so well.

"Oh, mighty Mother," I whispered, afraid to touch him lest he somehow not be, after all, breathing, lest he somehow not be real.

"Go ahead," Arlen urged.

The soft, soft feel of that rose-petal skin. . . . He was as solid as I. Gently, gently I lifted him, and he opened his eyes but did not cry, only crowed in baby wonder and reached out to pat my cheek. Touch of that tiny hand seemed all I would ever want of happiness. And oh, the faint, sweet fragrance of the little one's hair. . . . I stood in a daze of joy, holding him, joy too deep for tears or laughter, and Arlen put his arms around both of us, and bowed his head in gesture of wordless praise.

"Out," he said, and we wrapped the babe warmly and left the empty tomb and the candles burning down.

The rain had stopped, and the thunder, and the sun was shining through clouds. We stood outside the entry and gazed about us as if the whole world were made anew. Overhead arched a bright rainbow, the celestial serpent. The child babbled and reached out toward it.

"There," Arlen said. "His name is Davin, sky glory, the rainbow."

The little one looked at his father, owlish, his eyes round and innocent and the same greenish shade as Arlen's.

"Davin," I repeated.

And so his name was, all his life, even after his passage.

Food awaited us, dried fruit, Ophid's gift. We ate—little Davin ate eagerly. And by the time Ophid came for us, Arlen had sealed off the entry to the cenotaph. Forever empty that tomb would remain, and forever Lonn's.

# EPILOGUE

That was long ago. I am old now, and Arlen's russet hair has gone white, though he still works as hard as ever. We earned our way through honest toil after we left our treasure with Lonn, and Davin grew tall and honest and kindly like his father, with only a trace of something otherworld about him, something wise. He left when he was grown to join the sorcerers beyond the burning sea in their struggle against my marauding father Rahv. I have sometimes hoped he might have found Briony. . . . And we had three other sons, Arl and I, and two daughters, and found joy in them all.

We have never been visited by Lonn again, for which we are both glad and sorry. He was at once hero and scapegoat and grasping villain, greedy for more of life and love—are we not all? But all the misfortunes in my life seemed mild once I had Davin back. And the goddess has never withdrawn her favor

from us, Arl and me. Neither Rahv nor any other enemy has
ever troubled us here in our mountain haven, and I think none
ever will. We will live out our lives in peace in this place and
nod by the fire sometime in a final sleep, sometime when we
are very old. Together. Bound as by a chain of gold.